A NOVEL BY

WARREN DRIGGS

Old Scratch

Published by
Paradise Rim Books
Salt Lake City, UT

ISBN: 978-0-9987795-0-8
eISBN: 978-0-9987795-1-5

Book Design by GKS Creative, Nashville

Library of Congress Information is on file with the Publisher.

I'm a laying up sin and suffering for us both, I know.
He's full of the Old Scratch, but laws-a-me!
—Aunt Polly, "The Adventures of Tom Sawyer"

For Cee, who keeps my inner devil in check

1

SUSAN HAD A LOW OPINION OF ANYONE who didn't share her taste for the finest things in life. And the finest things in life, according to Susan, could only be measured in dollars and cents. Actually, more like treasury bills and gold bullion, for that's how she was raised. She forgot that she'd done absolutely nothing to earn her fortune. It came about exclusively from her conception, a conception that had been grudgingly offered by her mother. And because she'd been conceived by rich parents, she believed that she was special. I'd seen to that.

From Susan's elevated perch, she could see that poor people were simply the victims of bad investment strategies. In fact, some people appeared to have no strategy at all—they just got by on what they earned. And how shortsighted was *that*? They gave no thought to the newest IPO, or red-hot hedge fund. Can you imagine? They had no one to blame but themselves.

Susan was still a beautiful woman, having spent a good chunk of that comfy inheritance on creams, lotions, oils, and serums. She'd been lasered, exfoliated, and chemically peeled more times than she'd made lunch for her children, who were, mercifully, finally old enough to be out of the house. All the nipping and tucking had paid temporary dividends, too. But, regrettably, nothing could be done about all those miles under her hood—the rusted undercarriage. It was so depressing. When she looked in the mirror, she felt entitled to self-pity and regret that she hadn't gone to Dr. So & So instead. I'd seen to that, too.

She stepped back from the magnifying mirror which exaggerated every wrinkle (but she couldn't bear *not* looking into the damned thing) and let her towel drop to the tile floor. At fifty-eight-years old, she was tall and thin. Her hourglass shape was impressive, as was the sheer size and heft of her silicon girls. She spent four days a week with her ridiculously handsome personal trainer and had enough discipline to forego the crème brûlée. It showed, too. But rather than admire her beauty, she zeroed in on every flaw, even those wrinkles that belied her true age—evidence of maturation that should have produced more wisdom. However, that kind of wisdom belongs to those who gracefully yield to gravity; those who haven't fallen victim to pride, one of my favorite deadly sins.

The regression of Susan's beauty tormented her. How she longed for the days when her skin was tight and the only liver spots she saw were on the old ladies who played bridge at the Chestnut Hill Country Club.

She picked a dress fitting for the occasion—something understated in a $2,500 sort of way, for this was no time to flaunt. This was a time to show gratitude to the supporters and campaign workers who had worked to purchase the re-election of her husband, Republican Senator Kenneth Lawson of Pennsylvania. Twelve million dollars was spent (most of it from her personal trust) to be re-elected to the office that paid $174,000 per year.

Susan didn't care for politics. I actually enjoy the sport myself—all that self-righteous back-stabbing. She did, however, enjoy the prestige of marriage to a United States Senator. In fact, it had been her idea that Ken run for office in the first place. Well, technically, it'd been the idea of her father, the legendary financier, Phillip Rupert. He'd said Ken had the "look" to make it. And, as a fun bonus, his head was mostly empty, so it could be filled neatly to the brim with the designs of the rich who paid for his office.

Susan had been unhappily married to Ken for twenty-eight long and trying years, financing his ostentatious lifestyle and political career. She'd helped fill the gaps in his head, too; those vacancies that forever needed shoring up. Yes, she'd been married to him long enough to see his numerous flaws. But none of them were as galling as his obsessive phoniness. The way he desperately clung to his youth was more than she could reasonably bear.

I'm the devil. I like my job. Sure, there are times when there's no job satisfaction; when peace reigns, for example. But most of the time it's fairly easy. You all have these natural instincts to misbehave, to commit deadly sins every now and then. Who isn't tempted by a little Greed from time to time? Or how about some Lust, or Gluttony? And don't even get me started on the Wrath. Then there's your Envy, Pride, and Sloth to round out the Seven Deadlies. My job is to capitalize on those urges. I root out goodness and tarnish it. And, at the risk of a little self-flattery, I'm pretty good at it. A little prod here and a little nudge there. I watch you like fish in a tank, just swimming around and around in your bowl. I'll tap on the tank to see if I can get a reaction. Usually I can.

But here's the thing; I can't *make* anyone do something they don't want to do. "The devil made me do it." I appreciate the plug, I really do, but it's not true. I've encouraged you to misbehave, of course I have. I poke my thumb in all your pies, but I've never *forced* you to do a single thing. That's not to say I can't affect human behavior. I'm like a pebble in your shoe; small but relevant. Let's say you have a wrath issue with your neighbor and his goddamned barking dog. I'll make sure you tune into its bark so that you're really mad, so mad in fact that you'll kick it. And then I'll see to it that your neighbor (who would appreciate it if you'd mind your own goddamned business), lets his dog out a little earlier each morning to bark. I like creating fun little scenarios like that. They amuse me.

You all wear your costumes, but I can see through them. I'm not limited to the overhead view either; I also see things from the bottom up—the ugly underbelly. You barely hear my whisper or feel my nudge. But it's there all right. The Seven Deadlies always give me something to work with. Take Susan and Ken, for example. I can think of at least four Deadlies off the top of my head that were second nature to them. But they weren't slothful, I'll give them that, and they weren't gluttonous. They were too prideful to be gluttonous.

Ken tried to be humble, in public, but all the fawning made it difficult. He'd begun taking it for granted many years earlier when he met Susan. She was a grad student at Penn while he was grinding his way through the local community college, without any distinction whatsoever. Susan was charmed by his drop-dead handsomeness and "potential." Her parents thought his potential was a figment of her lustful imagination, but she'd insisted that Ken at least have *that*, lest he be unworthy of her.

When Susan became pregnant, Ken's potential was as necessary to her as the pre-nup was to her father—a filthy rich banker who had bestowed an enormous early inheritance upon his daughter. This gave Phillip Rupert (the rich father) much needed tax relief, and allowed Susan to express her devotion to him in his living years. You see, Rupert never bestowed a gift without calculating the repayment.

It remained a mystery how Ken was accepted to the Wharton School of Business. However, to those on the board of admissions, there was no mystery at all; Rupert's portrait hung in the foyer. To Ken's credit (and the classmate he'd cheated off), he did well enough to graduate. Shortly thereafter, he landed a high paying job as a "consultant" (another solved mystery) and began running in circles with big fish; the real mucky-mucks of Pennsylvanian business and politics.

As the luster of Ken's false modesty dimmed, so did Susan's adoration. However, in a moment of giddy inebriation on their third wedding anniversary, she tore the pre-nuptial agreement into pieces. I knew she'd come to regret this misguided moment of magnanimity when she sobered up. But as far as Ken was concerned, this was the most romantic thing Susan had ever done.

Ken's longing for power was on par with his lust. When power, fame, and money—the Trifecta of Aphrodisia—is packaged together as it was here, the opposite sex can be beguiled, even by an empty-headed civil servant like Ken. His chronic philandering clashed with his right-wing moral values platform, something that occurred to him (and his anxious staff), but only in passing.

I did all I could to make him morally blind to his hypocrisy. It wasn't very difficult.

"Susan!" he yelled from the marble foyer at the bottom of the impressive staircase, "The driver will be here in five minutes. Please be ready for once." Ken was a man who waited on no one, and especially not his wife who had begun to bore him long before their Wood anniversary.

"I'll be down when I'm ready." She was plainly irritated with him, too. This was a woman who took orders from no one, and especially not her husband who had begun to bore her well before their Cotton.

"Just this once it would be nice if you were on time. What in the hell are you doing up there anyway?"

"I'm getting ready."

"You've been getting ready for over an hour."

The driver arrived and waited with Ken. Susan could have been ready earlier, and indeed she was, but it pleased her to make Ken wait, to get him boiling in a way that disturbed his otherwise easy equilibrium.

Ken huffed and walked outside when Susan descended the stairway. He hardly even looked at her. She was satisfied, however, that the limo driver did a double take, resting his gaze for an extra count on her inspiring cleavage. She wouldn't acknowledge how handsome Ken looked, either—the humble, insincere civil servant who'd been honored by 51.7% of Pennsylvanians to serve another six years on their tab.

They settled into the backseat of the limousine. "How long must we stay tonight?" she asked.

"Susan," he said, pausing to emphasize how patient she forced him to be, "this is my party for winning the election, so we'll stay as long as we need to. And, please, don't give me the look that says we need to leave every time I look at you."

"But how would you know that look? You never look at me."

"Let's not start, Susan. Not now. Just try to enjoy the party."

"You mean the party I paid for, to honor the candidate my money elected?"

"How many times are you going to remind me it was your money, Susan? Give it a rest." Ken did have a point here; she reminded him of it constantly.

"I'll say it, Kenneth, for as long as it is my money." She used his full name when she was angry, hurt, or irritated. So, she called him Kenneth often.

This money business was a sore spot between them; a pesky, measurable fact. It *was* her money. It was his office, his fame, and his power; but her money allowed for all of it. This truth was the pebble in Ken's shoe, and every time she felt compelled to remind him of it, I made sure the pebble found a path directly to his heel.

"Listen, Susan, I know it's your money. How could I possibly forget? And you earned every penny of it, didn't you? So please, get off your high horse. It's very unbecoming." Ken had a point here, too. Susan had never threaded a needle or baked a rump roast, and the ironing board in the laundry room was new, without a single burn mark in the shape of a V. "Besides," Ken said, "your father knew the good I'd do in the Senate."

"The good you'd do in the Senate? Oh, please, Kenneth, at least spare me that. You are told when and how to vote. Anyone following a simple script could do what you do. So, please, Kenneth, don't patronize *me*."

"I'm not patronizing you. I'm only asking you to support me, for once." He regretted his choice of words—the bit about support, but she let it go.

After an uncomfortable silence in the backseat of the limo, he turned to face her. "Did you even vote for me?"

"I vote my conscience, Senator. Isn't that what you exhort all your loyal subjects to do?"

2

THE LIMO PULLED UNDER THE PORTICO of the Grand Hotel where the ballroom had been reserved. This was an invitation-only event—no riff raff allowed. The campaign staff had debated the invitation threshold, some arguing for a minimum donation of $500 and others insisting it be at least $2,000. It was finally resolved that only those patriots who cared about the direction the country was headed to the tune of $1,000, or more, were welcome.

The list was long but included no butchers, bakers, or candlestick makers. Common wage earners understood this and knew their place. The wealthy knew their place, too, and would gladly take the wheel to reduce crushing tax rates which forced them to spend millions on their schemes to trim the national treasury's share. The humbler citizenry could watch a video clip of the glitzy event on the local news, or read about the Senator's accomplishments in his glossy campaign literature that was mailed to "Current Resident" at a significant cost to the taxpayer.

Ken and Susan arrived fashionably late and were greeted

by enthusiastic applause when they entered the ballroom. The great Senator would eventually greet everyone there, even the cheapskates who paid the measly $1,000 minimum, for he was a consummate glad-hander. He trolled the crowd with a staff member at his elbow, whispering the name of each donor who approached him, allowing the Senator to greet them with a personal touch. Oh, he was *good.* He'd put his left manicured hand on top of the customary handshake to give it that extra homey touch—the one that said he cared.

"Hi, Dad." It was Rebecca, their twenty-three-year-old daughter. She had flown in for the event from Boston where she was in her seventh year of college, still vacillating on her major. Becky became "Rebecca" because Ken thought it might bolster his standing with the Jewish bankers. Even though Ken had anti-Semitic urges, he had the good judgment to keep them tamped down in public. It was only in private that he said things like, "The goddamned Jews think they own the place." I'm on board with hate. However, if I had my druthers, I'd prefer the kind that causes worldwide mayhem, but I don't scoff at a few insignificant murders either. Or, when things are really slow, even some hurt feelings.

Rebecca was ordinary looking; an unpleasant surprise given her parents' good looks. She was plump and her nose was too large for her face. Susan rode the poor girl constantly, reminding her that she was gaining weight. *Do you have any idea how many calories are in that thing?* But Rebecca had refused, *refused,* to go to the gym or do a jumping jack. However, aside from her looks, she was clearly her parents' daughter. Like her mother, she'd been born on third base and thought she'd hit a triple.

"Hi, Rebecca," Ken said. "When did you get in?"

"About an hour ago, and it was *awful.* Maybe Mom already told you, but I had to fly coach."

"Well, at least you made it. How's school going?"

"Finals are next week, but I might need to drop a few classes. The profs are so lame."

"You can only do your best."

"Yeah, I know. But I might need to transfer, or get a different major."

"Have you seen your brother?" Ken asked.

"Yeah, he's here somewhere," Rebecca said. "Probably off trying to talk someone out of voting for you. And you should see what he's wearing." Rebecca loved to criticize her brother who had developed his own convictions. And while those convictions caused friction in the Lawson household, John alone appeared to have them. However, before you roll out the red carpet for him, please know that his liberal sermonizing was done from the back pew, for he was a trust-funder, too.

John, who's hands were stuffed into the pockets of a hooded sweatshirt, half zipped, over a Led Zeppelin T-shirt, saw his dad approach. "Hey, Dad. Congratulations."

"Thank you." He looked down the length of his son. "I believe the invitation called for semi-formal attire."

John looked down at his clothes. "Oh, yeah, sorry."

"Be sure to say hello to your mother." This was Ken's way of dismissing his son, because John made him uncomfortable. Like most liberal do-gooders, John couldn't see the wisdom in war and low tax rates. He'd been infected with a liberal bias in college and it hadn't been properly treated, so it'd spread to his heart, where it was plainly visible, much to the chagrin of his conservative father.

John didn't share his sister's view of their super-duper birthright, either. In fact, he downplayed it around his socially liberal friends. He hadn't joined the Peace Corp, but he'd threatened it around his friends.

"So, how are you voting on the START treaty?"

"John, please, now isn't the time. This is a party. Please try to be happy for me and my friends."

"Your friends, dad, are friends for a reason."

Ken was rescued from a potentially ugly scene by Susan, who'd come over to welcome John. Ken believed his wife and son had a unique bond—a common unity of purpose to oppose everything he stood for.

Ken left them to wallow in their mutual disdain for his political legacy and spotted George Miles and his third wife, Chelsea (or was it his fourth?). What a pair they made. George was round, bald, pink, and chronically sweated, so his face was always shiny. It appeared that every movement he made was an exercise in physical fitness. His eyes were buggy, and his chin was sunken. I'll be honest, he looked like a toad. And, sadly, no matter how many times his young bride kissed him (and she did so reluctantly, on the cheek, and only in public), he remained a toad. But a very rich one, for George Miles was a seventy-year-old billionaire.

That George would land the gorgeous Chelsea, who was forty years younger, was no mystery. It was a bargain, plain and simple. Some wondered (out loud at times) why she'd agreed to marry him. They imagined how dreadful it must've been to share his bed. No, it couldn't have been pretty. But, as you like to say, if there's a will, there's a way! I've beguiled many of you to sell your soul for money, but once the deal is closed, there's usually the realization that you've overpaid.

George was wined and dined at every turn because he was rich. Admirers cocked their ears whenever he spoke, breathlessly awaiting words of financial wizardry. They complimented him about the dumbest things and laughed at his crude jokes (*Oh, yeah, now I get it,* then they'd practically bend over in hysterics). They bragged they had recently dined with George Miles. Yeah, *that* George Miles.

George had come to take it all deliciously for granted. He was so wealthy that he could have whatever he wanted without sacrifice. And when everything is essentially free, nothing has value. How sad is that? So, poor George valued very little; not his Gulfstream jet, not his yacht, and not his woman. Oh, he enjoyed them, for a time, but he didn't value them.

George and Chelsea had been married less than two years. Their post-honeymoon phase of growing discontent developed over the simplest things. For example, even though he was filthy rich, his farts still smelled. And the way Chelsea chewed with her mouth open had lost all its sex appeal. Who could have known that the gorgeous starlet he'd plucked from obscurity, the one who made every Y chromosome drool, snored like a sailor?

Ken approached the mismatched couple. "George, Chelsea, thanks so much for coming." His staff knew he needed no reminder who *they* were.

George extended his fleshy hand. "Ken. Congratulations. We look forward to six more years of your leadership in the senate."

"Thanks, George. My tax and spend opponents want to stifle job growth by raising taxes. I'm pleased we were able to fight them off this time, but they'll be back. I don't need to tell you this is a fight we can't afford to lose."

"You can count on my continued support, Senator." This

swanky affair was billed as a Thank You to those who had already given, but everyone knew (or at least should have known) this was actually the first fundraiser in the next re-election cycle.

"Well, hello, George and Kelsey." It was Susan, who'd drifted over when she saw her husband ogling Mrs. George Miles.

"I'm sorry, Mrs. Lawson," Chelsea said, "but my name is Chelsea, not Kelsey."

"Oh, of course," Susan said, as she did some ogling of her own. Most women, including Susan, emitted an envious scent when they saw Chelsea. But they were satisfied to know that she slept with a toad and would eventually deal with her own loose neck.

Another donor, who'd paid dearly for this access, approached Senator Lawson. "Senator, what can be done to stop Senate Bill 181? They'll try to ramrod it through next year."

It should be noted that the senator's staff was anxious about their boss's grasp of the issues, petrified of a gaffe. So, they guarded him closely. Out of necessity, however, Ken had learned a valuable political skill: the uncommon strategy of telling voters he didn't know everything. These infrequent admissions were disarming, for it was refreshing to hear a politician say, "I don't know." This was especially empowering for Senator Lawson who, indeed, knew very little.

3

JESSE SAMUELSON WAS A SMALL-TIME THIEF and meth addict who disappointed his parents with chronic regularity. It was bad enough that he'd stolen their cash, jewelry, and pill bottles; however, it got worse when the neighbors began missing power tools from their garages. When the neighbors' wrath finally trumped their pity for poor Gary and Ann Samuelson, they wrote a Neighborhood Letter, imploring the Samuelson's to "do something" or they'd be forced to call the police, something they emphasized (twice) in the letter that they were "reluctant to do as caring neighbors and friends."

The Samuelson's lived modestly so Jesse could attend private Catholic schools (not nearly enough to inoculate him from me, by the way). And, of course, he had to wear clothes that everybody who was anybody wore, and be the first in the neighborhood to have the latest X-Box game. It hadn't occurred to Jesse's parents that all this spoiling was rotting him. The ugly seeds they'd sown were now being reaped, and when the noxious weeds began to sprout, it was imperative for Ann to publicly acknowledge Gary's absence as a workaholic father as the cause for Jesse's behavior. It was equally imperative for Gary to publicly acknowledge that Ann's constant doting was to blame. While they blamed and fretted, Jesse was forever spared a single chore. When he turned twenty-two, his parents had finally had enough and kicked him out of the house.

Jesse was thin and smallish. He wore a beanie and had a barbed wire tattoo on his skinny bicep. His pants hung well below his waist, about mid-crack, which required him to walk bowlegged lest they fall to his ankles. He was determined to grow a beard, but what came out was wispy (at best), so he brushed it with his mom's mascara, which made the few whiskers look ridiculous.

Jesse felt victimized by his parents' callous disregard for his welfare. They'd kicked him out of his house? Because he'd borrowed a few bucks from them? They were his own parents for God's sake! The first few days on the street were scary. Jesse slept in the city park with bums who didn't shave and carried their worldly possessions in stolen shopping carts with wobbly wheels. Finding something to eat was a recurring problem. But a friend's dad owned a construction company that specialized in remodels. He needed some grunt labor, the kind Jesse could do once he developed a few callouses.

Jesse's first day on the job was dreadful. After what seemed like hours, he checked the time on his cell phone (of course his parents still paid for *that*) only to discover he'd been working a grand total of two hours. Jesse ran the numbers; he'd earned barely enough to buy lunch and a pack of cigarettes. But Jesse was no quitter, no sir—he stuck it out the whole day. He hadn't earned a callous, but he had a satisfying blister on his thumb for his effort.

He toiled all summer and fall, lawfully eking out enough

to get by (well, he'd shoplifted a few six-packs). He hung on to his job, living with another construction grunt on the crew named Slim.

Slim was tall—maybe 6'5" if he'd had better posture—but he hunched, embarrassed by his height. He'd always been a back-row kid in the class photo. He had a high forehead and pock marks from untreated acne. His mouth was a thin slit above his chin, so small that it could've been sewn shut with one suture. Slim was as skinny as his lips, which was surprising because all he did was eat. He was guilty of gluttony, but got away with it due to a metabolism completely out of whack. Slim's parents were absent most of the time (there was the bowling league, and then divorce court when his mom ran off with the guy at the *Snack 'N Bowl*). So, Slim bounced around with relatives.

Like Jesse, Slim wore his jeans so low that if he'd had an honest butt (which he didn't), the entire crack would've shown. A good six inches of his boxer shorts were exposed at all times. This required him to stand and walk with his legs slightly spread.

Slim invited Jesse to live with him at his aunt's house, along with a collection of other boarders (just about everyone in the clan without rent money). Aunt Eloise was a generous do-gooder who spread her welfare check around on family members who were down on their luck. There was her brother, Wayne, who roamed around muttering to himself. He sauntered through the house with a hairy pot gut that was mostly covered by a dirty tank top and pair of whitey-tighties (actually, they weren't very tight, having lost the elasticity in the leg holes, and neither were they very white). He looked like something that'd been dredged up in a police net.

No one knew what Uncle Wayne did all day, other than

wander the house scratching himself. He was slightly cross-eyed, which made it disconcerting to know which eye actually worked. So, naturally, people rotated their gaze while talking to him, sometimes looking at his left eye and sometimes at his right. Roughly fifty percent of the time they were staring at the eye that didn't work, which is quite insensitive when you think about it.

There were other boarders too, like Aunt Eloise's niece, who had three kids under the age of five. This young mother had no sense of smell (or shame), because the unchanged diapers made Jesse's eyes water. These kids would sit on the kitchen counter and throw Lucky Charms at each other, which were eventually eaten by three or four stray cats with bad gas. Their father lived elsewhere because he and the mother had been "working on their issues" for the past two years. He came around for most meals, however.

The final boarder was a thirty-year-old man with loose screws that caused him to shout odd things for no reason at all. *"Squirt the sofa!"* or *"Find the paint!"* This was distracting, but his curious fascination with feet was just downright weird. He'd lie on the sculptured shag and take the other residents' shoes off to sniff their feet, if they weren't paying proper attention.

That fall, Jesse caught a break doing a bathroom remodel for a rich old man and his hot young wife. The house was the largest one Jesse had ever seen, located in an area of town where Jesse had never been; the pricey Chestnut Hill neighborhood of Philadelphia. Special people lived in Chestnut Hill; privileged souls who wanted to believe they got there by yanking on their bootstraps—that it had nothing to do with their grandfather, the steel baron. That always amused me.

The bathroom in this mansion needed a remodel about as much as Mona Lisa needed her smile touched up. But if these zillionaires were willing to pay to have *this* color marble replaced with *that* color marble, then who was Jesse to quibble? Jesse correctly assumed the home had the finest of everything, and there was so much booze (the good stuff, too!) that the owners would never miss it in a million years.

While snooping, he also discovered a large stash of prescription drugs in the master bathroom. He'd pilfered as much as he dared—just a few pills from each bottle. As for the vodka, he filled his empty Gatorade bottle with Grey Goose and refilled their empty bottle with tap water. He'd considered the common courtesy of using their Evian, but just went with the tap in the interest of time.

Jesse justified this small theft on moral grounds. Uh-huh. These mansion dwellers had more money than God, so it wasn't like they were going to *suffer*.

Three weeks after finishing the job, Jesse's mouth watered as he thought back to the mansion remodel. He'd had the good judgment to crack a basement window in case he'd had the urge to re-fill his Gatorade bottle, or return for a few more pills. He'd had the bad judgment, however, to let Slim in on this potential bonanza.

At least Slim had a car—a beater with torn fabric seats and a cracked dashboard which exposed the foam padding underneath. The left rear-side window was missing and had been replaced by a black plastic garbage bag jerry-rigged into place with duct tape. The car couldn't possibly pass inspection, so Slim only drove it for emergencies. Emergencies ranged from a trip to 7-11 for a box of Frosted Flakes to a buddy's house to smoke weed.

On Tuesday afternoon, November 28th, Jesse and Slim drove to this latest emergency. They parked a block from George and Chelsea Miles' mansion, next to a silver Mercedes that had also been parked on the side of the road. Slim agreed to stay behind as a lookout, ignoring the fact that he had no cell phone or walkie-talkie to warn Jesse of potential disaster.

Jesse slipped through a gate that had been left open by the gardener, whose grimy pickup truck was parked on the gravel drive leading to the home. Jesse saw the gardener on the other side of the property. Mexican music blasted from a boom box in the bed of his pickup—music that sounds exactly the same to every Gringo, regardless of the song. I ought to pipe it through the suburbs of Hell on a never-ending loop.

The two-acre homestead was protected by a tall wrought iron fence. There were so many trees and shrubs that Jesse remained unseen by snobby neighbors who lived acres apart from each other; about one person for every eight thousand square feet (surely there's no greed in that). Jesse found the basement window, still cracked a quarter of an inch. He slid it open, slowly, slowly, and hopped inside. His shoes had damp mud on them from the garden (but not much, and the carpet was brown).

He waited, holding his breath, listening. There was no sound. He waited a few moments more. The refrigerator motor in the downstairs mini-bar kicked on. His heart raced like an overwound toy.

There'd been no cars parked in the driveway, but Jesse had seen enough movies to be quiet and vigilant. *And wipe off everything you touch!* He found the stairs and slowly climbed them, stopping and wincing with every creak. He made his way to the master bathroom via its back door on the stairway landing. The pain pills were still in the medicine cabinet, next to the Cialas and Vagicream. He figured the old man must've had a serious case of gout in addition to a limp dick, a thought that perplexed Jesse when he considered the gorgeous woman who owned the cream.

He closed the medicine cabinet with the tiniest click and began to leave when he heard voices. *Shit!* He froze. The voices were coming from the bedroom—light and playful, almost giggly. The door between the bathroom and bedroom was ajar. He peeked through the crack and saw the bed through the reflection of a full-length wall mirror.

What he saw made him groan with envy. The hot wife was sprawled on the bed, sexy and naked as a jay bird. The old man who looked like a toad was nowhere in sight. His replacement was a handsome, middle-aged man who looked vaguely familiar, but Jesse couldn't quite place him. Perhaps if Jesse had spent more time looking at *him* instead of *her* he might have made the connection. But, really, who could blame him for this rubber-necking? The local police captain would've done the same thing.

She was the most intoxicating thing Jesse had ever seen, and when she sat up and straddled the man, well, Jesse could see no use whatsoever for the bottle of Cialas in the cabinet behind him. He would've gladly forfeited all the loot he'd just stolen, plus a full year's wages to trade places with the man, for his lust was bubbling over like his 8th grade baking-soda volcano.

Jesse didn't want to leave—of course he didn't. He had fallen in love and didn't even know her favorite date movie. He wanted to burst through that door and tap the guy out. After drinking in one more view, one more long pull, he backed out of the bathroom like a crab. He hurried down the stairs, less stealthily than before, hoping the squeaking bed would drown out a squeaky stair. He hopped up and out of the window and into the garden mud, leaving the window cracked again, in case the urge to pilfer returned.

Slim was leaning against the trunk eating a bag of Cheetos when Jesse came running up. "Did you get the stuff?" he asked.

"Yeah, of course I did. Do I look stupid?" He showed Slim the stash which was visible in the clear plastic zip-lock bag Jesse had taken with him, proof that he was, indeed, not stupid. "But, dude, you won't believe what I just saw."

"What?"

"That chick was getting laid by some guy!"

"What chick?"

"Does it matter? The hot one. Who lives there. Who else would it be?"

"No fuckin' way!"

"Yes fuckin' way!"

"How'd you see it?" Slim was actually more interested in *what* Jesse had seen than how he'd seen it.

"Through the bedroom door. I saw the whole thing. Swear to God."

Slim began moving toward the house. "I gotta check this out."

Jesse grabbed his arm. "Are you crazy, dude? You can't go in there. They'll see you!"

"They didn't see you, did they?" And with that, Slim jerked his arm away and took off through the lilacs and hydrangeas at a reckless speed, led entirely by the radar of his loin.

Jesse waited, pacing by the car, certain Slim would be caught.

Just as he was about to start the car and scram, Slim was back, grinning lustfully.

"Did they see you?" Jesse asked.

"Holy crap, bro!"

"Yeah, I know, but do you think they heard you?"

"Dude, she was ridin' him like a buckin' bronco. You shoulda seen it!"

Jesse realized Slim was holding a jar of pickles. "Where did you get the pickles?"

"From their fridge, dude, where else? I was hungry."

4

CHELSEA MILES WAS ACTUALLY BORN PETUNIA TUCKER, the daughter of a flower child named Margaret who believed in free love. Margaret went by "Maggie" because Margaret sounded like a thick, middle-aged woman who wore a full fabric brassiere in the 1950's, and not the bra-less free spirit of the 1970's that she was.

Maggie's daughter, Petunia, also struggled with her given name. I'm sure you can't blame her. No one took her seriously with a name like Petunia. They made fun of her last name, too (you can imagine what kids would do with a name like Tucker), so she changed her name to Chelsea St. Claire. Now, where she came up with that name I haven't a clue. No one cared about her heritage anyway. In fact, her mother, Maggie, abandoned her as a child to experiment with communal living. In Guatemala of all places.

So, Petunia, aka Chelsea, was raised by her grandmother, a devout Christian who despised progress, and specifically the progress of women. Paranoid to a T, grandma was afraid of most everything—burglars, Russians, and atheists, to name a few. The front door had a regulation lock, plus two dead bolts and a safety chain. It took forever to open the door and whenever Petunia came in, she'd hear grandma from the other room: *Make sure the chain's on!* However, grandma loved her granddaughter and did her best to raise young Petunia with the same fear and guilt that had been drummed into her. *Fear God and His judgment!* God bless religion. It makes my job so much easier. Don't get me wrong, I'm tickled with the program. Where would I be without it? Out of a job, that's where.

Petunia was taught that boys were bad, and girls were worse. Grandma's lecture on the Facts of Life was abbreviated. Standing in the kitchen, clutching her bathrobe tightly to her chest, she told Petunia two things: your natural desire to fornicate is wicked, and if you do it, you'll wind up like "that Cookie Soinski." She never did say what'd happened to poor Cookie, but it must've been pretty bad.

Petunia first realized the power of her sex when she caught Mr. Fairbanks (her creepy math teacher who hid worn issues of Playboy under his mattress) looking down her blouse during an algebra test. She was confused, then angry, then determined. She used her Sex Power, first experimenting on that disturbed perv, Mr. Fairbanks, and then on boys her same age.

Petunia's grandmother constantly preached from the Bible (my favorite!), warning Petunia to "keep her candle lit under her bushel." It wasn't a direct quote from the Good Book (grandma had a tendency to ad lib when it suited her), but it was close enough. However, Petunia, the rebel that she was, chose to expose her bushel for all it was worth. All that nonsense about a well-lit bushel just might come in handy.

She formally changed her name from Petunia Tucker to

Chelsea St. Claire on her eighteenth birthday. This reduced grandma's life expectancy by several weekly sermons (How *could you* tarnish our family's good name? Why, we're direct descendants of the Pilgrims!). But Chelsea was an enterprising young woman who used her God-given light, and her bushel, to their maximum benefit.

First it was the shift manager at the Piggly Wiggly. Next was the pudgy, middle-aged dentist who advertised free cleanings. He'd hired her on the spot as a quasi-dental hygienist (even though she knew nothing about molars). She quickly grew bored with root canals, despite the fact that the dentist now thought he was Casanova. He'd promptly enrolled in CrossFit and had even begun to fake bake. What next? A Corvette? But his dull personality, preoccupation with gum disease, and modest bank account didn't stack up. So, Chelsea applied for a job at Global Munitions, a large corporation that supplied the Pentagon with all the ammo it needed to bomb sovereign nations to smithereens.

The CEO of Global Munitions was George Miles, toad-like but enormously wealthy. Indeed, he was one of the richest men in America. This challenge made the seduction of a dentist going through his mid-life crisis seem like child's play. Chelsea had done her homework and knew that Mr. Miles liked the ladies, and preferably ones half his age with well-lit bushels.

She was promoted to personal assistant to the personal assistant of George Miles (billionaires have all kinds of assistants). She eventually became the flight attendant on his Gulfstream IV jet. George, with Chelsea on board, zigged and zagged across the globe promoting the value of good ammo to friends and foes alike. On one trip, in the middle of the night at 40,000 feet, George succumbed to the bushel. His third marriage was crumbling and he needed a soft bosom to cry on. And whaddya know; by the time they touched down in Berlin, Chelsea had snared the Big Amphibian.

Chelsea was now unhappy in her marriage to George. It'd been flattering at first—all the fancy wine and hardly any costume jewelry. But she'd seen the looks on the faces of friends and strangers; looks that showed they'd done the math. She had exchanged her beauty, and comely bushel, for his money. Period. There was nothing particularly romantic about this exchange, but you do it all the time. George liked to believe it was his charm but, come on, he knew better.

And how did George feel about this bargain? He was happy with himself for a few months, or maybe a year, until that nagging complacency began rearing its ugly head (that was me!). There were other mermaids in the sea, beauties who could pull the Range Rover into the garage without scratching it, chew with their mouths closed for God's sake, and sleep without snoring. When Chelsea's sexy lingerie gave way to sensible flannel pajamas? Ugh, he wanted to renege.

So, when George saw the look in Senator Ken Lawson's eye the night of the Re-Election Party, the way he looked at Chelsea a fraction of a second too long, and the way she gazed back at him, he wasn't surprised, or crushed.

And then something deliciously nasty occurred. I won't tell you whether it surprised George, or not.

5

"GEORGE, HELLO, IT'S GOOD TO HEAR FROM YOU. Let me get rid of this call on the other line." A moment later, George Miles' personal lawyer was back on the line. "Sorry about that, George. Long time no hear. How are you, old friend?"

"Ted, I'm not well. I have an emergency matter. It's Chelsea. She's been murdered in our home."

"Oh my God, George. What happened? You say she's been *murdered*? *Chelsea*? My God, I'm so sorry. Are you okay?"

"It's awful."

"I don't know what to say. Do the police know who was responsible?"

"I just came home and found her lying on our bedroom floor. You're the first person I called."

"So you haven't called the police?"

"Not yet. I think she's been dead for some time. It looks like she was struck in the head. I'll call the police, but I wanted to talk to you first."

"Is there any reason to believe you might be a suspect?"

"I don't know, Ted. I was here yesterday afternoon for a few minutes, just long enough to pick up some papers. Maybe ten minutes. I didn't hear anything, so I assumed she wasn't home. Then I left for an overnight business trip to Chicago and just got back."

"That was yesterday?"

"Yes, and it's now, what," he looked at his watch, "two-thirty on Wednesday. I was last here about three-thirty yesterday afternoon."

"And Chelsea wasn't there?"

"I didn't see her. I assumed she wasn't home."

"Call the police immediately. If you have reason to believe you might be a suspect, say nothing. Let me know as soon as you've called them and I'll put you in contact with a criminal defense attorney."

George hung up with his lawyer and called 911. He was thoughtful about his demeanor, hoping to sound frantic, but not overly so, for he knew the recorded call would be replayed again and again for investigators. *I dunno, Sarg. He sounds pretty evasive to me.* George knew he'd be a prime suspect, because the husband always is. He carefully surveyed the scene before the police arrived. It was quiet; deathly so.

He decided to admit that he'd been there the previous afternoon for a few minutes, because a nosey neighbor might have seen him drive up. He had a partial alibi, but it was an ugly one—the high-priced "escort" (he was too sophisticated to gallivant with mere hookers) could only vouch for him from Tuesday night when he'd arrived at his Chicago hotel until Wednesday morning when she'd finally earned the full $3,500. George obviously didn't want to spill the beans about *her*, what with the love of his life having been smacked up the side of her head. And so recently.

George also decided to tell the police that a few pieces of jewelry had been stolen, along with a laptop from his home office. He thought it wise to inject the possibility of a burglar in the house that may have surprised Chelsea in the course of his thievery. There was no way the authorities could challenge him on the jewelry theft. But, to be on the safe side, he made a mental note to file an insurance claim. Those damned insurance companies were all a bunch of crooks anyway, so he felt justified in making the fraudulent claim.

Police cars and ambulance, sirens blasting, descended upon the estate like a swarm of bees. Detectives, lab techs, and photographers buzzed about the house and yard. There were rubber gloves everywhere. Professionals in coveralls were bent over with tweezers collecting all kinds of potentially incriminating evidence which was placed into plastic bags and labeled. The entire house was dusted for prints, even the toilet flusher handle (you never know).

Law enforcement would never admit it, of course, but there's more attention to detail when the victim is the beautiful young wife of a billionaire. There just is. You'd never see this many baggies at the crack house across town when a bottom-rung, tatted-up hooker gets strangled. Personally, I think they ought to just be honest about it. But listen to me, the devil, lecturing them on honesty.

The scene was grisly. Chelsea lay at the foot of the bed, face down, in a pool of waxy blood that covered a square yard of the cream-colored plush carpet. George had the passing thought that he'd recently spent $84 per yard for the carpet. Thank God they couldn't read his mind, he thought, because, really, how cold is *that*? The congealed blood was dark brown, too dark to look like blood. She hadn't been moved, or even covered by a sheet. Her arm was extended and her palm was twisted up. No one thought to inspect it, but her palm's life line was all wrong (any palm reader worth her salt would've predicted that Chelsea would live to see eighty). There was nothing wrong with her body, indeed it was a fabulous one, except that it was pale—pallor mortis having begun immediately upon death. And it was cold—algor mortis having gradually reduced her body heat to room temperature. Oh, and a piece of her skull was missing. But for these details, you might have thought she was merely sleeping.

The wall next to the bed was splattered with blood, like someone had dunked a paint brush into a Sherwin-Williams bucket of Cherries Jubilee, then treated it like an ordinary fly swatter, flicking the paint against the wall with each swat at an elusive fly. Because the random design of blood spatter happened to be on the wall of a billionaire, it might have passed for a Jackson Pollock, were it not so awful.

A shovel was found propped up against the brick wall just outside the rear door of the house. The shovel's blade was covered with blood and human tissue. So, naturally, the investigators assumed this had been the murder weapon.

The blood spatter expert determined that Chelsea had been standing a foot beyond the end of the king-size bed. She'd been facing her attacker who'd come in from the bedroom door. The attacker had been standing about four feet from Chelsea and had swung the shovel from his right, counter-clockwise, like a right-handed clean-up hitter. The blow had twisted Chelsea to her right, clockwise, and spun her to the floor, grazing the right side of her face on the end of the bed. She landed face down.

Notwithstanding the ugliness, there was good cheer and camaraderie between the investigators (they weren't cracking Knock Knock jokes, but they weren't kneeling over the toilet either). They'd seen worse than this before. One lab tech was complaining about the pass interference penalty in the Eagles recent loss, then casually said, "Hey, Stan, toss me another baggie, would ya? Looks like we've got a little more brain matter over here that I need to scoop up."

The investigators found a basement window had been cracked open, no more than half an inch, and footprints in the flower garden just outside the window. George overheard them say this was the likely point of entry for the intruder. He was confused. A basement window had been found cracked open? Maybe there really *had* been an intruder. And how lucky was *that*? After all, it was quite unlikely that George would have crawled through a basement window to murder his comely wife. Unless he'd been trying to throw them off.

After hundreds of photos were taken, from every conceivable angle, Chelsea's body was zipped up in a black body bag and taken by ambulance to the coroner's office for further study. The neighbors watched as the emergency vehicles drove away without lights and sirens, then gossiped about it.

The Medical Examiner's report revealed nothing new. Chelsea was dead alright; the cause being blunt trauma to the left side of her head, consistent with a single blow from the blade of a shovel swung with diabolical force. There were no other wounds, including defensive wounds, nor was there any skin under her manicured fingernails which might have suggested a struggle. There was something else, too: Petunia Tucker, aka Chelsea Miles, was pregnant.

Pinpointing the time of death is usually unnecessary, but sometimes it's critical. This was one of those critical times. The Medical Examiner's analysis began with the temperature of Chelsea's corpse. Once you die, your bodies cool about one degree per hour until you reach the temperature of your surroundings. By the time she was found, Chelsea was room temp. If she was like most women, she liked it warmer than that. They assumed her body temperature had been 98.6 degrees when her attacker entered the room. So, given the room-temperature of her corpse, they knew she'd been dead a minimum of seventeen hours, and probably more like twenty-four.

The front torso of her body looked like a full-frontal body bruise. It was dark purple, almost black. This wasn't caused by trauma, but rather the collection of several quarts of blood. Gravity drains the blood to the lowest part of the body once the heart stops pumping. The pooled blood causes permanent discoloration at about the ten-hour mark. Therefore, they knew she'd been dead for at least ten hours.

Chelsea's stomach contents didn't help pin down the time of her death either. All digestion stops in its tracks upon death. A ham sandwich will still be a chewed ham sandwich. If the medical examiner knew when she'd last eaten, he could figure out how long she'd been dead. However, he didn't know when she'd last eaten, and he couldn't ask her, so this was no help.

There were no insects roaming around her body either. Scientists can usually tell how long you've been dead by the size and type of insects feasting on your corpse. Different insects all take their turns, but at very specific times during the decomposition stages. Blowflies get there first (the greedy little bastards), usually within a few hours. Females lay their eggs on the body, especially around the natural orifices. The egg-stage lasts about a day, and once they hatch, the larva grows at a predictable rate. The insects are then measured by millimeter to determine how long they've been there feasting. Other insects come later, in stages, until the body dries up. Chelsea hadn't been dead long enough for the insect kingdom to congregate.

The best the Medical Examiner could come up with was that Chelsea Miles had been murdered at approximately three o'clock on Tuesday afternoon; give or take an hour or two.

6

GEORGE CALLED HIS LAWYER AGAIN to report on the investigation and to shed something else, another burden from his conscience.

"I called the police after we spoke. They were here at the house for hours. My God, they turned the place upside down."

"What did you tell them?"

"I told them I came home Tuesday afternoon about 3:30 to pick up some papers and left within ten minutes."

"And?"

"They asked me if I'd seen Chelsea and I told them I hadn't. They asked me what I did when I discovered her body the next day—if I'd called anyone or disturbed the scene in anyway."

"Did you tell them you'd spoken to me?"

"Yes, I knew they'd access my phone records, so I told them I called you first because you were a friend and good counsel to me."

"Anything else?"

"Yes, I told them some expensive jewelry and a laptop had been stolen."

"Is that true?"

"It may have been."

The lawyer decided to leave that alone. He didn't want to hear a confession, or evidence of obstruction of justice. "Did you give a formal statement?"

"No, I just answered their questions; like when I'd last seen her, the general state of my marriage, and so forth."

"I understand they're focusing on your gardener—the Hispanic, at least that's what's being reported. He hit her with a shovel? My God, George, it's horrible."

"That's my understanding, too. He was at the house all day Tuesday, and I assume his fingerprints will be all over the shovel."

"Is he here legally?"

"I'm afraid not."

"How did you pay him?"

"Cash."

"Did you know he was illegal when you hired him?"

"Yes, and I'm sure the press will punish me for it. I've supported candidates who want to secure our borders. What's wrong with that? I was only trying to help one of them, but you watch—they'll call me a racist. But you know I'm no bigot, Ted; it's just that there's so goddamned many of them streaming across the border. Good God, Ted, you know exactly what I'm talking about." This compassion was rich, because George *was* a racist; I'd seen it for years.

"How well did you know this Mexican?"

"Not well."

"Can you possibly imagine why he'd do this?"

"I've had a few suspicions about him, but I can't prove it."

"Based on what?"

"A few months ago I was supposed to have been out of town on business, but I came home early. It was late in the day, almost dark, and he was still here. They were out by the pool—Chelsea and he. They both acted flustered as if they were hiding something, like they'd been having an affair."

"You can't be serious. You honestly think Chelsea was having an affair with the Mexican landscaper?"

"I thought that was a possibility, yes."

"Then why didn't you fire him?"

"I told Chelsea about my suspicions and she laughed them off. When I threatened to have him fired, she accused me of being overly paranoid. Now I wish I had."

"But even if they were having a fling, why would he kill her?"

"I have no idea."

George poured a scotch on the rocks with his ear cocked to the phone (it was only nine o'clock in the morning, but these were trying times). The lawyer said, "I assumed it was a burglary situation. Chelsea stumbles onto a thief and he kills her. That was the implication from the initial reports."

"Maybe, but there's something else," George said. He hesitated, breathing into the phone. He swirled his drink and the ice clinked in the Waterford tumbler. "There was evidence of semen at the scene."

"Excuse me?"

"Yes, it appears my beloved wife was having sex in our bedroom before she was murdered."

"I'm sorry. I—"

"It was pathetic, Ted, to be surrounded by all those investigators discussing semen when they knew damned well it couldn't have been mine. I'd been out of town, remember? So, they whispered this juicy tidbit to spare the old man of his humiliation, knowing his beautiful wife, half his age, was having sex in their bedroom with someone else."

"I'm sorry, George. I don't know what to say."

"It's been awful." George believed his public humiliation was nearly on par with his wife's brutal murder. It was perfect.

"Have they tied the semen to the Mexican?"

"They'll try. But, Ted, I'm afraid the purpose of my call is to burden you with another secret."

"George, I am not a criminal defense attorney. If this disclosure you are about to make is related to the crime, you should discuss it with a criminal attorney."

"We go back a long way, Ted. I know this isn't your area of expertise, but I trust your judgment. And you are my lawyer, so I know you'll honor our attorney-client privilege."

"Of course I will, but—"

"I told the police I returned home at three-thirty to pick up some papers, and that I didn't think Chelsea was home. That is not true. Chelsea was home and she was very much alive."

"George, this information—"

"I walked into our bedroom and Chelsea was lying in bed, naked. The bed was a mess. Her bra and panties were on the floor."

"George, I urge you to contact a criminal attorney who can advise you—"

"I demanded to know who she'd been with, and do you know what she told me? She said—and I will quote her verbatim—she said 'it's none of your fucking business.' That's exactly what she said."

George's attorney was in an awkward spot. He would keep a dirty secret lest he be disbarred, but he feared his friend was about to confess something that he shouldn't.

"Chelsea stood up from the bed and reached for her panties. I expected her to be sorry, to be embarrassed, you know? But she wasn't. In fact, she ordered me to leave. Can you believe that? She ordered me to leave my own goddamned house! We argued and it was heated, as you can imagine. She told me, and I will quote her again, that she, quote 'would fuck whoever she wanted,' then she put on some flimsy teddy and lay back down on the bed."

"What did you—"

"I told her she was a two-bit whore and I left. I'd been in the house no more than ten minutes."

"I'm very sorry." Thankfully George hadn't confessed to bludgeoning poor Chelsea with the shovel.

"She wouldn't tell me who the guy was, but I have my suspicions."

"You think it was the landscaper?"

"No. I believe she'd been with a friend of mine. I believe she'd been with Senator Ken Lawson."

Silence on the lawyer's end of the line. Swirls of ice in the glass on George's end.

"After I left the house," George continued, "I drove straight to the hangar and flew to Chicago for a meeting. I spent the night and returned Wednesday afternoon when I found her body. That's when I called you."

"And you told none of this to the police?"

"Only that I'd come home to grab some papers and left after ten minutes, which is the truth. But, no, I didn't tell them we'd had a confrontation. As I said before, I told them I hadn't seen her and didn't think she was home."

The lawyer sat at his desk on the other end of town, resting his hand on top of his bald head. "Did you call Chelsea from Chicago?"

"I called her Tuesday night to tell her I wanted a divorce and didn't want to see her when I got home. But she didn't answer her cell and I didn't leave a message."

"There will be a record of the call."

"I suppose so."

"Why do you believe she'd been with Senator Lawson?"

"Call it a strong hunch. I know Lawson, and I knew my wife. I overheard a private conversation at a political function a few weeks ago. She told him something to the effect that 'Tuesday afternoon was amazing. Tuesdays are usually good for me.' Something along those lines."

"Have you discussed any of this with Senator Lawson?"

"No, and I don't want their relationship exposed, unless it becomes absolutely necessary. I'll deal with Lawson in my own way. And, Ted, you don't need to worry that he's under the threat of imminent harm. Quite to the contrary. He can help me now more than he could if he was dead, or in prison. He is about to become my most reliable seat in the Senate."

"George, I urge you to—"

"There's one more thing."

Ted didn't want to hear it.

"Chelsea," George said, "was pregnant."

"My God, George. I am so sorry."

"Don't be. I doubt the child was mine."

"How can you—"

"I can count on one hand the number of times we had sex in the last six months."

"How far along was she?"

"They say about four weeks."

George didn't care that Chelsea was dead, and especially now that he knew what a disloyal slut she'd been. He didn't think the baby was his anyway, although he knew it was possible. He might have remained married to her, going through the motions with steady monotony. However, as he reflected on the course of events, his position was now better than it'd been a week earlier—as long as he could escape a conviction. He now had marital freedom to spoil a new starlet who didn't snore in her flannel pajamas. He'd have a poker chip in the Senate, too, one he could play over and over again as long as his loyal friend, Senator Kenneth Lawson, held one of its coveted seats. George would force Lawson to become a passionate champion of military arsenals, and Global Munitions specifically.

7

JESSE AND SLIM SAT IN AUNT ELOISE'S messy living room two days later. The entire troop was there: Uncle Wayne, the kids that needed diaper changing, and the oddball who was lying on the floor untying Slim's shoes. Slim was distracted by a bowl of Sugar Smacks on his lap. The television was on, as it always was, and the local news was broadcasting tired stories of man's failures. No one was paying much attention to it.

"Ho-lee shit!" Slim yelled and pointed his spoon at the television.

"Ho-lee shit!" Jesse yelled and pointed to the television.

"Ho-lee shit!" They both yelled again, pointing. "Turn it up!" they said, directing their command to no one in particular.

They sat, speechless, watching the local reporter who stood in front of the Miles mansion, his hand pressed to his ear, a few feet in front of yellow police tape that cordoned off the property.

"*Chelsea Miles, the wife of billionaire George Miles, was found dead late yesterday in her home, the result of a brutal bludgeoning. She was discovered by her husband at approximately 5:00 pm yesterday evening. Authorities say she was murdered Tuesday afternoon at her home.*

"Friends and family have expressed shock at the news of the apparent homicide. An investigation is underway and detectives are releasing details of the murder as they are discovered. There are no official suspects according to Detective Robert Flygare of the Philadelphia Police Department, but the Miles landscape worker, Javier Flores, is a person of interest in the investigation."

"Ho-lee shit!" Jesse and Slim repeated, seemingly at a loss for any other response, comment, or thought.

"Senator Kenneth Lawson, a close personal friend of the family, has issued a statement expressing outrage at the brutal nature of this cowardly act and support for the family, pledging to commit whatever resources are necessary from the federal government to apprehend the perpetrator of this horrible crime."

"You think anybody seen us?" Slim whispered in Jesse's direction, without taking his eyes off the TV.

"No way, dude," Jesse whispered back out of the side of his mouth, for he couldn't take his eyes off the screen, either. "They'd be over us like flies on shit if they knew we were there."

"What're you guys whisperin' about?" It was Uncle Wayne who was passing through the room carrying a plunger. He wore his stained tee shirt and a pair of stretched-out underpants.

"Uh, it's nuthin'," said Slim. "We were just talkin' about work and stuff."

"Well, if you ain't doing nuthin' but sittin' there wastin' time, maybe you could give me a hand."

Jesse and Slim would have rather been arrested and tried for the cold-blooded murder of Chelsea Miles than follow Uncle Wayne into the bathroom with that plunger.

As Uncle Wayne left, he lifted the plunger over his shoulder and used it to scratch his back. Slim leaned closer to Jesse and whispered, "That yard guy we seen musta killed her right after we left. Holy shit, dude. We should go to the cops." Slim was processing this dilemma, but without the heady composure of Sherlock Holmes.

"Are you crazy!" Jesse said too loudly, and then looked around to be sure no one paid attention to what he'd said. "What would we tell 'em? That we were in there stealing drugs and shit and saw the missus gettin' laid? Are you fuckin' crazy? They'd blame *us* for killin' her. So don't be a stupid—we gotta think this through."

"Who was that guy anyways?" Slim asked.

"You mean the dude who was just on TV? I've heard of him. He's like somebody famous I think."

Just then, the television screen cut to video of Senator Lawson speaking to detectives at the scene.

"Ho-lee shit! That's him! That's the dude! He's a senator or something big. Ho-lee shit!"

In that very moment, I planted the careless seed of a plan that was already beginning to take root in Jesse's fried brain. The plan would need some refinement, to be sure, but it was devilish and had promise.

Javier Flores, the landscaper, spoke limited English, and Chelsea had no interest in learning Spanish (maybe French, but not Spanish). He thought she was pretty, and later admitted to spying on her while she lounged beside the backyard pool (hiding behind his trimming shears, drooling over the senorita, snipping one hydrangea leaf at a time). That's all he would admit to.

Javier had been born five hundred yards south of the border. If he'd squeezed out from the tight confines of his mother's womb just five hundred *and one* yards north, as the crow flies, his life would have been easier. However, as fate would have it, he was born to a life of poverty (it's not really fate—things don't just *happen*).

Javier had been illegally crossing the border for years. He'd find employment in el Norte as a laborer, but voluntarily return to Mexico long enough to get his wife pregnant (five times so far). He'd been returned by the INS, too, most recently for the theft of a lawnmower (he was innocent but, really, what did it matter; he was an illegal Mexican). Javier happened to be in Philadelphia because his cousin promised him work on a construction project there, but was left to fend for himself when his cousin was deported. He'd find temporary work, brandishing citizenship papers that were obviously fake. The employers would study the phony ID and then offer him work at thirty-five percent less than if the papers had been authentic.

Javier wasn't guilty of sloth, that Deadly Sin of leisure. He took second and third jobs, working eighty hours per week. He wasn't guilty of greed either (another favorite Deadly). He worked because he had to, living in a second story apartment with six other illegal laborers. He bought a used truck and landscaping tools and worked for the upper crust at low wages, sending whatever he could spare back to his family in Mexico. George Miles had hired him a year earlier, paying Javier in cash—a transaction that favored both of them, but did nothing for the national treasury.

He told investigators he'd been trimming the privet hedge

along the perimeter of the estate on the day Chelsea was murdered. He'd begun the day at eight o'clock and left about four-thirty. He didn't recall seeing any visitors at the house that day, except Mr. Miles who'd come home briefly that afternoon. Javier allowed that there may have been others, but he'd been preoccupied with the hedges and wasn't paying much attention to the house.

Detectives focused on Javier because the murder weapon appeared to be the shovel, the one found just outside the door of the house. Presumably the murderer had used that door to enter and leave the house (but, alas, there was the window in the basement, too). Chelsea's lovely blood and tissue were on the shovel, and so were Javier's fingerprints. However, Javier adamantly denied ever going into the house that day (or any day), and there was no evidence to contradict him. He told the detectives he'd used the shovel earlier that day and left it propped up just outside the door. He then trimmed the hedges on the other side of the property.

The detectives knew Javier had both the motive and opportunity to commit the crime. He was desperately poor, and might have sneaked in to steal something when Chelsea surprised him. Maybe, in a moment of fear, he'd instinctively swung the shovel at her. Therefore, he would remain a suspect, but the detectives weren't persuaded he was their man. At least not yet.

8

IT WAS A CHALLENGE FOR SENATOR LAWSON to pander to the media under these trying circumstances. There he was, feigning outrage at the murder of his dear friend's wife, standing smack dab in front of the home where he'd been banging her just the day before. He was in front of the cameras, unscripted, and nervous as hell. But the Senator was good in front of any lens, so he furrowed his brow and pledged to sock it to the monster who'd committed this appalling crime.

Susan was waiting for Ken when, two gin and tonics later, he finally came home. His enthusiasm to deal with her was negligible.

"I heard." Susan stood in the master bedroom. Her hair was pulled back, yanked into place by a clip on the back of her head. Cold cream was smeared on her face.

"It's devastating," Ken said. "George is beside himself."

"And you?" she asked.

"What's that supposed to mean?"

"What do you think it's supposed to mean?"

"Susan," he frowned. "I'm not in the mood to play games with you. Not tonight."

"Are you sad for your sugar daddy's loss of his, what, fifth wife? Or are you just sad that she won't be around to stroke your insatiable ego?"

"You've said a lot of insensitive things to me, Susan," he said with practiced wounded pride. "But that is obscene, even for you."

"No, Ken, what is obscene is the way you've run to the front lines with cameras flashing to capitalize on this tragedy, claiming you give a shit about poor George. But I wouldn't worry too much about him, Ken. He'll buy another one soon enough."

"You're a cold bitch, Susan."

"Then it must gall you to know that this cold bitch has paid dearly to have earned the right to disrespect you as much as I do."

Senator Lawson called a meeting of his staff early the next morning. He wanted to strategize how Javier Flores, the landscape worker, might provide an opportunity to rail, yet again, on rampant illegal immigration. This blatant politicizing of Chelsea Miles's murder was upsetting to his staff, but as their boss's political fortunes went, so went theirs. So, they soldiered on, doing the peoples work, pretending to respect the Self-Righteous Lion of the Senate.

Staffer Paul McDonald said: "Let's issue a press release suggesting violent crime is directly tied to illegal immigration. We can probably find some statistics somewhere." McDonald was Lawson's most outspoken and bigoted aide. In addition to his committed homophobia, he was opposed to all things foreign, especially foreigners. He was unaware of a link between immigration and violent crime, but the choir he preached to didn't care. Their heads were buried so deep in the sand that they rarely came up for air, which led to malnourished thinking. This, of course, suit me fine.

"But we don't even know if this Flores guy was the killer?" said staffer Ann Lee.

"He must be," said McDonald. "Otherwise the cops wouldn't have identified him in the first place." McDonald was a big "where there's smoke" guy.

"I agree with Paul," said Senator Lawson. "The Mexican probably did it. But let's stress our commitment to the judicial process—that all men are innocent until proven guilty. But let's also work in something about how law enforcement costs are high because of these Illegals, even if it turns out this Gonzales or Hernandez amigo didn't do it."

Personally, I prefer this kind of thinking, but your enlightened citizenry might shudder to know who is actually running the Land of the Free and the Home of the Brave.

"I'll prepare something for your review, Senator," said McDonald.

"I'd like to see it before it's released," Ann said, mindful of her political future as someone to be taken seriously.

After the meeting broke up, the Senator began calling people who might know the status of the investigation. What had they learned? Was there any breeze blowing his way? If so, he would immediately volunteer to the police that he'd seen Chelsea the afternoon she was murdered. It would be criminal suicide not to. However, if there was no evidence to implicate him (and he was fairly certain there wasn't), volunteering anything now would do him in, politically and otherwise.

The investigation focused on Javier Flores. However, Flores's statement that he'd seen Señor Miles come home that afternoon was potentially disastrous. Lawson's sources reported that George said he'd come home to pick up some papers that afternoon and immediately left town (to ink the deal on a large cache of explosives with a conglomerate of arms dealers, all of whom were earnestly committed to the Second Amendment). What had George seen in those few minutes when he'd come back to the house? What did he know? He thought about calling George, but decided to keep his mouth shut until he knew more.

Senator Lawson also learned from his sources that George claimed some jewelry had been stolen. The investigators had discovered a partially opened basement window and some footprints in the flower bed just outside the window. The burglars (there were two sets of footprints in the dirt), must've gained access through that window, because there was no sign of forced entry.

Lawson had racked his brain for two days now. What evidence had he left behind? He knew this would be no run-of-the-mill murder investigation—not when the victim was the wife of a billionaire arms dealer with political ties. Could they identify his semen, a stray hair, or a fingerprint? Or how about something he'd absentmindedly left behind, like an official United States Senate business card, a cuff link, or a dirty sock?

A misstep here might land him on death row. He was scared, anxious, and confused. However, one emotion he did *not* feel was sadness for the lost life of Petunia Tucker, aka Chelsea St. Claire Miles. The sex had been good, but he had his own crosses to bear.

Senator Lawson's fundamental problem was the challenge to

act wisely when he could rely on no one but himself. This was unchartered territory for the charismatic but shallow thinker. He was helplessly on his own. And, with all due respect to the Self-Righteous Lion of the Senate, he was no match for me.

9

JESSE WOKE EARLY THE NEXT DAY. He couldn't sleep because his mind was racing (this was rare, for his infertile mind lacked imagination and sleep was rarely uninterrupted by thoughtful analysis). He was determined to formulate a foolproof plan that would make him rich.

He left the bedroom that he shared with Slim, and walked to the kitchen. He was startled to see one of the small children dressed only in a two-pound diaper sitting on the kitchen counter with his feet in the sink. The little boy had dragged a chair over and used it to climb onto the counter. He was turning the water faucet on and off, a simple activity that appeared to give him joy. The child's mother was still sleeping, and his father was still working on his issues in the quiet comfort of his own apartment across town.

Jesse felt sorry for this boy whose name he didn't know. For all he knew, the poor kid didn't even have a name. It appeared he just went by "Hey!" and "Knock it off!" Me, I felt nothing.

He stepped onto the linoleum floor with his bare feet. It was sticky, like someone had spilled orange juice and hadn't bothered to wipe it up. The child looked him over and returned to his preoccupation with the faucet. Jesse found nothing in the refrigerator except a few wilted carrots, one leftover hot dog in a bag, and some AAA batteries that were there for no apparent reason. It was tough keeping food in the house with Slim around.

Jesse found a piece of white lined paper, the kind you find in a three-ring school binder. He tested three different pens from a chipped ceramic coffee mug by the phone before finding one that worked, and then sat on the plaid sofa that faced the kitchen. Like any good plan, it was wise to write it down, lest a critical component be overlooked. He wrote a sentence and crossed it out. This needed to be just right. Jesse, never a wordsmith (that ugly, coffee-breathed Mrs. Harrow had given him a D+ in English), labored over the phraseology until it set the perfect tone, one that would inspire his reader to action!

Slim walked in. His hair was sticking straight up so that his head look like a whiskered dandelion. He wore only boxer shorts, the chronic morning exuberance of his loin still evident. He didn't seem embarrassed by this feature. Jesse, however, was plainly troubled to look in his direction.

"What are you doin' up so early?" Slim yawned and scratched his head.

"Just thinking about what we should do. About the murder and all."

Slim saw the boy at the sink and put his finger to his lips. "*Shhhh!* You want the whole world to hear?" he whispered at a higher volume than normal speech. "Shit dude, this place could be crawlin' with bugs! Haven't you seen any of them shows?" He poured Cheerios into a bowl, and then walked over to the sink and interrupted the boy's fun just long enough to run cold tap water over his cereal. He then sat on the sofa next to Jesse and began eating.

"So, what's up?" Slim asked.

This was a terribly awkward conversation for Jesse, sitting next to his partner in crime who wore only a pair of tattered boxer shorts, eating a bowl of Cheerios soaking in water. In addition to all of that, there was the nameless child with a wet diaper sitting on the kitchen counter with his feet in the sink. Nevertheless, it was under these unusual circumstances that Jesse proposed his plan for everlasting prosperity.

"Okay, here's what I'm thinking." Jesse proceeded to lay out the details of a plan that was simple, but sketchy. He grabbed a clean piece of paper and, using his best penmanship, wrote:

This is BLACKMAIL. We saw what you did to the Miles lady. We here with are going to DEMAND $10,000 or we will go straight to the police. Just THINK about it. We will be in touch in a few days. We'll probably call you.

He handed the note to Slim who read it carefully, making sure there was nothing they'd missed. "Maybe we should hold out for, like, twenty grand instead."

"Yeah, I was thinking the same thing," said Jesse. "But if you ask for too much the FBI gets all involved. I'm not worried about the local cops, but the FBI is a lot smarter. Besides, ten grand for doing nothing? We wouldn't have to work for a long time." One hoped that a good public education might have produced a higher standard of behavior, or at least a shrewder capitalist.

"Yeah, okay. Good thinkin' on that. I guess we split it even, huh?"

"Well," said Jesse, "I saw them first, and I'm doing all the work so I get seven and you get three."

"No way, dude. I saw them longer than you did."

"Okay. I get six then."

"I guess I can live with that, especially if that means I get four." Slim wanted to be crystal clear on the terms, because he knew this criminal enterprise was fraught with peril.

"Seems you're getting four grand," Jesse said, "you need to figure out how to get his address."

"Yeah, I'll mail it today."

"Then we wait a few days and send him another letter after he's had a chance to think it over."

Before they stood, their business now completed, Slim treated Jesse to a large burp—a robust celebratory toast to put a seal on everything that'd been said. The recycled smell of Cheerios hung in the air.

10

SLIM SLID THE LETTER INTO THE ENVELOPE and walked it to the mailbox a block from Aunt Eloise's house. It arrived on Capitol Hill, along with thousands of other letters from angry citizens. From there it was scanned for suspicious bombs or powders and then on to Senator Lawson's office in the Dirksen Senate Office Building.

It may have surprised Jesse and Slim to know that Senator Lawson didn't read these letters. Pimple-faced interns skimmed them, pasting the kookiest ones on the fridge in the breakroom. But, alas, for some strange reason (Ha!), Jesse's letter made its way directly to Senator Lawson's desk, unopened. No one was more pleased by that happy fluke than Lawson himself, because if anyone else had opened it, the senator would've had an awful lot of explaining to do.

Senator Lawson opened the letter and read. *What the—!* He read it again. *There'd been no one in the house that day!* He'd parked his silver Mercedes down the street. Had someone seen him go in, or out? No, he was sure of it. So, who *were* these people? The letter said "we," so there was more than one. *How had they seen him? And, oh my God, what had they seen?*

He read the note at least ten more times. No, this was *not* good. There must've been something more to the threat, some sort of trick, because they'd only demanded $10,000. Was this a joke? If so, these jokesters had information that would crucify him.

Lawson was not so dense to know that withholding evidence was a crime—a felony no less. Even a numbskull would know Lawson's testimony would be important. "Who, *me*? You wanted *my* statement? Really? Humph. All I did was screw her brains out before she took a spade to the noggin. Sure, my hair and semen are probably all over the place, but I doubt there's any on the shovel."

He put the letter back into the envelope and stared at it. His mind raced but wasn't going anywhere. He put it in the bottom drawer of his desk and locked it. His hands were shaking. Lawson rarely drank during the day (unless you considered lunch, or anything after 4:00 pm as "the day"). He needed something to calm his nerves, but he was scheduled to attend a committee meeting at the Capitol. The chairman of the committee was a pompous liberal Democrat (he wouldn't have been so pompous if he'd been a Republican) who was Ivy League and looked down his self-righteous nose at those with a mere *public* education. He even wore a bow tie, and only an insufferable liberal would do that.

Senator Lawson decided to make an appearance at the meeting and then feign a contagious illness. He grabbed his briefcase and slipped out of the office, taking the elevator to the basement floor where an underground tunnel connected the Senate Office Building to the Capitol. Most of the senators were driven back and forth in the tunnel on golf carts by caddies who wore suits and ties (*I gave Ted Kennedy a ride today! Swear it.*). This time,

Lawson walked because he needed time to think, and he did that best on his feet.

When he arrived at the committee meeting, he told his fellow colleagues he'd been fighting a stomach bug (it was churning, after all).

"You should go home."

"Yes, Senator, you must get your rest." These were treacherous Democrats who didn't want to catch anything because of the abysmal state of health care in America, and they didn't want Lawson there anyway.

"Thank you, Senators, but it is important that I participate."

"No, really, we insist. We'll have our staffs send you the minutes," they said, subtly stepping back from him and wiping their hands on their pant legs.

"Are you sure?" Lawson said, then winced and clutched his stomach for affect.

"Yes, we're sure, Senator. We need you to regain your strength."

"Thank you." He coughed again for good measure, as if the bug had suddenly spread to his lungs. "You may be right," he said as he left; clutching, coughing (and now even limping), until he was out of sight. He drove to an exclusive bar in Georgetown, where the indulged had been making back-room deals for decades on the taxpayer's dime. He was shown to a private table. Midway through his second vodka tonic he decided he had to bring someone else in on his dilemma, to help him think. His greatest fear (among many great fears) was that his blackmailers would send another letter that *would* be opened by his staff. He couldn't let that happen.

The only choice was Paul McDonald, his bulldog legislative aide. McDonald was shrewd and marginally principled. He had talent for not letting moral imperative clutter his thinking, and I loved him for it. Yes, Paul could be trusted. His office was also next to the mailroom, so he could comb through the mail the moment it arrived.

He called McDonald on his cell, who agreed to meet him at the bar. Ken was on his third drink by the time he arrived. Paul took off his coat and sat at the table across from Ken.

"Paul, I trust you more than anyone else on my staff. I hope you know that."

"Thank you for that confidence, Senator. We need men like you in these times of moral uncertainty."

"There's something I'm going to share with you that is very personal, that is extraordinarily private. It cannot be divulged to anyone."

"I understand."

"I'll just get right to it. I had an inappropriate relationship with another woman."

"I see." Paul didn't consider this to be newsworthy—not with Lawson.

"This was a one-time thing, and I regret it."

"Uh-huh."

"It was a physical relationship."

"I see."

"And it was inappropriate."

"Uh-huh."

"And I deeply regret it."

"Uh-huh."

"And it won't happen again."

"Okay."

"Unfortunately," Ken said as he stared down at his drink,

"this relationship has become more complicated than a simple misjudgment on my part."

"Uh-huh."

"It involves the wife of an influential donor."

"Oh."

Ken took another sip as McDonald waited for the rest of the story. He assumed there was more, because the good Senator wouldn't have bought him a drink to disclose a simple roll in the hay. That was a routine occurrence—the worst kept secret in Washington.

"So, whew," Ken said and ran both hands through his hair. "The woman . . . it was Chelsea Miles." There, he'd said it.

"*Chelsea Miles*?"

"I'm afraid so."

"When did this . . . event . . . take place?"

"Paul, it was the day she was murdered."

McDonald sat across from the Senator, speechless. Horrified. "Are you . . . *serious*?"

"Yes, Paul, I may be in legal jeopardy." The obvious was still an art with Ken.

"Did . . . were you . . . involved in the, the . . . I mean were you . . .?"

"No, Paul, I didn't kill her if that's what you're asking." He said this with enough practiced conviction to temporarily sooth McDonald's panic.

"Have you told the authorities?"

"No, Paul, I have not. You're the only person who knows of this. And it must stay that way, for obvious reasons."

They both looked down at their drinks. McDonald shifted in his chair, loosened his tie and unfastened the top button of his shirt. He was a devout Christian and the Senator's mangy affair was an ugly sin. But Senator Lawson was a committed Christian, too—fighting the liberals who wanted to take God out of schools, and even out of *Christmas!* The liberals, if left unchecked, would turn America into a modern-day Sodom and Gomorrah, because evil prevails when good men do nothing. Therefore, McDonald had pity for Lawson. He'd been a victim, yes, that's what he was—a victim who'd made a terrible mistake. But his political enemies would pounce, blowing this unfortunate one-time indiscretion completely out of proportion for their own nefarious purposes.

"I understand, Senator. What can I do to help?"

"Thank you, Paul. I've always known I could count on you. But, I'm afraid it has become more complicated."

"I see."

"I've received an anonymous letter."

"You have?"

"It was written by someone who knows I was with Chelsea the afternoon she was murdered."

McDonald looked down at his drink. This was not happening.

"Paul, I need to find out who these people are, and exactly what they saw. If I go to the authorities, I'll be ruined. We all will. We've got to find these shameless monsters."

McDonald put his head down in something of a nod, but it remained there, staring at his drink, but not really seeing it.

"Do you see why I need your help?"

"I'm not sure what you want me to do, Senator."

Lawson didn't know either. "You know, there's the illegal Mexican with the criminal record. Felony theft I believe."

"Okay."

"Is there anything we can do with him?"

"Like what?" asked McDonald.

"I don't know, but let's think along those lines."

"What lines?"

"Maybe indirectly help the authorities make their case."

"Uh, I'm not sure how we'd do that." McDonald didn't like where this was going.

"Let's just keep thinking. In the meantime, the blackmailers said they'd be sending me another letter."

"Oh."

"They're smart and they mean business."

"Sounds like it."

"They're probably connected to our political enemies somehow."

"Yeah, you're probably right."

"They've demanded money."

"How much do they want?"

"Ten thousand."

This confused McDonald. "Ten thousand? As in ten thousand dollars? That's it?"

"Yes, and that has me worried. These are sophisticated people, Paul. They followed me and got inside somehow. No one has any information about them, not even the police. We're dealing with a well-connected group who is determined to bring us down, and all that we stand for. It's obviously not about the money. Surely they have other, larger, designs."

"I agree it couldn't be about the money," McDonald said. "They would have demanded a hundred times that much, or more."

"Let's go back to the office and I'll show you the letter. They'll probably contact me again the same way. I need you to stay by the mailroom and go through it the moment it arrives until we get another message from them. Then we can decide how to respond."

"Okay."

"Thanks, Paul. We're in this thing together and I appreciate your loyalty."

Now they were in this thing together? They were? McDonald threw back the rest of his drink.

11

THE TRADE WINDS CAUGHT THE UNHAPPY NEWS that Chelsea, aka Petunia, had died and blew it all the way to Guatemala where Maggie, Chelsea's mother, had settled. Maggie lived in a commune where everyone she slept with, or canned beets with, shared what they had with each other. These aging hippies had limited cunning, and even less ambition. They actually boasted about having lost sight of the Jones'. They pretended this was based on high-minded principle, but I happen to know it was just petty sloth.

Maggie had grown weary of sharing pickled cucumbers with other sagging socialists. When she heard the terrible news about her daughter (and that she'd been married to a billionaire), she scrounged the airfare, promising to return at the end of her grieving. She bummed a ride in the bed of a marijuana grower's pick-up to the airport, and caught a flight to Philadelphia. Maggie convinced herself that communal living had never been her cup of tea anyway. She was tired of old hippies playing the guitar all day, pretending to be Bob Dylan.

And, seriously, how many corporate conspiracies could there actually be?

She dreamed that from that day forward the only potatoes she'd eat would be au gratin style, or an ingredient in the world's finest vodkas. She'd sold out to the American dream (and so quickly!) with hardly a nudge from me. But Maggie would soon discover that George Miles would've made a terrible socialist. The ironclad pre-nup he'd insisted on was proof of that.

Maggie was short and pleasantly overweight. Her generation eschewed bras as a symbol of female subjugation, so her large twin ottomans hung loose for years without the burden of fabric hoists. And it showed—her pendulous breasts swayed nearly to her navel. Maybe she'd get a reduction and have some other work done now that she was going to be rich. Oh, the things she would do! Fillers, lipo, quick lifts, and more! Things that would have been anathema to her just a week earlier.

Maggie's black hair was long and straight, with straggly gray tresses that made her look like a long-haired skunk. Her skin had been exposed to the equatorial sun for so long that it looked like wrinkled hide. She occasionally shaved her legs and arm pits, but was a slacker in the grooming department. Besides, Gillette and Dove were part of a greedy conspiracy to coerce gullible people into buying things they didn't need (those darned capitalists).

Maggie was a product of the 60's (great decade for me). Her mother (Chelsea's frantic evangelical grandmother) fretted over Maggie's anti-war music, forbidding her from playing it on the plastic console in the living room. All these mangy peaceniks were destroying this Christian nation! Maggie didn't like going to church either (and what kid doesn't like *that*?). So, she and her mother fought. When Maggie marched in support of the Equal

Rights Amendment, her mother flipped out. Women's Lib was an affront to family values and grandma wouldn't tolerate the insidious sin of equality to infiltrate her home. She kicked her daughter out of the house, taking a public stand for family values.

All these years later, grandma was losing her marbles, living in a "value-priced" nursing home. She lived on the third floor, affectionately called the Reminiscent Wing (because it sounded better than the Nobody's Home Wing). She'd taken her favorite picture of Jesus with her where it hung above her bed. Jesus looked sad and worn out, as if all humankind had so disappointed him. Poor grandma slipped quickly into dementia, but not before giving her last few dollars to the church.

There was a small graveside service for Chelsea. She didn't have many girlfriends (she'd been too busy out-sleeping them to the top, and they'd resented her for it). However, several of George's friends attended, including Ken and Susan Lawson (Susan went to be the bigger person, hoping the magnanimous gesture would wound Ken even more). Most of the attendees assumed, privately of course, that George would have another accessory soon enough; probably before Global Munitions' next quarterly board meeting. Pretty callous to think such a thing, I know, and especially at Chelsea's service, but that's what they thought.

Maggie arrived in Philadelphia in time to attend the service. She was layered with all the clothes she owned because winter in Philly was unlike the weather in Guatemala. The other mourners thought she was a curious homeless person. None of them (including George) even knew that Chelsea *had* a mother. Maggie elbowed her way to the front row and stood next to George, just a few feet from the casket where Chelsea lay, stiff as a Barbie doll.

"Hi," she said to George. "I'm Petunia's mother."

"Excuse me?" George asked as he looked for the funeral director to remove this transient from the premises.

"I'm Maggie, Petunia's mother," she repeated, and stuck out her chubby hand. "I think she goes by Chelsea now. We've been very close and I was devastated to hear the news. I came just as soon as I could. But I'm here now and ready to help."

"Oh. Well, Mrs. . . .?"

"Just call me Maggie."

"Very well. My name is George. I was Chelsea's husband. Thank you for coming, but as you can see, the arrangements have already been made."

"Sure, but whenever family dies it's good to be together. To give each other support. At least we'll have each other to lean on, and I want you to know that I'll be here with you for as long as it takes."

"Well, thank you for that." George kept looking over her shoulder for the funeral director. Chelsea had mentioned her mother once, something about her ditching out and moving to Central America.

Maggie linked her arm through George's and patted him on the arm with her free hand. There was a cheap silver ring on every finger, even her thumb. She looked at the minister and nodded that it was time to begin.

Detectives Rob Flygare and Roger Olson watched the service from a distance. They were there to observe any unusual guests, perhaps even the killer. They saw nothing out of the ordinary, except for the squatty homeless woman who'd butted her way to the front and stood next to George Miles, himself a prime suspect.

The detectives had seen photos of Chelsea before her murder and hated the fact that this man, who could easily have been her father, and who looked like a toad, had actually been her husband. They allowed themselves a private moment of self-pity for their meager salaries which would never be enough to lure a woman like Chelsea to *their* beds. This self-pity made them hope that George would be proven guilty, which might somehow even the score.

Following the benediction, George tried to extricate himself from Maggie's grip, but she hung on like a barnacle.

"I know, George dear, that it must be difficult for you, meeting your family—your mother-in-law—like this. I probably should have called ahead to give you time to make arrangements."

"Arrangements?"

"Well, I'm afraid Petunia was the only family I had. Now that she's gone, I'd hoped we could bring the family together."

"I'm sorry, but I'm afraid we'll have to deal with this loss separately. But it was a pleasure to meet you." He broke free and began walking away.

"But, George," she said. "I dropped everything the second I heard. I haven't even had a moment's thought about where I'll stay because I've been so worked up about Petunia."

"Would you like my secretary to book you a room for a few days?"

"Well, yes, that would be lovely. At least until the financial matters are resolved. I'm just not that familiar with those sorts of things."

"I'm afraid there isn't much to resolve," George said, irritated by his growing awareness of Maggie's real purpose.

"But surely there's the question of her assets. I believe I'm her only heir. Of course, there's her grandma, my mother, but she has all-timers."

"I'm afraid Chelsea had no assets. I hope you will forgive my bluntness, but I was her husband, and *I* am her principal heir. However, that legal distinction is unimportant because, as I mentioned, Chelsea has no assets that I am aware of other than the personal property I bought her."

"But . . . I thought . . . well, I thought you'd have given her . . . ."

"I have given her a great deal of personal property. But, of course, that now belongs to me."

"Are you saying that, as her mother, I am entitled to *nothing*? Is that what you're saying? Because it's very hurtful." Maggie was being roused from dreams of cosmetic lifts and destination spas.

"As a courtesy, I will pay for you to stay a few days and your travel expenses to return to your home."

Maggie's wrath was peaking. This man, this . . . this *toad*, had the audacity to deny her what should've been rightfully hers; a large portion of his wealth. His notorious indifference to her plight was galling. Her comrades at the commune were right—rich Americans had a gimme gimme gimme attitude. Here was a rich American, her very *son-in-law* no less, who stepped all over her. Why? Because she was a woman and didn't play by their good-ol'-boy rules, that's why. Let them have their filthy lucre. She would return to the commune where devotion to family and generosity meant something.

12

"HI, MOM, IT'S ME."

"Hello, Rebecca. I enjoyed seeing you the other night at your father's re-election party. How's school going?"

"It's okay."

"Is something the matter?"

Ken and Susan's privileged daughter, the one who'd bravely overcome her hour-long flight in coach, was pregnant. It occurred in the usual way. The Boy was a feral, one-track-minder who happened to be the president of his fraternity. He barely even knew Rebecca and didn't like her much. For that reason, The Boy felt victimized for being placed in this position. Why had he been so drunk? Why had they let this girl into the party? And why, for God's sake, wasn't she on the pill? Rebecca called him for a week with no response. She was crushed.

"I'm pregnant, mom."

"Oh my God, Rebecca! Are you sure?"

"Of course I'm sure."

"Who's the father? Have we met him?"

"No, mom, you haven't."

"Does he know who your father is? I didn't even know you were dating anyone. How could you have been so careless?"

"No, mom, I don't think he knows who my father is, and I doubt he cares."

"Please don't tell me he wants you to *keep* it."

"Don't worry, mom. He doesn't."

Susan preached for a few more minutes; mostly a belated sermon on teen promiscuity. Her therapist was helping with her relationships, but he wasn't helping much. Susan was in therapy because that's what you do—you go to therapy. You and your sofas, droning on and on to small bearded men about your mothers and childhoods. Don't you get tired of it? I mean, please, enough with the drama.

Rebecca was always asked if she had any "prospects", because she knew her parents were afraid she'd never have one. *So, dating anyone?* She'd lie to save face, and to get them off her back. But now, even the father of her fetus wasn't a prospect. A few days later, she decided to have an abortion. She'd known from the beginning it was inevitable, but she wanted to wait, as if the choice were really hers. This should have empowered her, but instead she felt powerless, like she'd really had no choice at all.

She called her mom again.

"Mom, I'm not sure where to go. I'll be in Philadelphia next week for Christmas break. Maybe I should go to Dr. Carlisle."

"Oh dear God, Rebecca. Dr. Carlisle has been our family doctor for years and is a friend of your fathers."

"I know. That's why I'd go to him."

"But, Rebecca, I wouldn't want him to know any of our family's dirty secrets."

"Dirty secrets, mom?"

"I just don't want to involve anyone we know. That's all."

"Because you're ashamed for me?"

"Of course not. You know what I mean."

"Well, then where can I go?"

"Can't you just go to Planned Parenthood up there in Boston?"

"But, mom, Planned Parenthood doesn't perform abortions."

"But they could refer you to someone there."

"You mean to make sure it's nowhere near dad's senate district."

"Rebecca, stop it. You know that's not what I meant."

"Well, then what *did* you mean?"

"I'm just thinking of you. I want it to be easier for you, Rebecca."

"Will you go with me? I haven't told a soul and I don't want to go by myself."

"Oh, Rebecca. You know I would, but people know me because of all the media surrounding your father. If they recognized me the press would have a field day at your expense. And I don't want that for you."

"Of course not."

Rebecca drove herself to the clinic. While she was undergoing the wrenching ordeal of her young life, The Boy was at the frat house, knocking down another Pabst Blue Ribbon.

13

"THE DUCK IS EXCELLENT, SIR."

"No, I'm in the mood for something redder, something meatier. Give me the filet and let's have it rare. Oh, and I'll have another one of these," he said, pointing to his gin and tonic. This was just another day for the fine senator of Pennsylvania to be wined and dined. Even political foes curried his favor, pretending to respect him.

This time it was friends from the oil and gas industry picking up the tab at Café Milano, one of Georgetown's most expensive restaurants. These were the constituents Senator Lawson was most comfortable with; the upper 1% of rich, white people. They were the ones who donated, so they had his ear, and could buy his lunch. Lawson knew this and his pride levels spiked (but we all know what goeth before the fall, don't we?). After lighthearted talk amongst the boys about Nancy Pelosi's plastic surgery and Hillary's lumpy thighs, it was time to get down to business. It was time to earn the expensive meal.

"Now, gentlemen, how can I help you?"

"Well, Senator," said Lobby Man #1. "We've got the Sierra Club breathing down our necks on those off-shore drilling leases. And that mess in the Gulf was a public relations nightmare. Even Fox News showed oil gushing from that damned pipe. Some birds and fish died, and we feel terrible about it, but the liberal media overplayed it." Lobby Man #1 saw the wisdom in oil, and I agree with him. It's been good to me—I can probably squeeze a few more wars out of the sludge.

"We need to kill the Clean Air Initiative Act," said Lobby Man #2. "The suppliers would take a big hit with all the bureaucratic red tape. I don't need to remind you they're some of your biggest supporters."

"The Chairman of the Energy Committee," said Lawson "opposes free enterprise. When Congress reconvenes we'll regain the majority, so there'll be new leadership. If I get the chairmanship I can probably derail the bill." A savvy derailment would save them millions of dollars, dollars that could be better spent on his future campaigns.

"Senator, there is another matter we'd like to mention," said Lobby Man #3. "We understand your son is an outspoken environmentalist. We care about the environment, too, but these tree huggers have crossed the line. Again, we respect your son's right to express his views, but we heard he's been hired by the Sierra Club."

The Sierra Club? This was something the Senator didn't know.

"We believe," said Lobby Man #2, "they're paying him for political gain and nothing more." Oh, that was rich.

The Senator and his son saw the world through different blinders. Ken arrived at his convictions after polling his core constituency. John, on the other hand, hadn't been seduced by the lure of power and PAC money (he only had to answer to the trustee of his trust fund). Therefore, he mistakenly believed his convictions were pure. That was rich, too.

The latest sparring between father and son had been over campaign financing. "So, dad, what did you think about the recent Supreme Court ruling allowing corporations to give unlimited money to political campaigns?"

"I thought it was right on. I suppose you'll complain about it, along with every other law that helps corporations make America the greatest nation on earth." Lawson had only read the dumbed-down version of the opinion—but the gist had been explained to him by a lawyer on his staff.

"I figured you'd say that," John said.

"Listen, John, I don't want to fight about this. It's the law of the land and I support it."

The Lawson family was doing battle on all fronts, but most of the skirmishes were personal (or secret), so they couldn't rally around each other, even if they'd wanted to. There was the increasing friction between Ken and John. That was no secret. But Rebecca's abortion was, and so was the fact that Susan was now lustfully fornicating with Jeff, her hunky personal trainer.

It had all started when Jeff, a fitness junkie, spotted Susan at *Fit & Tone*, the trendy gym in town that pampered members with post-workout smoothies for only $399 per month. He spotted Susan doing a downward facing dog. Because she was attractive, and because he'd done yoga a few times, Jeff felt qualified to stand closely behind her, to give a quick pointer. Jeff was young and tan, so Susan felt obliged to let him.

Soon Susan was primping for her workouts. She didn't wear heels, but neither did she wear those cheap Russell Athletic sweats. She didn't work out too hard at the gym, either, lest she actually sweat. Instead, she worked out on her treadmill at home, then showered and got dolled up for the gym, hoping to see Jeff there.

Jeff was no different. He'd do a short workout to get a light sheen of sweat because he thought it made his muscles look more toned. Then he trolled the gym, ogling women spreading their legs on the thigh machines. That's when he saw Susan and made his move. Within a few days he was training her three times per week. Soon, they were doing the downward dog in private, surrounded by designer gym clothes strewn about the floor of his one-bedroom apartment with a pantry full of protein powder and peanut butter.

Susan easily rationalized this bi-weekly dalliance. She knew that Ken explored more than farm subsidy legislation during the four days a week he spent in Washington D.C. Well, she didn't *know* it, know it. But she had a darn good hunch. In fact, it was remarkable that Ken's sexual exploits hadn't been outed by the press (or by an intern looking for her fifteen minutes). Ken was not partisan where sex was concerned, either. He'd even do it with a Democrat from time to time, but that was about the only time he crossed the aisle.

The Lawson family had its private struggles, all right. And last, but certainly not least, was the Senator's potential to be the lead story on CNN, ABC, CSPAN, and ESPN. He'd be the international face of infamy. Even his allies would scatter like he had the bird flu.

Senator Lawson couldn't control where the investigation led, or what evidence might dribble out. I hoped it would dribble in his direction so I could watch the media salivate over his carcass like famished vultures.

14

JESSE AND SLIM WERE EXCITED about their forthcoming bounty. Slim was especially antsy because of the urgent deadline for the Nigerian investment scheme he'd seen on the internet. It promised a return of $24,000,000 if he sent $2,000 cash to an off-shore bank. Even a dunce could see that was a darn good return. They needed to strike quickly though, because they could say sayonara to the money once the senator was in the slammer. So, after waiting four days, it was time to implement The Plan.

When they opened a P.O. Box at the post office, they were required to put a name on the account (of course, they were too savvy to put their own). Slim had recently seen a news story on T. Boone Pickens, a rich oil man who'd turned coat on the oil industry, actively promoting clean air alternatives. Mr. Pickens was also nicknamed Slim—Slim Pickens. They decided to open the account under Slim Boon Pick, and were assigned box number 789.

The boys had seen scary movies where the axe murderer wrote his threatening notes with letters cut from magazines. Using an old issue of Aunt Eloise's Ladies Home Journal, they glued cut-out letters to a piece of the same white-lined paper. By the time they were finished, the note was a dry, wrinkled mess of glue and paste, but it would do the job. It read:

THE time is uP. It's all Oiled aNd ReadY.

Put the money in unmarked bills

and send it to PO Box 789 in pHiladelphia.

Don't try anytHing fancy Or the world

WilL knOw wHat you did.

Slim addressed an envelope, put the note inside, licked it, and walked it down to the mailbox. They figured it would take about three days to arrive, plus a few more days for Lawson to round up that much cash. Ten grand didn't grow on trees—they had to be patient.

They pleasantly mulled over their upcoming fortune on the walk back to Aunt Eloise's. There was a long list of everything they'd buy. Aunt Eloise would also be paid the overdue rent and the kids might each get a tricycle (or maybe they could share one). The twenty-nine-year-old misfit with the foot fetish deserved something, too (but what? they wondered). They decided not to give Uncle Wayne anything because he was just too weird.

Ann Lee was troubled; there was that nagging feeling from an unknown source. She'd been on Senator Lawson's staff for several years and had an uncanny sense when something smelled fishy, and she'd caught a whiff of fish. It had to do with Paul McDonald, her ideological nemesis on the staff. He wasn't acting his normal self.

Ann's grandparents had immigrated from Korea, which is apropos of nothing, really. But McDonald was wary of anyone who was not certifiably Caucasian. The first time she'd met him he asked what she "was". Uh, human? She was too annoyed to explain her heritage, the halves and the wholes. Besides, no one really cared (except people like McDonald—who stretched his eyes to slits with his fingers and said "Ah so" to Yang Chung every time he saw him in junior high). It may have surprised McDonald, but how was she supposed to know if everyone in China uses chopsticks?

Ann was smarter than anyone else on the staff (she tried not be arrogant about it, but it'd leak from time to time). She was a policy wonk, a political junky, who took all that nonsense so seriously. She'd thought about running for office, but the thought of constantly panhandling for money? Ugh. So, she became a backgrounder, like a roadie who works backstage. She was never the headliner.

Lawson wanted to hire her because she was Korean (well, actually, she was 100% American and had never been to Korea). Woman? Check. Diversity? Check. No one could say *he* was sexist or racist. Ann was a Republican, but she didn't share her boss's views on the sacred trilogy of the right wing: Guns, Gays, and God. No siree, Ann believed she was morally superior to those folks (this is so much fun to watch). She fancied herself as a counter-balance to McDonald, who was as far right as they came.

She pictured McDonald as a miniature devil dressed in red tights, with horns. He'd be perched on Lawson's shoulder, holding a pitchfork, whispering naughty things (I have no idea where the whole horns and pitchfork came from. Seriously? Horns?). Ann, of course, would be the heroine on his other shoulder, dressed in white with a radiating halo. Rich.

Lately, Ann was on alert because McDonald was conspiring with the Senator more than usual, and in hushed tones. He was also acting strangely when it came to the mail. Ordinarily the mail was toxic; it meant more work. But there he was, loitering around the mailroom for nearly a week, pouncing on it the moment it arrived. This worried her.

The Senator wasn't himself, either. He was preoccupied with the Chelsea Miles murder and it looked like he hadn't slept in days. This should've been a happy time for him. He'd just been re-elected over a snobby liberal who, inexplicably, wanted to ban assault weapons from churches (What next? Ban the Ten Commandments?). Moreover, the GOP had picked up three more seats in the senate to give them a majority. This meant Lawson would have more power, perhaps even a committee chairmanship. So, why so blue?

If the two of them were up to something, Ann would eventually figure it out.

15

JAVIER FLORES HAD EVERY RIGHT to be worried. Whether he was guilty or not was entirely beside the point. He'd be toast if the Federales had any evidence against him. The illegal immigrants were blamed for all the mischief—thievery, drug dealing, and hogging all the coveted jobs, like lawnmowing and maid service. White people were getting screwed.

The police had told him that he was under investigation and wasn't to leave. Now there's a fun twist! Here he was, an illegal immigrant guilty of something awful, or not, and he was told *not* to leave. Javier had no alibi, and no money to pay a lawyer, so they'd assign him a lousy bi-lingual public defender. He'd be doomed. Therefore, he decided to sneak back to Mexico. That was another fun twist. He'd sneak *back* to Meheeco. He gathered his few belongings, sold his old pickup to a friend, and bought a bus ticket to El Paso, next to the Mexican border and his home in Ciudad Juarez.

Javier walked across the border without incident, looking every bit like he belonged to the south of it. He hailed a rusted taxi to his house in western Juarez, out where the poor people lived. This was the largest section in town, by far.

He arrived late, after the children had already fallen asleep. The familiar smells of re-fried beans, corn tortillas, and jalapenos shot through his nostrils. It felt good to be home. His wife was still awake, doing laundry at the sink. She was a good woman, raising five children on a skimpy budget without complaint. Oh, I tried, believe me, but I couldn't even get a spark of greed, or envy. I'll grudgingly acknowledge goodness when I see it.

She fell into her husband's arms, then quickly pulled away. "Why you are home? We no expect you too soon. Do you lose job? You are so sick?"

"I leave mi trabajo in El Norte because they say I do somethеen muy bad." Javier told her about the murder, insisting he had nothing to do with it (it made no sense to confess to all the spying behind the hydrangeas). She led him to their bed, next to another bed which held their sleeping children, and quietly made love to him, privately rooting against a sixth conception. The only protection they had, their only defense, was the image of Mother Mary hanging on the peeling plaster wall above their bed. If they were embarrassed that she spied on them doing what she'd done immaculately, they didn't show it.

Flygare and Olson, the lead detectives on the Miles murder, were being pressured to name a suspect. And now one of the primary persons of interest had gone missing? Javier Flores couldn't be found? This was bad. They hadn't had enough evidence to arrest him, yet, but they'd scolded him, reminding him to standby in case they wanted to put him in jail.

They'd meant to get a semen sample from Javier, but someone had dropped the ball. What a dumb blunder *that* was! No one in the rundown apartment where Javier had been staying knew where he'd gone (or they wouldn't fess up). The detectives figured Javier had skedaddled back to Mexico.

The detectives had their hunches about who the murderer was, and they didn't think it was Javier. They thought it was the husband, George Miles. His story about the missing jewelry and laptop were too convenient, and there was no other evidence of burglary. He'd been evasive, and even contradictory over his descriptions of the missing items.

"How the hell did he know the bracelet was missing if he couldn't even describe it?" asked Flygare. "That woman had a million of 'em."

The investigators had asked George for a semen sample the day after the murder. "I will certainly cooperate in the investigation," he'd said "but now is not the time, gentlemen, with my wife so recently murdered." And, really, who could have blamed him? It would've been rugged coming up with a semen sample under those circumstances, even for a younger man who'd been wired to plant his seed with obsessive regularity.

The detectives didn't force the issue at the time. They knew George would be hard to lose. Billionaires tend to leave large tracks wherever they go. But Javier was another matter. If Javier's semen matched the gob they'd found in Chelsea, bingo, they had their man. If not, they'd put him at the bottom of the list.

George had indirectly implied the semen wasn't his, because he insisted he'd only been home ten minutes and didn't see his wife during that time. Once they got his semen sample, he'd be caught in a damning lie if it belonged to him. On the other hand, if it *wasn't* his, then he had a motive for murdering his wife. For what more compelling motive could there be? Enraged husband returns home to find his wife in the afterglow of illicit coitus not-at-all-interruptus?

There were at least three main holes in this tidy theory. First, George's fingerprints weren't on the shovel. Secondly, even assuming George wanted to kill Chelsea in a fit of rage, why would he go outside and get a shovel to do it? Even if he had, he'd have needed a pair of gloves, too. And, finally, how could they arrest George until they pinned down the owner of the sperm, who himself would be an obvious suspect.

Even though George had no criminal record, the cops figured he was probably guilty of *something* in his past, but he'd never been convicted of anything, and certainly nothing as sinister as pasting someone in the noggin with a spade. Let me emphasize here that the *cops* had no record on him. The rap sheet I had on him was long enough to roast him in sulphur.

The State's Finest were not about to go arresting the billionaire on mere hunches. He would have an Olympian legal team. They needed more evidence. In the meantime, George would remain at the top of their list of suspects until they could eliminate him.

George decided it was time to get a criminal defense attorney when the detectives renewed their request for a semen sample. Ted had recommended William Sperry, one of the most notorious defense attorneys in the country, with offices in Philadelphia. Sperry was respected by the prosecutor's office, but not well liked (he was no peach to work with). He was George's age, and refused to retire because he relished a good fight. If the Commonwealth wanted to hang his client, they'd have to earn it. No concessions and no plea bargains.

"George, it's a pleasure to meet you," said Sperry.

"Likewise. Ted highly recommended you." It was unusual for George to meet on someone else's turf—people usually came to him. But now he sat in Sperry's office with a spectacular view of the city. A telescope stood in the corner, pointing in the general direction of the Liberty Bell. The Harvard diploma hung on the wall, handsomely framed, like the crest of a nobleman (it would've been in the bottom drawer if it'd been from Montana State).

George filled Sperry in on the extent of the investigation as he understood it. He told him more of the truth than he'd told the cops: that he'd unexpectedly come home to grab some papers, found his wife in the sack, demanded to know who she'd been with, called her a bitch, and left. He told Sperry that the investigators hadn't taken a detailed statement from him, but he'd cooperated so far, except for providing the semen sample they'd requested.

"I know it wasn't my semen," George said. "So, I assume they'll claim I had a motive to kill my wife—out of rage."

"They are probably entitled to the sample," Sperry said. "You were presumably the last one to see her alive, and the one who discovered her. Besides, you've already told them you didn't have sex with her, and didn't even see her. Therefore, the only danger in submitting a sample would be if it was yours after all. If it was, the police will pounce on the discrepancy in your story."

"It wasn't mine. Trust me."

"Do you have any idea whose it might have been?"

"I have some thoughts on the matter, yes."

"Would you care to share them with me? I am your attorney now and I consider the attorney-client privilege to be inviolate."

"I believe Senator Ken Lawson was sleeping with my wife."

There was a lengthy pause as Sperry digested that revelation. Sperry was rarely at a loss for words; he used them profusely to earn his comfy living. "George, that evidence is important." Sperry was also a master at stating the obvious at several hundred dollars per hour.

"But," said George "for my own reasons, I don't want the police to focus on Lawson. Unless, of course, it turns out he is guilty of killing my wife. But, honestly, I don't think he is. Therefore, unless I say otherwise, I want my belief on that subject to be kept private. As far as I know, the police have absolutely no idea the two of them were lovers."

"I hope you'll reconsider your position. It won't serve you well if you wait too long to come forward with information that connects Senator Lawson to the crime."

"I understand," said George. "In the meantime, how should we respond to the investigators who keep pestering me for a semen sample?"

"Let me give that some thought, but I'm inclined to allow it at this point."

After more discussion about the case and the process that George could expect, he got up to leave.

"Excuse me, George, for bringing up the sensitive subject of my fee, but it's important that we have an understanding from the outset. My fee is $800 per hour. In addition, you will be billed for my paralegal and researcher's time at $200 per hour. This may require a considerable amount of time, especially if you are arrested. For that reason, I request an initial retainer of $200,000. We can re-evaluate the expenses as the case develops. However, if this case were to go to trial, I expect the fees and costs could approach two million dollars, depending on the expert witnesses we'll need."

"Send me a bill," George said, like this was the cost of a parking fine.

Voluntary arrangements were made with George to obtain the semen sample. He arrived, without fanfare, at the lab where the sample was to be given. Thankfully there were no camera crews to record this humbling event, and no stop watch. He was given a plastic jar, lid, and paper bag. As a teenager, such a request, especially with the aid of a stolen Playboy, would've been a walk in the park. "*Oh, it spilled? Shoot, no problem, hand me another jar and I'll be back in a jiffy. No, better yet, hand me two in case it spills again.*" But now, well, now he'd really need to hunker down.

It wasn't easy sitting there on the toilet seat of an industrial bathroom with linoleum on the floor (George wasn't accustomed to seeing linoleum anywhere). The fluorescent lights removed any semblance of romance. There wasn't even a scented candle, or mood music, just a worn issue of Cosmopolitan. Did they expect him to achieve success over an article titled "How to Build a Lasting Emotional Relationship"? Or a photo spread of Barbara Walters' new gown and hair style? He also knew the staff was just outside the door, wondering what was taking so long. The pressure! And when he thought about why he was doing it (because his wife had just been brutally murdered with a *shovel* and he was a potential suspect), well, you can imagine how it didn't inspire eroticism.

When he had finally, and mercifully, accomplished the objective, he opened the door holding the paper bag with the jar inside it. There was no applause (but there was a collective sigh of relief from all concerned). His shame was complete when the young nurse took the bag from him at arm's length and told him he was free to go. Free to go and do what? Have a cigarette in the lobby?

There were no surprises when the lab results came in, just another level of awkward intrigue. The semen found inside Chelsea's vajayjay did not belong to her husband. Unfortunately for George, this revelation did not eliminate him as a suspect, for they knew he'd returned home at the approximate time of her death. And now they had a motive.

16

THE LETTER ARRIVED ON THE FIFTH DAY and Paul McDonald was there to retrieve it. He snatched it up like a winning lottery ticket, clutching it with a grip reserved only for his paycheck and NRA card. He walked into Senator Lawson's office and closed the door.

"We got it! We got another letter!" He realized, too late, that he was using that pesky pronoun "we", as if this letter and all it represented was now his problem, too.

"Let me see it." Lawson held out his shaking hand and took the envelope. It was written in the same handwriting as the previous envelope, with no return address. He opened it like a hand grenade with the pin out, and removed the piece of paper. He read it quickly to himself and then out loud for McDonald's benefit. On the second reading, his worst fears were realized. Aside from the phrase that "the world will know what you did," which shook him to his core, there was another phrase that hit him even harder:

It's all Oiled aNd ReadY.

It was now abundantly clear these blackmailers were backed by the rabid do-gooders in the environmentalist movement. The oil reference was a blatant slap in the face. They must have been sophisticated and well-funded to have tracked him to Chelsea's house without being detected.

The two men sat in silence, fretting over each syllable. It was McDonald who finally spoke. "Senator, I think we need to cooperate with them. It's only $10,000. They'll expose this if we don't."

"They'll probably expose it anyway. These liberal bastards will do everything they can to bring me down. They don't have a moral bone in their bodies. This time it's a measly ten grand. But what about next time?"

McDonald didn't know if this was a question he was supposed to answer, or not. Finally, he said, "Do we have a better option?" (now throwing out the "we" with reckless abandon). "We need to put this fire out. These people aren't playing games. We'll have to deal with the next threat when it comes."

"Bullshit!" Lawson slammed his fist on the desk, causing his prized 4" by 6" photo of him shaking hands with Ronald Reagan to topple over. "That is *exactly* what they're doing—playing games. They're putting their own selfish interests ahead of the country. They'll stop at nothing!"

"So what do you suggest?"

"Where would we get the money?" Lawson asked. "The campaign fund? Is that the safest way to play this? Or do you recommend I take it from my personal account?"

"Let's take it out of the campaign fund. We can hide it better than a $10,000 cash withdrawal from your personal account." Paul's only solace was that it wasn't his money.

Lawson instructed McDonald to get the cash and do exactly as Jesse and Slim had demanded; those sophisticated, left-wing, tree-hugging, oil-hating, liberal bastards. McDonald put the cash in an envelope and addressed it to the post office box in Philadelphia. Before mailing it, however, he returned to the Senator's office.

"Listen, Senator, we might have an opportunity to find out who's behind this blackmail."

"How?"

"We hire a private detective to camp out near that post office box and watch it like a hawk. He can photograph and follow the person who picks it up. We could turn the tables on them and do a little blackmailing of our own."

"Yeah, I like it. Blackmailing is a serious crime, so let's give them some of their own medicine." Senator Lawson's duplicitous thinking pleased me. "But I can't be in the loop—you better handle all the arrangements."

"Let me see what I can do." Oh my, poor McDonald was now substituting "me" for "we."

McDonald hired a private eye to do the surveillance. When the blackmailers came for the package he was to photograph and follow them, but remain hidden at all costs. McDonald hired him through a go-between to be sure their man didn't know the relevance of this mission, or who had hired him.

Lawson felt better just knowing they were taking action.

Ken had grown up with an abusive father who drank hard and took his mediocre fortune out on his wife and children. Ken had two older brothers who'd earned their GED's by the skin of their teeth. No one in the family had been to college, and when Ken floated the idea, his father had poo-pooed it. "Why spend all that money on some highfalutin college? All they do is fill your head with crap. Go get yourself a real job to get a leg up on those sissy college boys."

Ken bucked the family trend. His girlfriend attended the local community college and he enrolled, too. He almost dropped out when the girl dumped him. That's when he met Susan Rupert. She was stunning and always got what she wanted, by force of will, or her daddy's wallet. And, for better or worse, she wanted Ken. To be worthy of her, however, she insisted he transfer to a better college.

Susan looked down on Ken's backward family. They could barely articulate the difference between a cab and a chardonnay. Talk about embarrassing. She dragged him from blue-collar servitude, luring him with the insidious addiction to money, and instilling in him the precious commodity of entitlement. I understand. I was there when she'd been lured in, too. You all take your little monetary schemes so seriously, as if they make you superior (even when it is simply handed to you without any scheming on your part at all). By the time he'd been on the Rupert family jet, spent weekends in Martha's Vineyard, and her daddy had pulled strings to get him into Wharton, Ken had been so thoroughly seduced that he scarcely remembered from whence he'd come. Priceless.

Their early years of marriage had been good enough, but it began to unravel when Ken started taking credit for things. This irritated Susan because he'd been nothing without her, *nothing*, and now he'd had the gall to talk down to her.

The children, John and Rebecca, brought them closer, for a time. They had a full-time nanny *and* housekeeper which spared them from actually raising the little monsters (How do the little people *do* it?). But there developed a budding discontent between them. I was there when Susan instructed Ken in all the ways he should change. And I was there when Ken instructed her to keep her goddamned mouth shut.

Susan's third pregnancy was a surprise because they'd had sex so infrequently (with each other). They were each privately relieved by the miscarriage, and then upset at the other for showing such calloused indifference to the loss of their child.

Susan rued the day that she'd torn up the pre-nuptial agreement her father had paid so handsomely to create. She'd considered divorce many times over the years, but there were the children to consider, and the estate (half of it anyway). And even though she was loath to admit it, Ken's political career gave her some national cachet. But when he'd tell crowds at campaign events about the sanctity of marriage, then look at her so lovingly, like he couldn't wait to go home and snuggle? Or how he was monogamy's champion? It made her want to barf.

The audacity of the man, Susan thought, especially given what had happened a year earlier. She'd found a prescription bottle of Zovirax in Ken's sock drawer (she'd been snooping for something else). She discovered it was medication for the treatment of genital herpes. This did not please her. It was bad enough that Ken violated the Christian principles he publicly embraced, but to bring home sores on his penis?

She'd been luxuriating in her wrath all day, waiting for him to come home, feeling morally superior because she'd dodged a nasty STD from her own dalliances. Fortunately, they hadn't had sex for a long time, both of them finding excuses, much to the other's relief. When Ken walked in the door she threw the bottle of pills at him. "You're a disgusting pig!"

"Are you drunk? Get a hold of yourself!"

"You'll screw anything that moves and now you have herpes. If it weren't so pathetic, it would be funny."

Ken didn't know the source of his herpes; it could have been one several young women who'd caught his fancy. Their motivation consisted of basic lust *(Oh, Ken, you're so handsome, and so big!).* There was also your basic pride *(Uh, yeah, I just bagged Senator Lawson).* There was even your basic greed *(That'll be $500, big boy).*

Ken had beaten himself up over his carelessness, for now he was doing battle with the itchy little sores. In fact, he had the itchy sensation at that very moment, brought on by the mere thought of his polka-dotted love dart. However, he had the rare good judgment not to scratch it in front of Susan.

Susan was measured in her tone for dramatic emphasis. "You will *never* have sex with me again. Do you hear me? *Never!*"

"Don't flatter yourself. You're my wife and I'll have sex with you whenever I want. So, stop with the drama. It's quite unbecoming."

"You will never touch me again."

Ken did not appreciate being threatened by Susan in this way. He grabbed her by the shoulders.

"Keep your hands off me!"

"Stop me."

He threw her down. He was losing it, his wrath swelling.

"Ken! Stop it! I'll call the police!"

He sat on top of her and ripped off her shirt. She screamed. She had just sent the maid home and they were alone in the house. He pinned her arms down with his knees. "You think you can tell *me* what I can't do? I'll do whatever I want, and you'll keep your ugly mouth shut!"

He raped her.

In the days following the rape, Ken was playing defense. He thought she'd get over it soon enough. He'd overreacted, sure, but it wasn't *that* bad. Rape schmape. Let her go on a little shopping spree if that's what it took. Her loathing, however, was palpable. She'd considered divorce but hadn't been able to rally for such an expensive public spectacle. It would have cost her millions, not to mention her satisfied roost among the politically powerful. So, she soldiered on with her boy toys by day and attended public functions with Ken by night.

Susan knew the flavor of Ken's young tarts. So, the first time she met Chelsea, she knew something was brewing between them.

"It must be fabulous being married to Senator Lawson," Chelsea had gushed to Susan at a charity event where the tables sold for $25,000 (plus, they made you look like a total cheapskate if you didn't bid on the Scotland golf package, or the weekend at Sun Valley).

"Well, I suppose there are certain advantages. But it looks like you haven't done too badly for yourself," Susan said, nodding in The Toad's direction. "I always thought George would settle down with an educated woman who was more his age." Susan knew Chelsea had earned the dubious privilege of marriage to the billionaire only because of her voluptuous DNA. Duh. She'd also heard about Chelsea's modest upbringing, and how her given name had been Petunia. Petunia. How perfect.

"And I'm sure your marriage to Senator Lawson is a joyous one."

"We are very happy," said Susan.

"I'm glad to hear that," said Chelsea. "I can only imagine what it must be like. You do nothing, but you're allowed to circle the edges of his world."

Ken had no wish to divorce. It wouldn't look good for his political career, one that might lead to a run for President (there had already been whispers of an exploratory committee!). He'd dismissed the role of Susan's silver ladle, slurping the bounty of its plentiful scoops as further evidence of his worth. All the while, she kept treating him to rants about how he owed her everything. He couldn't stand her.

It was no wonder that he couldn't confide in her that he was being blackmailed for sleeping with, and then nearly beheading, his latest mistress.

17

SENATOR LAWSON WAS IN A PICKLE. The oil company lobbyists were antsy, leaning on him to publicly oppose the Clean Air Initiative Act. His puppeteers had given him millions of dollars, and now they wanted their money's worth. This was normally a no-brainer—he would do it with gusto, like any good patriot. But if he publicly opposed it, those nasty, tree-hugging environmentalists might expose his involvement in the murder. They'd take his behavior with the late Chelsea Miles completely out of proportion to smear his family values reputation. On the other hand, he couldn't actually *support* the bill. Are you kidding? His supporters would have him committed (*Why, he's gone pure loco!*). He'd be tried for treason within their corporate board rooms. Hence, all the stalling until he could find out who was blackmailing him.

Dan Leonard parked across the street from the post office in a blue mini-van with tinted windows. Inside he had the latest hi-tech surveillance equipment. He hadn't been told who'd hired him, only that it was someone who wished to remain anonymous. He'd been paid $2,500 to photograph and identify the person who went to P.O. Box 789.

His usual assignment was to tail cheating spouses. He'd lost count of the number of divorces he'd contributed to over the years. There would've been even more, but I happen to know he'd occasionally sell out to make an extra buck. For example, let's say he'd been hired by a wife to follow her cheating slime-ball of a husband. He'd approach the misunderstood husband with the money shots of him and his secretary on the second-floor balcony of the Days Inn, looking a bit disheveled in that post-coital sort of way. The cheating husband would pay double whatever his wife had paid to make the photos disappear.

The husband would rail against his wife (*"She had me tailed? She doesn't trust me? I can't believe this shit!")*. Dan would commiserate with the poor guy for a while (*"Yeah, I know, can you believe women these days?"*). Then Dan would propose a solution. For an extra two thousand dollars, Dan would report back to the nosey wife that her husband had actually been sneaking away from the office to donate blood. It was a win-win-win when both spouses paid. The wife was relieved that her husband was civic-minded enough to donate blood, the husband escaped with half the stemware, and Dan was able to make his own alimony payments (the result of being on the other side of the lens a few years earlier).

Dan arrived before the post office opened and peered through the windows. A set of glass doors led to a vestibule, and ultimately to a hallway where the post office boxes lined the wall. He returned to his mini-van and parked in a space that provided a view through the glass doorway to the wall of P.O. boxes.

His stakeouts usually involved long periods of boredom punctuated by moments of adrenalin. *Okay, there you are.* Click. *Now turn around.* Click. *Okay, good, good.* Click. Click. *Now smile for the camera. Come on now; how about a smug post-coital grin. Atta boy.* Click. *Just a couple more for the missus. Excellent.* Click. Click. *Sorry buddy but you're going to have a shitty night.* Click. *Okay, how about one more with the Motel 6 sign in the background. Perfect.* Click. *Now say goodbye to half your 401K. Good. Good.* Click. *Sorry pal, just doin' my job.* Click.

His high-powered binoculars zoomed in on box 789. These were expensive Swarovski binoculars. He'd given the goods to several angry spouses to afford them. They were a lot better than the ones Santa had given him when he was fourteen. He'd worn out that pair spying on the neighbors, and particularly Kathy Johansen, the eighteen-year-old next-door neighbor.

Dan's vigilance was impressive, at first, but within an hour his binoculars turned toward any attractive woman who walked by. He would insist, of course, that he wasn't a common pervert. Nothing happened that first day, which was fine by him. The longer it took, the more money he'd make, so what did he care if the renter didn't march up to the box whistling Dixie, then turn and say cheese for the camera? He waited until the post office closed before going home to report to the anonymous employer who'd left only a cell phone number.

Actually, he did have something to report. He'd learned through gum-shoe detective work who had rented the box.

"Hello?"

"Yeah, this is Dan Leonard, the guy you hired to scope out the post office."

"What can you tell me?"

"Well, nobody came to that box today, I can tell you that."

"Did you find out who rented it?"

"Yeah, it was rented about five days ago to a guy named, let me see, it was a weird name so I had to write it down. Hang on." There was shuffling in the background. "Okay, here it is, 'Slim Boon Pick.' That's b-o-o-n and the last name is p-i-c-k."

"Call me as soon as you have anything else to report."

"Sure thing. Hey, mind telling me who this guy is?"

"I do," said the anonymous man before hanging up.

The next day was a long one. That morning, he'd stopped to buy a sandwich and Big Gulp before resuming the surveillance. He didn't arrive at the post office until a half hour after it had opened (he'd pretend he'd arrived early so he could pad his bill). He parked in the same spot, maybe fifty yards from the glass doors, and settled in for the wait.

By two o'clock that afternoon no one had come within ten feet of the radioactive post office box. He'd drained the Big Gulp and had to pee. There'd been times when he'd peed into an empty milk carton, so as not to leave his post, but today he walked into the post office to use the bathroom.

There were two twenty-year-old kids standing in front of the urinals. One of them wore a beanie and low-riding jeans. The other was tall and skinny with a pock-marked face. He was stooped over, eating a bag of Fritos while he stood peeing. Dan overheard their brief conversation.

"Dude, relax. It'll be here soon. Okay?"

"It better be 'cause that deal on the computer ain't gonna last too long. And Aunt Eloise is givin' me heat for the rent."

Dan didn't think much of their conversation, but happened to follow them out of the restroom (they hadn't washed their hands) when they approached the post office boxes. They went directly to number 789. The shorter one, the one with the beanie, produced a key, opened the box, and removed a thick envelope.

"No way, dude! It worked!" he said to his friend.

"Fuckin A!"

Dan was unsure what to do. He'd left his camera back in the minivan. He had no pen or paper, either. *Shit! Shit! Shit!* He considered running back to the van, but these guys were already at the door with a spring in their step. He decided to follow them. They apparently had no car—they'd walked from wherever they'd come. Dan followed them on foot, furious with himself for having left the camera behind. He wasn't close enough to hear their conversation. If he had, it might have saved him a lot of extra time—time he could have used to go retrieve his camera.

"Dude, let's go to Adam's for some blow. Do us some celebratin'!"

"Slim, you gotta slow down on that shit, dude. We gotta think clearly, man."

"Yeah, but maybe it'd make us more alert."

This logic was sensible, so they headed the opposite direction to Adam's. Dan followed them there and waited outside, across the street and two houses down. It was freezing cold which justified padding his bill even more, notwithstanding his boneheaded blunder of leaving his camera behind. He waited, shivering without a coat. Two hours later, the boys emerged from the house. The shorter one was still clutching the envelope (imperceptibly thinner). They walked back the way they'd come and eventually entered a large, square, dilapidated house. Dan waited outside until dark, committed the address to memory, and walked back to the post office. His van sat alone in the parking lot with a parking ticket on the windshield. This called for more padding.

He called the anonymous employer to give him a sugar-coated report.

"What happened?"

"Well, they picked up the package around fourteen-hundred-hours."

"You mean 2:00 o'clock?"

"Yeah."

"Okay, you said 'they?'"

"Yeah, two punks, probably in their early twenties."

"Where did they go?"

"A couple places actually. But I think I know where they live."

"Okay. Are you there now?"

"Yeah," Dan lied. "I am sitting in a van across the street from the house." At least he was driving there.

"Stay there until you see them again and get back to me. In the meantime, email photos of the house and the two guys as soon as we hang up."

"Uh, well, I, uh, I didn't get any photos yet." Dan said and then hurriedly described the two before he could be interrupted, to show that he'd been paying good attention.

"You didn't get any *photos*? What in the hell are you talking about!"

"Well, I decided to go inside the post office to make sure I didn't miss them. I didn't want to take my camera in because that might look suspicious. It was just a professional judgment call."

Dan squeezed his eyes shut and winced because it was about the dumbest thing he could've said, or done.

There was silence on the other end of the line and finally the caller said, "Get me photos as soon as you can, dammit! And no more screw ups."

Dan promised there would be no more judgment calls and hung up. He shivered all night in his van across the street from Aunt Eloise's. He had nothing new to report by morning.

Paul McDonald told Senator Lawson about the two punks who'd picked up the money. This confused both men. Cheech and Chong must've been front men for the group that was orchestrating the blackmail. Lawson had been horrified to learn the box had been rented to "Slim Boon Pick." This was a clear reference to oil tycoon, Slim Boone Pickens, the renegade turn-coat. Yet another ominous sign that they were dealing with sophisticated left-wing extremists.

Once their man on the scene (the dimwit who'd forgotten his freaking *camera*) could get some photographs and ID on these two, they'd know what they were dealing with. In the meantime, Lawson would keep stalling on his principled opposition to the Clean Air Initiative.

18

SCOTT BENJAMIN WAS A YOUNG LAWYER in the Philadelphia County Prosecutors Office. He'd gone to law school because he thought it sounded cool (he had pride issues, just like the rest of you). Now he sat in a plush cubicle earning less than a shoe cobbler. However, because he was a lawyer, most people thought he was rich. Scott was average looking I suppose, but the past ten years had put him on the soft side of lean. He wasn't gluttonous, at least not yet, but he was on the cusp of a Deadly. His forehead had become a fivehead; receding just enough to give him the look of a dad.

His wife, Theresa, became pregnant with Libby in college, waddling to her finals and scribbling in the blue book with her legs resting on the next seat. She thought pregnancy, for all the hype, had been a fraud (it's Eve's curse, you know—all the pain—but she got exactly what she deserved for eating that apple). Nausea, lethargy, and swollenness caused Theresa to question the ways of nature (again, blame Eve, that gullible, half-dressed floozy prancing around the garden frolicking with snakes like me). When she became pregnant with Mia, her nursing career went bye-bye.

"Honey, will you please bathe the girls and get them to bed?" She was halfway down the hall before Scott could respond. By the time the girls were bathed and ready for bed, Scott was exhausted, too. It had been a big day.

"Daddy, can I have a drink?" Libby asked.

"Me too," said Mia. This was transparent stalling, for they weren't thirsty. Scott stood in front of the refrigerator that was plastered with art work—stick figures with extra-long torsos and pencil-thin legs practically doing the Chinese splits. Scott was the tallest figure, with a round head and three hairs sticking up on top. Theresa stood next to him, anorexic, with long stringy hair that flipped up at the end. The two girls stood next to her in the line. Their long stringy hair flipped up at the end, too (it's just the way you draw a girl).

Theresa was almost asleep by the time he got in bed. He reached over and touched her shoulder.

"Not tonight, okay? I'm *so* tired."

"You don't need to do anything," he whispered. "It'll be quick—you won't feel a thing."

"That's pathetic," she mumbled. "How was your day?"

"Good. We finally won that Ponzi scheme case. Remember the guy who stole millions from his family and friends and blamed them for not stopping him?"

"Sleaze ball." Theresa was so tired she could barely speak.

"No kidding. But the big news is I was put on that Miles murder case. Stew Franks asked me to second chair it. He said I could have a couple witnesses."

She rolled over. "Seriously? That's awesome."

"It's going to be huge."

They lay in the dark a few minutes when she finally whispered, "Okay, fine, but let's make it quick. I'm really tired."

19

DAN LEONARD SPENT A SLEEPLESS NIGHT parked across the street from Aunt Eloise's boarding house, freezing. He needed to stay awake too, in case one of the low-riding punks chose to take a midnight stroll. He'd peed on the neighbor's shrub in the middle of the night.

The anonymous employer called him the next morning to check for progress. Dan's frozen cell phone felt like an ice cube on his ear. He believed this martyrdom ought to be rewarded, so he resolved to pad his bill even more. There'd still been no activity inside the house. He called his girlfriend to pass the time, then began a crossword puzzle (but had no idea what you called a "young kilt wearer," so he gave up). He drove around the block and parked in front of a different house, because the neighbor might become suspicious of some guy sitting outside his house in a freezing minivan doing crossword puzzles, and peeing in the bushes.

Aunt Eloise's front door finally opened and the tall one emerged, alone. He wore the same clothes as the day before, walking with legs spread to keep his pants up. Did he not have a belt, or even a rope?

Dan was in a quandary; did he follow Cheech and leave Chong at the house unwatched? He pulled out his camera and began shooting. Because he'd taken no photos the day before, he overdid it that morning, treating his camera like a semi-automatic weapon. He started the van and followed Slim to a 7-11 a few blocks away. Slim came out a few minutes later with a bag of groceries in one hand and a half-eaten candy bar in the other.

Slim had already blown through a chunk of his $4,000. He'd paid Aunt Eloise the overdue rent with the proud airs of a rich merchant bestowing a tip on the boardinghouse wench. She'd taken the wad of cash and shoved it down her 40-DDD bra where even the most nefarious criminal would dare not go to retrieve it. She didn't count it in front of Slim, pretending not to care about the money, but one minute later she slipped into the bathroom and greedily did so.

Jesse was counting his money, too. He'd spent some on the coke at Adam's house, and contributed to the Aunt Eloise rent fund (but Slim had taken all the credit). And, in a fit of giddy prosperity, the boys agreed to give Uncle Wayne $50 each (Jesse had initially argued that he should contribute less, because Uncle Wayne was technically Slim's blood).

Dan needed a photo of Jesse before he reported back to the anonymous caller. He finally got his chance that afternoon when they left for Adam's house to snort more coke. After all, what else would they do with the money, *save it*? Dan watched them through his camera's lens, clicking photos for every two steps they took.

He followed them to Adam's in his minivan, waited a few minutes, and then drove back to Aunt Eloise's. He parked in front and walked up to the door. The porch was icy, even though an opened bag of ice melt sat next to the door with a Scooby Doo plastic cup in it. He knocked and the door was opened by a middle-aged man who wore a dirty white tank top. There was something not quite right with this man, something about his eyes which weren't in sync with each other. Behind him, Dan could see another younger man lying on the living room floor sniffing a pair of shoes. Something wasn't right with him either.

"Excuse me," Dan said, "I'm looking for two young men who live here."

"Yeah."

"Are they home? May I speak to them?"

"They was here, but they just left."

"Do you know how I can get a hold of them?"

Uncle Wayne just looked at him.

"I met them a few days ago," Dan continued. "They gave me their address and phone number but I've misplaced the number. I run a construction company and they said they might be interested in doing some work for me."

"Oh."

"Who's at the door?" a woman yelled from beyond the living room. "And close the damned thing for Pete's sake, it's freezin'!"

"Somebody's lookin' for Slim and Jesse," he yelled over his shoulder.

"Well, tell him they ain't here," Aunt Eloise yelled back.

"They ain't here," Uncle Wayne said.

"Shoot," Dan said, "they just told me their names were Slim and Jesse, but I didn't get a last name."

"Slim just goes by 'Slim' and I don't know what Jesse goes by."

"You don't know their last names?"

"They probably have one, but I can't think what it is," Uncle Wayne said. "Let me go check." He closed the door on Dan who stood shivering on the porch. He wasn't sure if the odd man was going to return or not. Just as he was about to knock again, the door opened to Aunt Eloise. She was holding "Knock It Off!" on her hip.

"You say you got some work for the boys?"

"Well, I might. I just need their full names and a contact number so I can reach them."

"Well, Slim, that's my nephew, he's a good hard worker. Anyways, his last name is Monson. Need me to spell it?"

"No, that's alright."

"Okay then and Jesse, let's see, Jesse's last name is . . ." she looked up to the sky as if an angel might reveal it to her. "I think its Samuel, or Samuels. Hold it, I think its Samuelson. Yeah, I'm positive that's it. I'm like eighty percent sure."

Learning a possible cell phone number ultimately became too much of a challenge. *Dammit, Wayne, I said shut up while I'm thinkin!" "Why don't you shut up?" "'Cause it's my house, that's why! Okay, now whaddya say you needed again, the phone number, was it?* Dan excused himself, figuring he had mined as much information as he could.

Jesse and Slim were thrilled to see that Adam had stocked up on more cocaine. They were in paradise (which isn't all it's cracked up to be, by the way). Adam had also invited two girls over who liked to party. The boys wanted to impress the girls with their wads of cash, and what better way than giving them crisp bills to roll for good snorting?

The two girls, Desiree and Shauntay, hadn't done well on their ACTs. They were squeezed into size-two animal print skirts, when they really needed a size eight. Their muffin tops drooped over their skirts which were too short. They wore stilettos, halter tops, and gobs of makeup (it looked like it'd been applied with an industrial paint brush). Their hair was big, and stiff, as if it'd been jerry-rigged together by a sophisticated network of hidden pipe cleaners.

"He was, like, totally into me," Desiree was saying.

"Are you *kidding*? He was, like, totally hitting on you, and you were all, like, totally ignoring him," said Shauntay.

"I was wearing that one top you liked. But I was all, like, totally fat yesterday."

"He's, like, totally obsessed with you. But now Krystan says he likes her."

"I know. And I'm all, like, are you *serious*? He's into *me*. And she's all, like, 'no way, fat bitch.' She totally grosses me out."

Jesse and Slim lost interest when it became obvious the girls were all, like, totally absorbed in their drama and weren't going to drop their animal-print skirts. Eventually, the girls became intellectually exhausted and began using their hundred dollar bills. It was a blizzard of cocaine. I'm all, like, totally serious.

The next day the girls were long gone, and so was the money. The boys were, like, totally bummed. They were, like, way depressed. All they had to show for their once-in-a-lifetime jackpot was a runny nose.

20

STEWART FRANKS CALLED A MEETING to discuss the Miles' murder investigation. Stew was the lead prosecutor for capital cases. He was busy because you tend to kill each other, a lot. And there's usually a Deadly involved. Wrath and Greed are probably the most common culprits. But there's also your Lust, Envy, and Pride (you rarely murder each other because of Sloth or Gluttony, but it happens).

Stew had risen to the top in the prosecutor's office by virtue of his seniority, and not his brains, or trial skills. He'd campaigned for this position for twenty years. They finally promoted him, hoping he'd retire soon thereafter. However, those hopes were dashed when the promotion ratcheted up his pride. He began dying his hair and putting product in it. He even used teeth whitening strips. His wife was convinced he was having an affair.

The informal meeting was held in the prosecutor's conference room. They sat around the table: Scott Benjamin as the number two man on the team, and the two detectives, Flygare and Olson. Stew was eager to stand before a phalanx of microphones to assure the citizenry that justice would prevail! However, before he could preen behind the handsome wood podium with the state seal, he needed something to report—something that showed he was about to nail the goddamned miscreant who'd brazenly taken Chelsea's life with a swinging spade.

"So, gentlemen," Stew asked, just as he took a bite of bagel, "where are we?"

"As you know, Mr. Franks—"

"Call me Stew."

"Very well," said Flygare. "As you know, Stew, we have three primary persons of interest. We think the evidence against the husband is fairly strong. We have motive. His wife had sex with another man shortly before he came home that afternoon. So, we ought to assume he knew about it."

"Okay," said Stew, as he chewed while the others pretended not to see the piece of bagel on his lip.

"We also have opportunity," said Detective Olson. "Miles was the last one who saw her alive. He also found her body."

"But shouldn't we be focusing on the sperm donor?" asked Scott. "He's undoubtedly relevant."

"Yeah, we know," said Olson.

"She was pregnant, and Miles claims the baby wasn't his."

"Yeah, we know," said Olson.

"So, assuming husband is telling the truth—the sperm donor has got to be a prime suspect."

"Yeah, we know," said Olson.

"And husband's fingerprints weren't on the murder weapon."

"Yeah, we know," said Olson.

"And it seems illogical that he'd go outside to grab a shovel to kill her."

"Yeah, we know," said Olson.

"And he didn't wipe his prints off the handle because the landscaper's prints would've been wiped off, too. And they weren't."

"Yeah, we know," said Olson.

"Okay, so we don't have enough to arrest the husband," said Stew. "Who else do we have?" The gob of whatever it was still hovered precariously on his upper lip. Each of the others waited for someone else to gesture toward his mouth, or say something. *Uh, Stew, uh, you have a little . . . no, the other side, yeah, there, you got it.*

"We have the landscaper," said Flygare. "This Javier Flores guy. His fingerprints were on the murder weapon and he was there when the murder took place."

"Motive?" Stew asked. It was now clear that the dangling thing was, at least partially, cream cheese, which acted as a bonding agent to his lip.

"We don't really have motive," said Flygare. "We wanted to get a semen sample but we've lost track of him."

"But if it *was* his semen, then he'd probably be our guy," Stew said as he took another bite, which the others hoped would dislodge the dangler. It held firm.

"Yeah, we know," said Olson.

"So we lost an important person of interest to the investigation."

"Yeah, we know," said Olson.

"We let him get away."

"Yeah, we know," said Olson.

"He's probably in Mexico by now."

"Yeah, we know," said Olson, who finally looked Stew dead in the eye and motioned to his lip.

"So, who's the third suspect?" Stew asked. "You said there were three."

"The lover."

"But we don't know who he is," said Stew.

"Yeah, we know," said Olson.

"So, we don't have much to go on."

"Yeah, we know," said Olson.

"We need to find that Flores guy."

"Yeah, we know," said Olson.

"What about the thief?" asked Scott. "Someone came in through that downstairs window, and the husband said some jewelry and a laptop was stolen."

"Yeah, we know," said Olson.

"So, there's also the possibility that an unknown burglar killed her."

"Yeah, we know," said Olson.

"So, we're really looking at a minimum of four suspects; five if there's another sperm donor out there who got her pregnant, besides the guy she had sex with that afternoon."

"Yeah, we know," said Olson.

"There may be even more than that."

"Yeah, we know," said Olson.

If all you heard was Olson's responses, you might think they knew a lot.

Dan now had the names and photos (too many, really) of the post office box renters, so he was eager to make a report.

"What have you learned?"

"I've got photos which I'll email to you in a minute. I also got their names. The shorter one you'll see is a guy named Jesse Samuelson, and the tall one goes by Slim Monson. I checked the county records and neither of them own any property, cars; nothing. I don't even think they're employed."

"Anything to suggest they're tech savvy?"

"Uh, to be honest, these two don't look savvy about anything."

"Any connections to political causes or any interests like, say, oil and gas, or some environmental cause?"

"*These guys?* Doesn't seem like it to me."

"Keep on them. I want to know who they talk to and where they go."

"Yeah, okay, but for how long?"

"Until I say otherwise."

"Listen, buddy, I appreciate the work and all, but I have other clients. I can't follow these punks around for the rest of my life. You understand."

"I'll send you another $5,000. That ought to be enough for another week or so."

"Okay, yeah, I guess I can do that." Dan was no longer annoyed. "Is there anything in particular you want me to watch for?"

"I just want to know where they go and who they talk to."

Dan was tired of these guys, on both ends of the transaction. But he'd follow them to hell and back if the money was good enough. So far, the money was good—not hell and back good, but good.

Jesse realized they'd made a mistake—they should've asked for more money. If this senator guy had been willing to send them ten grand that easily, he'd probably send more. Where was the downside? They'd never go to the cops, but he didn't need to know that. If they came forward with what they knew, they'd only get in trouble themselves. Geez, the cops might blame *them.* And if the senator guy really had murdered her, the cops would figure it out soon enough.

"Slim, I think we ought to give it another shot."

"Whaddya mean?"

"What do you think I mean, you idiot? We need more money from the Congress guy. What else would I mean?"

"I can't read your mind, dude."

"Only this time, we go big."

"How big."

"Twenty grand big."

Slim whistled. "We splittin' it equal this time?"

"The lead guy always gets more."

"Then I'll be the lead guy this time," said Slim.

"Hey, if you're going to be a jerk about it, I guess we can just split it even."

Jesse began composing a note the old-fashioned way (i.e. sans cut-out pasted letters which was too much work), while Slim leaned over his shoulder eating a bag of Doritos. Jesse tried to be patient, but the Nacho Cheese on Slim's breath was annoying, and so were the bawling kids in the other room. He needed to get out of this place. So, in a moment of grand audacity, he decided right then and there to ask for $50,000.

It's us again. This time we here with want $50,000. We know you've got it too. And then our business is finished and we won't bother you anymore. So no funny business. Just do it like you did last time.

Slim read along. "Ho-lee shit, dude! Fifty grand? Are you shittin' me?" He raised his hand for a high five, but Jesse left him hanging because he was concentrating so hard on the letter.

"Yeah, he needs to know we mean business."

"Maybe we should say we've got photos or something. That'd scare the shit out of him."

"Yeah, I was thinking the same thing," said Jesse, who was not thinking the same thing at all (but couldn't allow Slim to think he'd come up with something the lead guy hadn't already thought of). "I was going to add that, but then I thought maybe he'd want to see them before he paid."

"If he wants to see them, we'll charge him again for that, too." Slim was beating Jesse to every punch.

"Yeah, I thought of that, too," said Jesse.

The third in the trilogy of blackmail notes was amended to include the bold assertion that they had photos. It was addressed and mailed as the others had been.

Dan Leonard watched them leave the house again, clutching a letter and then dropping it in the mail box. He called the anonymous employer to report what he'd seen.

Senator Lawson was on the phone in his office when Paul McDonald tapped on the door and opened it slightly. Lawson waved him in and pointed to a chair.

"Listen, Susan," Lawson made an exasperated look for McDonald's sake, "I don't really care." Susan must've had the last word because a moment later Lawson hung up without saying another word.

"Sorry to bother you, sir, but I heard from our investigator."

"Go on."

"He says the blackmailers are unemployed punks. Says he doesn't think they're tied to anyone with the least bit of sophistication."

"Then how in the hell did they see me? I just don't get it."

"We may never know, sir, but he said they just dropped a letter in the mailbox. If it comes to us, I guess it's good and bad."

"Good?"

"Well, at least it would appear they're acting on their own. But they might want more money."

"Little bastards! I want to find out what they know and how the hell they know it. You got that? I want these punks interrogated!"

"I have our man on the ground following them for at least another week and he'll keep us posted. I think we should wait a few more days to see what happens."

"Okay," said Lawson, "but keep your eye on the mail. In the meantime, I'll assume they're not affiliated with the goddamn environmentalists and issue a statement that the Clean Air Act is bad for American business, and bad for national security."

Senator Lawson had the impressive agility to find a national security threat in almost anything. He'd stumbled onto the strategy to ensure his opponents measured their responses carefully, otherwise he'd brand them soft on terrorism. *What, you don't think national security is important? Then fine, go ahead and vote for the Clean Air Act, and empower the jihadist Muslims while you're at it. Be my guest. But it'll be your fault if there's another terrorist attack.* This rhetoric, for some reason, resonated with about 35% of voters.

21

ANN LEE HAD OVERHEARD PAUL MCDONALD ask the receptionist three times if the mail had come that morning. Something was up. He told the receptionist to let him know as soon as it came. But what McDonald didn't know was that McKayla's loyalties were with Ann, who'd actually made an effort to know her, whereas McDonald still alternatively called her Melinda, Melissa, or McKenna. Therefore, she'd buzzed Ann as soon as she saw the mailman come.

Ann hurried to the mailroom and frantically searched the stack of mail for anything that looked unusual. There was an envelope with the address handwritten by someone with poor penmanship, and no return address. She decided to take her chance on that one and slipped it into her blouse, just as Paul charged into the room.

"What are you doing in here?" McDonald asked.

"What do you think I'm doing in here? I'm looking to see if I won the million-dollar sweepstakes. What are *you* doing in here?"

"It's none of your business."

Ann left the mailroom, but hid partially behind the copy machine to see if Paul left with any mail. He didn't. Either she held the prize in her blouse, or nothing had come. She was eager to get back to her office because one corner of the letter was jabbing her rib.

She closed her door and opened the letter, carefully peeling up the flap so it could be re-sealed, unnoticed.

It's us again. This time we here with want $50,000. We know you've got it too. And then our business is finished and we won't bother you anymore. So no funny business. Just do it like you did last time. We have photos too.

No doubt she'd grabbed the correct envelope. She read it again. Her heart raced. This wasn't just another kook imploring the senator to drop an A Bomb on the entire Middle East. She made a copy of the note and placed the original back in the envelope. She sealed the flap with a glue stick, and walked back to the mailroom, slipping it into the stack of mail.

A few minutes later she buzzed McKayla at the front desk.

"Say, McKayla, will you do me another big favor?"

"Sure. What's up?"

"Can you buzz Paul McDonald and tell him another small batch of mail just came, in case he might be interested?"

"I don't know what's going on here, but I'll tell him."

A minute later she saw McDonald rush to the mailroom and come out clutching an envelope. He headed to Senator Lawson's office.

McDonald handed the envelope to his boss who opened it and removed the letter.

"Shit!" Lawson said. He leaned back in his chair, horrified. They had *photos*? Are you kidding? For a brief moment, Lawson actually wondered to himself how he looked in the photos. Did he look fat? Did his bald spot show? Did he look out of breath?

"And now they want fifty grand? What next?" asked Lawson. "We can't keep giving in to these crooks. They sound like bozos. Read that again, the part about 'here with.' Are they serious? They're either complete morons or they're playing a game."

"If they were with an environmental group," said McDonald, "I think we'd know by now. Maybe we've misjudged them. Maybe they're just a couple of losers. Our guy on the ground said they don't even have jobs."

"Well, I'm not giving them fifty grand. If I do, they'll just keep blackmailing me. We need to confront them."

"So what do you think?" asked McDonald. "You want to get somebody to interrogate them?"

"We don't have a choice. This could go on forever." Lawson kept saying "we". Poor McDonald was waist deep in this mess without even having seen Chelsea do her thing. It didn't seem fair.

"Okay," said McDonald, "but I don't think we should use our same guy. He's a private detective, not an interrogator."

"You find someone, Paul. He can't know that I'm involved, and he needs to be paid from funds that can't be traced to me." Naturally. "And I don't want him causing serious injury to these guys, unless they don't cooperate."

McDonald called a guy who knew a guy, who knew a guy, who knew a guy that came highly recommended. And the guy who would now be known as The Guy was an ex-con that coaxed information from people. The coaxing was enhanced by 275 pounds of meanness and sparse conscience.

The Guy's given name was Glen. He'd served time in three different states for violent crimes (he'd actually committed them too—he'd never been framed). Glen rarely worked alone because, as strange as it may sound, he didn't know how to drive a vehicle. So, he brought in his partner, Whitey. His instructions were clear: corner these guys and find out what they know.

Whitey was the smart one, having earned his GED by threatening the teachers who finally awarded him the coveted diploma. Whitey was actually black, with tattoos all over his body that didn't show up well on his skin. Most people wouldn't have suffered all that pain for such a marginal payoff, but Whitey had a high pain threshold. He'd hardly winced each time his nose had been broken.

Glen and Whitey were given the photos and address for Jesse and Slim. They drove Whitey's panel van from Washington D.C. to Philadelphia the next day. The van had no rear windows and *A-1 Locksmith* was written on the side. There were no seats in the back, just your basic tools of the trade: duct tape, rope, handcuffs, guns, and brass knuckles.

They drove past Aunt Eloise's house a few times, and then to the outskirts of the city where they rented a small storage shed. It was a dirty, unpainted, cinderblock cell. A string dangled from a light bulb in the center of the shed, which was empty, except for an upright piano that the previous renter had left behind because it was too heavy to move. It was cold inside and there was a two-inch gap between the cement floor and the wall on one side. The shed's only access was a garage door that could be locked from the outside with a padlock. The exterior surroundings were poorly lit with no security except for a chain-link gate at the perimeter of the property.

Glen and Whitey returned to Aunt Eloise's by dusk and parked a few doors down the road. They settled in, expecting to wait. A few minutes later, Jesse and Slim left the house and got into an old car with a plastic garbage bag covering the rear-side window. The tall skinny one drove and the kid with the beanie rode shotgun. Glen and Whitey pulled away from the curb and followed them. Slim pulled into a Taco Bell parking lot a mile later. The Interrogators pulled the van into the empty space next to Slim's car and waited for the boys to return with their chimichangas.

Jesse and Slim came back out fifteen minutes later.

Glen rolled down his passenger-side window. "Hey, you guys know where we can get some weed?"

"Maybe," said Slim (he wisely carried an auxiliary baggie in his glove box).

"We'll pay a premium if it's decent shit."

Slim walked over to the van and Jesse followed him. If these big dudes in the van were willing to pay a premium for his run-of-the-mill weed, then cowabunga!

"Yeah," Glen said. "We're from out of town and want a smoke."

"I'll sell you a joint for twenty bucks," said Slim.

"I said we wanted to smoke, not get hosed."

"Hey, that's what it costs, dude."

"Let's see it," Whitey said, as both he and Glen got out of the van.

The four of them stood between the two cars when suddenly Glen grabbed Slim's skinny arm and stuck a gun in his chest. Whitey did the same to Jesse. "Get in the van. *Now!*"

"Holy shit, dude, you can have it!" Slim was naturally terrified. "I don't care—just take it!"

"Shut up or we'll blow your fuckin' brains out!" The boys were shoved into the open sliding door of the van and Glen jumped in behind them, his gun aimed at their heads as they curled in the back of the empty van, as far away from the gun as they could possibly get. Whitey ran around to the driver's seat and they sped away.

22

THE BOYS COULDN'T SEE WHERE THEY WERE GOING because there were no windows in the van. Their kidnappers said nothing, other than "Shut the fuck up!" whenever Jesse posed a reasonable question, like "What do you want from us?" Slim was in petrified shock. What had he been *thinking*? Twenty bucks for some average weed? Stupid! Stupid! Stupid!

They drove for half an hour. It was dark outside by the time they finally stopped. Glen got out of the sliding door, his gun still aimed at the boys. They didn't know what they'd done to earn this horror ride, other than slightly overcharge these crazy freaks for some mediocre ganja.

Glen ordered Slim out of the van at gunpoint. Slim moved like a ninety-year-old man, practically bent in half at the waist. "Please don't kill me, please don't kill me, please don't kill me." This request didn't reflect poorly on his manliness—no one wants to be shot. After Glen and Slim got out, Jesse dared to sit up in the back of the van and looked out the front windshield. He saw they were parked in front of a storage shed.

Whitey remained at the wheel, staring at Jesse through the rear-view mirror, expertly switching his toothpick from one side of his mouth to the other. He admonished Jesse not to try anything cute or he'd blow his brains out. This command was overkill, because Jesse couldn't think of a single cute thing to say, or do.

Through the windshield, Jesse saw Glen bend down and open a padlock at the bottom of the small garage door, and lift it open. It was dark inside the shed, but the headlights from the van illuminated an old upright piano at the back of the otherwise bare room. Glen, with his gun still aimed at Slim's head, pulled a string in the middle of the room and a light bulb came on. He shoved Slim up against the piano, and, from inside, pulled down the garage door.

Jesse was freaking out in the back of the van. His bosom buddy was about to be executed, gangster style, and he'd be next. Inside the shed, Glen ordered Slim to sit down on the cement floor with his back to the piano, facing the front of the shed. Glen pulled a roll of duct tape from his jacket, yanked Slim's hands behind him, and wrapped his wrists to the piano leg. He then stood above Slim and put the gun in his jacket's pocket. This gave Slim no small amount of relief.

"Okay," Glen calmly said, "you're gonna tell me everything you know about how you seen him. Once you tell me everything, I'll let you live. If you don't, then I'll kill you. It's that simple. Okay?" Glen was so calm and matter-of-fact about the whole thing. However, Slim knew Glen would shoot him if he didn't get what he wanted.

"I don't know what you're talking about. How I seen *who*?"

Glen's kick to Slim's chest was instant and violent. Slim's hopes for survival vanished. He couldn't breathe.

"I will ask you again," Glen said. "Tell me about the letters."

Slim now understood what Glen was talking about (and realized he should have demanded a full 50% share from Jesse), but he couldn't speak. He tried, but the pain in his chest and lack of air made speaking impossible. He nodded his head, to show he'd respond helpfully as soon as he could breathe again.

In the back of the van, Jesse's eyes had adjusted to his surroundings. There was an industrial yellow flashlight lying a few feet from him, next to a coil of rope. Just then, Whitey's cell phone rang. He stared at the caller ID for a few more rings, then finally sighed and pushed the button to speak, like he might as well get it over with.

"Whitey here."

Jesse eyed the flashlight. They were going to kill him, so why not take a chance? He had nothing to lose. Whitey became annoyed at the caller, arguing over a late utility payment. Jesse inched toward the flashlight and gripped it with his right hand. It felt heavy, maybe three or four pounds. He was about five feet behind and slightly to the right of Whitey who was still sitting in the driver's seat. Whitey kept glancing at Jesse through the rearview mirror, but was invested in the telephone call.

Jesse slid forward to the point where he could have reached Whitey's right shoulder. He slowly raised himself to his knees so that he was kneeling on the corrugated metal floor of the van. The flashlight was heavy in his right hand. He held his breath.

One. Two. Three.

He swung the flashlight with all his might, striking Whitey on the right side of his skull, just above the ear. It sounded like he'd struck a pumpkin with a five iron. Whitey dropped the cell phone and slumped forward in his seat against the steering wheel.

Jesse jumped from the sliding rear door and ran. He didn't look back. He had no idea where he was, or where he was running to. He didn't stop until his lungs were about to explode. Only then did he dare to look back. No one was following him. He was standing in the middle of a dark road. Up ahead he saw the lights of a gas station and convenience store. He took off running again.

He waited outside in the shadows of the convenience store. He could see the employee at the cash register was a middle-aged female. There was no one else in the store. Should he call the police? If so, he'd be arrested as a thief who was trying to blackmail a United States Senator. Maybe he should make an anonymous call to the police to save Slim; telling them to go immediately to the storage shed. But he needed an address.

He took a deep breath to steady himself, and walked into the store. He pulled his beanie down nearly to his eyebrows, standing as he was in a well-lit fishbowl.

"Hey, um, I'm sorta lost. What street is this?"

"Listen, buddy, we got video cameras everywhere. This is River Road and cops patrol out here all the time."

"Yeah, I know, but, like, what's the address?"

"Why do you need the address?"

"I need to call a cab."

The clerk looked him over and finally gave him the address. Jesse left and returned to the shadows again. He dialed 911 on his cell and hung up. He needed to think this through. Who were those thugs and what did they want? Was it possible they were undercover cops? He'd heard about rogue cops doing strange and cruel things. But over some weed? Seriously?

Jesse could see the city lights to the east and began walking. Whenever he'd see headlights he'd hide behind a street-side bush, or sign. It was 11:00 p.m. by then, and cold. He walked for another two hours. He finally got his bearings when he came upon a familiar commercial area.

Meanwhile, Glen had grown impatient with Slim's inability to speak. He slapped him a few times but Slim couldn't provide the answers Glen felt entitled to. He decided to get the information from the other kid in the van, instead. He lifted the garage door from inside and stepped out into the cold. The headlights from the van temporarily blinded him, making it impossible to see through the windshield and into the van. He walked to the passenger's side and saw that the sliding door was open. Then he saw Whitey slumped over the steering wheel. *Shit!*

Glen ran around to the other side of the van and yanked the driver's door open. Whitey didn't move. He shook him and Whitey mumbled. He saw that he'd been hit in the side of the head. Glen went back to the shed to tell Slim that he'd be back to kill him if his buddy didn't survive. Slim didn't know what he was talking about. His buddy? *What* buddy? Glen turned off the light and left the shed, closing the garage door behind him.

Glen picked Whitey up from the driver's seat, carried him around to the open sliding door, laid him down next to the coiled rope, and slid the door closed. He then sat in the driver's seat and dialed the anonymous employer on his cell. No answer. Shit! He needed to get out of there, and he needed to get Whitey to a hospital. But, alas, he didn't know how to drive. He turned the key and the engine started, followed by a loud screeching sound because he didn't release the key. He divined the R stood for reverse. He pulled the gear lever down and haltingly backed away from the shed.

Luckily, he was in a large empty parking lot because he drove like a drunken six-year-old. He stomped on the gas pedal and then hit the brake with equal force. Whitey was spared serious whiplash only because he was lying down in the back. Glen drove out of the parking lot and headed down the road. He was unable to use his cell and drive at the same time (at this moment, it would've been difficult for him to chew gum).

He pulled the van up to the hospital and screeched to a stop. Medical personnel came out to help. They saw a large man hunched over the steering wheel, gripping it so hard they feared he might bend it. Beads of sweat were pouring down his face. They assumed he was having a heart attack. However, he told them he was fine; it was the guy in the back that needed help.

They brought a stretcher out and removed Whitey from the van. Glen was told to park the van and come inside. Glen, however, didn't know how to park, and didn't want to go inside. So, he left the van where it was, haphazardly parked near the emergency entrance, and walked away.

He kept trying to call the anonymous number but there was no answer. He found a Denny's a block from the hospital and sat drinking black coffee, considering his options. Where in the hell did the kid with the beanie go? And how in the hell had he overcome Whitey's strength, and gun?

Slim was finally able to breathe, but his chest felt like the piano had landed on top of him. He was pretty sure he had a cracked sternum (or whatever that bone between his ribs was called). It was dark and freezing cold, too. His arms and shoulders ached from being pulled behind him and his wrists were on fire. He heard a scratching sound on the floor and realized there was a rat in the room that had crawled through the crack.

For one of the first times in his life, Slim wasn't hungry—he was too scared to be hungry. If the men didn't return to kill him, he knew he'd die anyway. No one knew he was here except Jesse, who was probably dead by now. After two more hours, he prayed they'd return to finish him off.

Dan Leonard had been parked a few doors down from Aunt Eloise's house when Jesse and Slim got into the old car with plastic taped over the rear-side window. He was about to follow them when an A-1 Locksmith van parked in front of him pulled out first. He assumed this was a coincidence, but the van followed the boys to Taco Bell. It pulled in next to their car while the two boys were inside eating tacos.

Dan parked his minivan on the opposite side of the parking lot. When Jesse and Slim returned to their car, he saw how they were thrown into the back of the A-1 van. What in the hell was going on? He followed them because that had been his assignment. How was he supposed to know that Paul McDonald, the anonymous caller, had forgotten to call him off the case once they'd hired The Interrogators? He wasn't supposed to see any of this. Of course, I was thrilled.

He followed the van at a safe distance to the outskirts of town. The van passed through an opened chain link gate to a rundown storage facility. He parked several hundred yards away and watched The Interrogators remove the tall one from the van and take him inside one of the storage sheds. After a few minutes, he saw the smaller one, the one with the beanie, take off running from the van with no one following him. Now what was he supposed to do? Should he stay where he was, or should he follow Jesse? He'd already taken plenty of photos of the A-1 van and the huge men who drove it. He'd also taken photos of the storage shed, and now he was shooting photos of Jesse running away.

Dan decided to stay where he was. He called the anonymous number for further instructions. There was no answer. He waited until he saw the large man come out of the shed and lift the driver to the back of the van. Presumably the driver had been shot or wounded by Jesse, who'd then skedaddled. He watched the van lurch and weave its way through the deserted parking lot. Obviously, the man who was now at the wheel had also been seriously wounded and was barely able to drive. He called again. Still no answer. *Shit!*

He followed the van to the hospital. Clearly the driver was suffering a medical emergency because he didn't stop for red lights, or even drive on the correct side of the road at times, weaving in a herky-jerky manner until he reached the hospital. Dan photographed the medical personnel lifting Whitey to the stretcher, and the driver who'd simply walked away from the van without any apparent injury or illness. He followed the man to Denny's and waited outside in the parking lot until he could reach the anonymous caller for further instructions.

23

JESSE STUMBLED INTO AN ALL-NIGHT WENDY'S at 4:00 a.m., cold and exhausted. The cops scared him, but not as much as the goons who were trying to kill him. He'd concluded they must have been hired to track him down because of the blackmail letters. There was no other reasonable explanation (I mean, who kills over an illegal drug trade? Right?). He decided to turn himself over to the protection of the cops, and who would've dreamed twenty-four hours earlier that he'd find comfort in *that*?

At least the cops wouldn't kill him. But, yikes, they might frame him for murder. He'd been a burglar in the house the very day Chelsea had been murdered and his fingerprints were probably all over the place, including the basement window and medicine cabinet. Ugh, his fingerprints were even on the tube of Vagicream. How humiliating. He'd live out the rest of his days in solitary confinement, known only as the infamous Vagicream Killer.

That infamy was still preferable to being tortured to death by Glen and Whitey. And what *about* Whitey, anyway? Had he killed him with the flashlight? If so, there would be no doubt who'd wielded the murder weapon—his fingerprints were all over the freaking flashlight, too. And here was a scary thought: what if Glen and Whitey were undercover cops? *Vagicream Killer Goes on Cop Killing Spree.* Oh my.

It was 4:30 a.m. when he dialed 911. He told the operator he had just witnessed an abduction and possible murder. The dispatcher assured him a police officer would arrive at Wendy's shortly. Jesse felt relief for the first time in ten hours. Of course, he could kiss the $50,000 goodbye, and he'd probably go to jail, but at least he'd be alive. He hoped he hadn't waited too long to save poor Slim.

The officer arrived at the Wendy's parking lot without lights or sirens. Jesse walked out with his arms raised, an admirable act of surrender. It was still dark outside and his breath was visible from the cold.

"Are you the young man who called about an abduction and possible homicide?"

"Yeah, that's me. I need to talk."

"It's cold outside, son. Why don't you have a seat in my car."

Jesse sat in the warm patrol car and leaned his head back, prepared to unload his sorry tale. Before he could do his unloading, the policeman asked his name and other background information. Jesse was finally allowed to unburden his soul of criminal mischief. It would have made more sense if he'd started at the beginning—if he'd gone all the way back to the remodel job and the pill thievery. But for now, he told the cop that he and Slim had been minding their own business when they were abducted in the Taco Bell parking lot and taken to the storage shed from whence he had escaped.

The officer was less frantic than Jesse thought he ought to be. The officer also ignored the constant interruptions that streamed through the radio. More than once Jesse wanted to ask him, *Hey, do you need to get that?* or *Shouldn't we get moving?* When Jesse had finished his woeful tale, the policeman picked up the radio to ask for backup, and they headed to the storage shed facility. Jesse, who rarely wore a seat belt, had the good judgment to buckle up, for he didn't want to compound his criminality, not smack dab in front of the cop at a time like this.

Jesse couldn't remember exactly which unit Slim had been taken to. They all looked identical. They drove slowly by when Jesse spotted the flashlight lying on the pavement. "It's this one here!"

Another squad car arrived and parked next to them. The two officers got out and conferred, and then came back and opened Jesse's passenger door. "You sure this is where it was?"

"I'm positive. Look, the padlock isn't even locked. You can open it and see."

The sun was not yet up but the sky had lightened in that pre-dawn way. The officers lifted the door and shined their flash-lights inside. Slim was sitting spread eagle on the ground, his hands tied behind his back to a piano leg. They thought he was dead, but he raised his head and whispered, "Please don't kill me."

Dan Leonard had drifted off to sleep but awoke to see the flashing lights of two police cars parked directly in front of the shed. He was about to drive toward them, to offer his eyewit-ness account, when he realized he'd been secretly following the kidnapped duo, too. He picked up his cell and called the number again. This time Paul answered.

"Sorry, I see you tried to call a few times. My phone was on silent."

"Listen, buddy, I don't know what the hell you got me into, but I'm sitting in a parking lot in front of a bunch of storage sheds. The two guys I've been following were kidnapped and brought here last night. I think the kidnappers already killed one of them, the tall skinny one, and the other one escaped. I don't know where the hell he is. Now the cops are at the storage shed. I have it all on my camera."

Silence on the other end of the line. This could not be happening, thought McDonald. He had forgotten to take Dan Leonard off the surveillance! *Shit! Shit! Shit!* And now he'd not only seen, but photographed the abduction and the . . . *murder*? Did he say one of them had been *murdered*? Oh, dear God. No, no, no, this was all wrong.

"Get the hell out of there!" McDonald screamed into the phone. "Now! You can't be seen!"

Dan knew the situation had spiraled out of control, and he didn't like it a bit. This justified a whopping padded bill.

They took Slim by ambulance to the same hospital where Whitey was recovering from a skull fracture. The officer drove Jesse directly to the police station. Jesse probably should have demanded a lawyer (you and your lawyers) before the dirty secrets started spilling out, but he wanted it over with. Besides, it's not like he'd *killed* anybody (well, there was the undercover cop, or whoever the hell he was, who might be dead). Sure, he'd probably have to re-pay the ten grand, or at least pay taxes on it. And he was guilty of a breaking and entering, which wouldn't look good on his resumé. But he was alive and grateful for it.

Jesse was led down a corridor to an interrogation room with one of those one-way mirrors. He passed an Asian woman who sat in the reception area, fingering the pleat of her dress, waiting to spill her own guts no doubt. She'd probably had a restless night herself, Jesse thought—debating whether or not to tell the truth, the whole truth, and nothing but the truth.

Ann Lee had the same thought as she saw Jesse being led back to a room for questioning. She wondered what he'd done, and whether he'd had the same night of tossing and turning. Maybe the kid with the beanie and low riding jeans felt the same sense of relief that she did, now that she was about to unburden her secret, a secret that would overheat giddy television news anchors to near sexual excitement. I could see the imminent pain. Who couldn't?

Ann had considered confronting Senator Lawson about the note, but he would've denied there was anything to it. And Paul McDonald? Are you kidding? So, she decided to spill the beans. If Lawson and the rest of the staff chose to blame her, so be it. She would do the right thing and let the sacred annals of history be her judge. Good for her!

Jesse was led to an austere room with metal furniture. As soon as he sat down he started spewing forth confessions and apologies to the local policeman with alarming gusto. When he got to the part where he saw Chelsea Miles in bed with Senator Lawson, the local cop knew this kid was disclosing a blockbuster. However, before calling in Flygare and Olson, who worked at a precinct across town, he patiently endured Jesse's exhaustive narrative of the sex scene (twice actually—to be sure he got it right). He just wanted to be thorough. Uh-huh.

When Flygare and Olson arrived, they told Jesse to start over from the beginning, which he did, spending ample time on *exactly* what he'd seen through the crack in the bathroom door. Neither detective interrupted him.

Jesse took them through his now regrettable decision (for which he was truly sorry) to blackmail the senator. A lengthy written statement was prepared and Jesse signed it. He was then taken for fingerprints. A few strands of his hair were also plucked. They didn't ask him for a semen sample (which would've been pleasantly given) because now they knew who the sperm donor had been. Fingerprint analysis would later show that Jesse's prints were found on the basement window and medicine cabinet.

The detectives didn't believe Jesse was involved in Chelsea's murder—he'd been too forthright, gushing forth damning (and embarrassing) admissions (he admitted to smelling the tube of Vagicream, for example). But they needed to hold him so they'd know where to find him for further questioning. Therefore, he was booked into jail for breaking and entering.

The detectives waited until they were safely behind closed doors before doing a chest bump.

"*Senator Ken Effing Lawson?* Are you *shitting* me?"

"Un-freaking-believable. If that's really Lawson's jiz . . . ." He lowered his voice to a professional tone. "We need to move before Lawson finds out we're on to him. If I know Stew Franks, he'll call a press conference as soon as this leaks, so we'll need to rein him in. One bad move here, and we could be screwed."

There was a knock on the door.

"Yeah, what is it?"

"Sorry to bother you," said the local cop, "but there's someone here who wants to give a statement. I think it's something you'll wanna hear. She says she's on Senator Lawson's staff and needs to speak to someone right away. Says it's important."

The detectives stared at each other. "Put her in the conference room next door. We'll be right in."

24

AN HOUR EARLIER, right after McDonald hung up with Dan Leonard, his cell phone had rung again. This time it'd been Glen, and Glen wasn't happy.

"I've been trying to call you all night! We got some serious shit going down here!"

"I know," said McDonald. "My phone hasn't been working. What's going on?"

"I'm sitting at Denny's having a cup of coffee."

"So where are you now?"

"I just told you; I'm having a cup of coffee at Denny's." Glen understood neither the nuance, nor basic rules of sarcasm.

"Where are they—the two punks? Please tell me you have them."

"No, I don't have them! And I don't know where they are. This is a total clusterfuck! Me and my partner, a guy named Whitey, we separated them to get a straight answer. I dragged the tall one into a storage shed and tied him up. He didn't give me any information so I went back to get the other one, but the little son of a bitch was gone. He'd tried to kill Whitey, and then took off."

"He got *away*? You're telling me Jesse got *away*?"

"Whitey was guarding him in the van but the little prick must've hit him in the head and took off. I swear to God I'm gonna kill the little son of a bitch!"

"So what did you do with the other one—the kid in the storage shed? Where's he now?"

"I left him tied up in there so I could take Whitey to the hospital. What else was I supposed to do?"

"So he's still tied up in the shed? Are you *serious*?"

"I guess so," answered Glen.

"You *guess* so?"

The waitress came by with the coffee pot and Glen waved her away. On the other end of the line, McDonald was trying to process the unimaginable.

"Listen to me," McDonald said. "The one who got away has probably gone to the police and they've probably found the kid in the shed by now. Where's your van?"

"I left it in front of the hospital when I dropped Whitey off."

"You just *left it there*? Why in the hell did you do that? It's going to have evidence all over it!"

"Because I don't know how to drive, that's why."

McDonald was speechless. They'd hired someone who couldn't *drive*? This was disastrous. Jesse was on the run and would probably go to the police. He would easily identify this Whitey guy who was now in the hospital. It would all be traced back to McDonald and the Senator. Jesse would tell the cops about Lawson's ill-timed tryst with Chelsea—on the afternoon she was *murdered* for God's sake. This kid apparently had photos, too. No, this was very bad indeed. And it was so much fun!

The police tracked down Whitey before his cranial swelling had reached its peak. They'd put a call out to all hospitals in the area asking if they'd treated a large black man with a goose egg on the right side of his noggin. Within ten minutes they'd located his whereabouts at Mercy Philadelphia Hospital. They asked Jesse to accompany them to the hospital to get a positive ID, but Jesse begged them not to take him anywhere near the man.

Oil and gas Lobbyists #1, #2, and #3 were seated in a richly furnished conference room next to Senator Lawson's private office when Paul McDonald poked his head in.

"I'm sorry to interrupt you, sir, but there's an urgent matter that requires your attention."

"If you'll excuse me, gentlemen," Lawson said.

Lawson said nothing on the short walk to his private office; McDonald trailing him like a well-trained hound. They closed the door. He sat at his desk, bracing himself for bad news. This was virgin territory for him, for he always won. If he couldn't charm his way into winning, he'd buy his way into winning. If he couldn't buy his way into winning, he'd coerce his way into winning. If none of that worked, he'd always been able to blame someone else. However, he couldn't control this situation through charm, money, coercion, or blame. It was all very tragic.

"I'm afraid I have some awful news. I received two calls. The first was from the private investigator we hired to follow your two blackmailers. The second was from The Interrogators, the ones we hired to confront the blackmailers."

"Go on."

"The Interrogators found the two and took them to a remote area for questioning. However, they didn't get much information, so we still don't know how they came to learn of your . . . 'liaison' with Mrs. Miles."

"Well, tell them to keep at it. They'll talk eventually."

"I'm afraid that's the bad news, Senator. It seems that one of them was able to escape. The other one might be dead in a storage shed where they were being questioned."

"What!"

"See, our private investigator, the one we hired first, was still following them when they were abducted by The Interrogators. He saw the entire course of events."

"What in God's name! I thought you called him off!"

"We apparently forgot to do that."

"For God's sake! Where's the private investigator now – the first one?"

"I told him to get away from anywhere he could be found and traced back to us."

"And where are the so-called "Interrogators" as you like to call them? The second ones you hired."

"One is in the hospital. Apparently, he was injured during a confrontation with the punks they were questioning. The other one is hiding out, waiting for further instructions from you."

"From me? From *me*?" screeched Lawson. "I will not take responsibility for this fiasco! This was your doing, and you will see to it that I'm not involved in any way. I thought I'd made that clear."

"But, with all due respect, sir, we talked about this at length. I don't think either of them can be traced back to this office." Paul's failure to stop this "we" business in its tracks was now bearing the ugly fruits of betrayal.

"You don't *think*? You better be right or I'll see to it that you never work another day on The Hill!" The senator refused to grasp the likelihood that within days, or perhaps hours, he wouldn't be working on The Hill, either.

As McDonald passed the receptionist's desk, he was informed that Ann Lee would not be in until later that afternoon. Apparently, she had some important business to take care of in Philadelphia.

While Jesse was being booked into jail, Slim was recuperating in the hospital, sitting up in bed eating Jello. He was grateful for the uniformed guard standing outside his hospital door. When Slim was released from the hospital later that afternoon, he was escorted directly to jail (and hopefully to solitary confinement until both Glen and Whitey had died from natural causes).

Ann was satisfied that she'd done the right thing as she left the Philadelphia police station that morning. She didn't know what had led to the note, of course, but it was bad news if a senior member of congress was being blackmailed. What if a madman was on the loose? It was best to let the cops know. And if the senator had done something sinister for which he could be blackmailed? Perhaps it was just as well that be discovered, too.

The detectives asked her to keep this information secret. She'd agreed because she knew McDonald would sabotage an investigation if he and the senator had been up to something fishy, which now seemed likely.

Flygare pulled her aside as she was leaving. "Ms. Lee, do you happen to know if Senator Lawson has any travel plans scheduled within the next week?"

"Not that I know of, but I'll let you know when I get back to the office." She was relieved to know they were probably arranging for his security until they could get to the bottom of this threat.

25

DAN LEONARD DECIDED this would be a darned good time to get out of Dodge. He was tired of the winter anyway, so he bought a ticket to Miami. He'd been there before and knew where the Cuban senoritas were. This very knowledge had contributed to his divorce. However, before he left town, he did a little digging of his own to find out who'd hired him. His telephone number tracing software came in handy (you couldn't just plug in the number to get the owner's shoe size and social security number, but you could get the basics). A few hours later, he had the name of Paul McDonald, a name he didn't recognize.

McDonald's Facebook profile was sad. His photo revealed a forty-two-year-old, awkwardly posed in a suit and tie, holding a miniature poodle with a bow in its hair. McDonald was single, liked to read mystery novels, and listen to Air Supply. He was a devout Christian who worked in Washington D.C. as a legislative aide to a senator from Pennsylvania.

Whether McDonald had hired Dan for something connected to his work was anyone's guess. But, whatever it was, it had gone south. Dan didn't really care; he'd been paid (in cash) and made it a point not to become involved in matters he was investigating.

Stew Franks was giddy. It looked like Senator Lawson would be arrested for the murder of Chelsea Miles. And how cool was *that*? We're talking national headlines and Stew would be the one to announce it. He tried to be humble—tried to pretend it wasn't about him, but rather about justice for the people! He fantasized about the way the press would hang on his every word. He'd been thoroughly seduced by the potential stardom. It was time for another meeting with Scott Benjamin and the two detectives.

"Gentlemen, what do you think?" Stew asked them. "Do we have enough to arrest him?" This was no time for idle chit chat. The people needed to be told!

"I think we're close," said Flygare.

"We need samples of his hair, semen, and fingerprints," said Olson. "I think Lawson's our man, but don't forget; just a week ago we thought it was the husband. We need to be careful here."

"I know, I know," said Stew. "But let's assume, hypothetically (Stew was big on hypotheticals), that the hair and semen match. The unidentified fingerprints at the scene will probably belong to Lawson, too. Making those assumptions, do we have enough?" Stew wanted *so much* for it to be enough. He would've pawned his soul to me for a pittance for the chance to stand behind the podium for the big announcement.

"But we still have the murder weapon problem," said Scott.

"That's not insurmountable," said Stew.

"You don't think it's a problem that the only prints on the murder weapon belong to the landscaper?" asked Scott. He had pride issues, too, and didn't want to be caught by the courtroom artist with his mouth hanging open as the *real* killer stepped forward to proclaim that the fingerprints were his, and his alone!

"Well," said Olson, "there's a partial print on the shovel that appears to match a thumb print on the nightstand clock. But it's only a partial print, and it's not definitive."

"Well, that's huge," said Stew stating the obvious, "especially if it's Lawson's."

"I agree—*if* it matches," said Scott. "But it's a poor print, and only a partial one at that. It would be more corroborative than conclusive. But, yeah, at least it would preclude the defense from *excluding* Lawson."

"Right. That's what I'm saying," said Stew.

"But there's still the problem of motive. Why would Lawson kill her?"

"Maybe," said Flygare, "she threatened to expose their relationship, and he lost it. Maybe she tells him she's pregnant and was going in for a paternity test and he freaked out."

"Okay," said Scott. "But why would he use a shovel? I mean, think about it. A *shovel*? You've just had sex with your lover. She threatens to expose you, or blackmail you, or whatever. And, by the way, she wouldn't have any reason to blackmail him for money—she's married to a billionaire, after all. But, anyway, let's say she threatens to make the relationship public. Why would Lawson go outside and grab a shovel? It makes no sense."

"But if that partial print on the shovel belongs to him?" asked Flygare.

"Then I think we've got him," said Scott. "It still wouldn't make sense, but we'd nail him. But why would there only be a partial print on the handle? Wouldn't there be a lot of prints on it?"

"That's a good point," said Stew. "But if he didn't do it, why would there be *any* of his prints on the shovel?" This was also a good point and Stew was proud of himself for having made it.

"Maybe he wiped them off the shovel handle but mistakenly left one," said Olson.

"But if he had the hindsight to do that, why wouldn't he wipe down the rest of the room, like the clock?" asked Scott. *Somebody* had to be the devil's advocate here.

"Maybe he did. Maybe he wiped the room and just overlooked the clock."

"Sure, that's possible. But if he wiped down the shovel to remove his prints, why are the landscaper's prints still all over it?" asked Scott.

No one responded. Some things are not fully understood, except, of course, by me.

"Okay," said Stew, eager to keep their enthusiasm high, "how do we go about getting the samples we need from Lawson?"

"We meet with him, on his turf," said Flygare. "We let him know that we have reason to believe he was with Chelsea that day, and we need to eliminate him as a suspect. We tell him if he cooperates, and the samples exonerate him, we'll keep this private."

"And if he doesn't agree to cooperate?" asked Stew.

"Then we tell him we'll get the samples the old-fashioned way—with a subpoena. And we'll see to it that it's made public."

They figured Lawson would hire some damn attorney who didn't give a shit about justice. But, ultimately, they'd get the evidence, and when they did, there'd be an ugly 8" by 10" photo of

Lawson on the cover of *Time*. The accompanying article wouldn't be pretty either.

The detectives decided to confront Lawson without warning. They drove from Philadelphia to Washington D.C., arriving mid-afternoon. They took the elevator to Lawson's lair on the fifth floor of the Dirksen Senate Office Building. The receptionist told them Senator Lawson was in the office, but was a busy man and couldn't just drop everything to chat. Flygare and Olson were insistent.

"Senator," McKayla said into the phone, "I'm sorry to interrupt you, sir, but I have two gentlemen here to see you." She couldn't have known that she'd soon be fielding calls from Detroit to Bangladesh. "Yes, I know," she semi-whispered into the phone, "but they're from the Philadelphia police department and said it was urgent." She looked up at them hovering over her desk. "They are rather insistent."

The detectives imagined the emotion on the other end of the line just a few yards from where they stood. This was their pay-off for earning less than the public servant in the next room; the one who was probably soiling himself at that very moment. McKayla told the detectives that Senator Lawson would see them, and asked them to sit in the waiting room. A moment later, a middle-aged man, who looked like the kind of guy who'd listen to Air Supply, walked briskly past them and into the senator's office.

They waited in the reception area; beneath an impressive oil painting of Robert Morris with a plaque reminding those who gazed upon his homely countenance that he was the first senator from Pennsylvania. On the opposite wall hung a painting of the seat's current occupant. Lawson looked sharp, his manicured hand resting upon a replica of the Liberty Bell. He looked nothing like a felon.

Five minutes later, Mr. Air Supply left the Senator's office and Lawson emerged. He strode with feigned confidence over to the two detectives and stuck out his clammy hand.

"Ken Lawson," he said. "I'm sorry to have kept you waiting. I have a terribly busy schedule and wasn't expecting you." He looked at his watch for effect. "So, how can I help you gentlemen?"

"My name is Robert Flygare and this is my partner, Roger Olson. We just need a few moments of your time. Perhaps it would be best if we met in private."

"I want to be as helpful as I can, but I'm afraid I don't have much time." He looked at watch again.

"Well," said Flygare, "I don't think this is something you'd want to discuss here in the waiting room. I really don't."

"Very well then, why don't we step into my office?"

The senator's office was decorated in Basic Kenneth Lawson. It didn't look like the humble sanctuary of a public servant. His desk was gigantic, unlike the stainless-steel relic the detectives had to *share*. It was adorned in Classic Ostentation, a fitting testament to his compulsive narcissism. Photos of Ken with famous leaders and celebrities were plastered on the cherry-wood paneling. A few family photos were sprinkled in here and there. Who said he wasn't a family values candidate?

A large Bible was opened on a book stand in the corner. Flygare wanted to blow the dust from the page that was opened to the Ten Commandments. The righteous senator should've brushed up on them before recklessly violating Number Six (Thou shalt not kill), Number Seven (Thou shalt not commit adultery), Number Nine (Thou shalt not bear false witness), and Number Ten (Thou shalt not covet thy neighbor's wife). Fortunately, these no-no's had all been committed on a Tuesday afternoon, and not the Sabbath Day (saving him from a violation of Number Four).

He sat behind his desk and motioned for the detectives to sit in the leather "constituent" chairs where precious few constituents actually sat. Lawson's chair was raised so that his knees barely fit underneath the top drawer of his desk.

"So, how can I help you, Detectives?"

"We're here to ask you a few questions about Chelsea Miles. We understand she was a friend of yours."

"Yes, yes, she was. I have been a good friend of George, her husband, for some time. It was a shock to hear of her murder."

"Senator, we'll get right to the point," said Flygare. "Some evidence has surfaced that suggests you were very close to Mrs. Miles."

"Well, I suppose that's true. We had become good friends."

"How good?"

"We saw them socially from time to time."

"When did you last see her?"

"Oh my goodness, I don't recall off the top of my head."

"Uh-huh."

The detectives sat in comfortable silence while Senator Lawson squirmed and got even clammier.

"Our evidence suggests that you had become physically intimate with her."

"I would be curious to know the source of that evidence, Detective. I need not remind you that is an inflammatory accusation."

"It is indeed. Even more inflammatory is the evidence that suggests you were with her the afternoon she was murdered."

"Again, Detective, I will not sit here and listen to these accusations without knowing their source."

"Senator, I'll be blunt," said Flygare. "Will you provide us with samples of your hair, semen, and fingerprints?"

"This is ridiculous!"

"You're not legally required to do so, at least not yet. However, we have probable cause to believe you were with Chelsea Miles, in her bedroom, on the afternoon she was murdered. Our evidence is strong, sir. If you choose not to voluntarily cooperate, we'll get the court to issue a subpoena immediately."

"What kind of witch hunt—" Lawson stood. "I am a United States Senator, for God's sake!"

"If you wish to prolong this, by all means go ahead." There was no rush in the delivery.

They say that before you die, your entire life flashes before your eyes, all the secret Deadlies and dreadful little boo-boos. This amuses me. Lawson's video would've been riveting.

"I will consider it to aide in the investigation," Lawson said, which was big of him. "However, I'm not prepared to do so at this time. I'd like to consult with counsel before making any commitment to you *gentlemen*." He tried to be tough, but it fell flat, if you ask me. He braced his hands on the desk to steady them, the color having drained from his face. "Now, if you'll excuse me, I believe our business is finished here."

"Here's my card," said Flygare. "Please let me hear from you by the end of the day. Hopefully you'll see the wisdom in cooperating with us." Lawson wanted to reach across the desk and knock the smirk off his face, especially when he said: "If a formal subpoena is required, we may not be able to keep it from the press. You know how pushy they are."

The detectives saw themselves out and Lawson slumped back to his chair, numb. McDonald, who'd been pacing in the hallway, came in. Lawson stared through him.

"How did it go? What did they want?"

"I need a lawyer. They think I murdered Chelsea Miles."

26

KEN LAWSON WAS A LITTLE DEVIL. He was ruthless like most conquerors are, zeroing in on his target with discipline, notwithstanding his mediocre IQ. Indeed, for these audacious souls, a higher level of intelligence is actually a disadvantage because it makes them cautious, which doesn't play to their strength. Ken was smart in an unconventional way, maneuvering well in the glib and nuanced world of politics. I sort of liked him.

It took him a few minutes to recalibrate to the new reality. He needed a lawyer. He knew plenty of them, crawling as they did through the gutters of Washington D.C., but he didn't want one of those greedy bastards, who'd salivate to get the case for their own ego, eager to capitalize on his one little indiscretion. Instead, he called one of his best friends from his days at the community college.

Andrew Bradshaw was different. He wore mismatched socks, and the knot in his tie was always off to one side, like a noose. He dyed his gray hair to look brown, but, regrettably, it came out orange (he had no wife to tell him how ridiculous it looked).

He squinted when he read because he'd forget to use his reading glasses that rested permanently next to his receding hairline. He was gangly and loose jointed, like his puppeteer was two sheets to the wind.

Bradshaw was successful, but didn't act like it. He was honest and principled (but lest you get the idea that he was without sin, I can tell you the court reporters folded their arms over their thin blouses when he was around, and he refused to pay his parking tickets because he hated the mayor for some reason).

Both Bradshaw and Lawson had good instincts. The fundamental difference between them, however, was that Bradshaw had a top-notch brain. He knew every ounce of the law, every nook and cranny. He recognized that knowing the law and being a good lawyer were vastly different things. Quoting the judicial code, word for word, is waaaay overrated.

When they were in college, Bradshaw had refused to believe he wasn't cool enough to hang with Lawson's rich and handsome crowd. You know; *that* nauseating crowd. Bradshaw wound up in criminal defense because he understood the causes of crime (and it's not all me, by the way). His humble roots had been planted on the other side of the tracks and he'd never seen the need to yank them up and transplant them in more affluent soil—the soil that receives most of the fertilizer. In other words, he'd never hobnobbed with the beautiful people at Martha's Vineyard.

"Andy, this is Ken."

"Well, I'll be damned. Hello there, old friend! How's the family?"

"Andy, I need help."

"Oh, I'm sorry to hear that. I've got a hearing in twenty minutes, but I know the judge and he can wait. What's up?"

"I'm in serious trouble, Andy, and you're the first person I could think to call."

"Hang on; let me close my door," said Bradshaw. He was back on the line seconds later. "Talk to me."

"I'm sure you've read about the Chelsea Miles murder?"

"Of course."

"I'm afraid I may be arrested."

"Arrested for what? For the *murder*?"

"Yeah, and I didn't do it."

Lawson's profession of innocence meant nothing to Bradshaw. Guilty men rarely gush forth with the truth. Go ahead, blame it on me, I'm used to it.

"What evidence do they have?"

"Andy, I did something really stupid. I got involved with Chelsea. We had a fling. That's all it was. I'd been over to her house the afternoon she was murdered. They know about that visit. Don't ask me how, but they do. Two detectives just came by and they want samples of my hair and fingerprints. They want a semen sample, too. Shit, Andy, I'm fucked, absolutely fucked. What am I going to do?"

"Where are you right now?"

"I'm in my office in D.C. This couldn't have come at a worse time."

"How soon can you get to Philadelphia?"

"I can't just leave. I need to clean up my calendar and talk to Susan." He leaned his head back and ran his hand through his hair, leaving it there on top of his head. The mere thought of Susan made him nauseous. "I can be there tomorrow morning."

"Does she know about any of this?"

"Not yet."

"Okay, let me call the County Prosecutors office. I can probably buy us another day. In the meantime, I don't want you talking to anyone. We probably have spousal immunity if you need to discuss it with Susan. But no one else. I mean it, Ken. No one."

Ken would've rather passed three large kidney stones soaked in Tabasco sauce than have this conversation with Susan. He didn't care that he'd hurt her, but he didn't want to give her the satisfaction that he'd erred, and done so in such a publicly humiliating way.

"Well, you're home early," Susan said when he walked in. "I guess the will of the people is finished."

"Susan, please, I need to talk to you."

"I'm listening," she said as she continued sorting the sweaters in her closet, her back to him.

"It's about Chelsea Miles."

This got her attention. I saw the flinch. She put the stack of expensive sweaters she'd hardly worn in the Good Will pile, then turned around to face him, stone-faced.

"I was having an affair with her." There, he'd said it. That was the hardest part. Susan didn't respond. She arranged her face into a look of pitiful resignation for his pathetic weakness.

"Unfortunately, we met at her house the day she was murdered." He waited for a response, but still nothing.

"Somehow the police found out about our meeting that day. They think I murdered her."

He'd expected her to flip out, but she said nothing. She just looked at him with . . . with what? Contempt?

"Aren't you going to say anything?" he asked.

Nothing.

"I didn't kill her, whether you want to believe it or not."

Susan turned and began sorting another pile of cashmere.

"Goddammit, Susan, do you even care?"

Susan did care. She cared because she'd be dragged through the mud of gossip, too. And, worse than that, she'd be pitied. *Look, there's the Senator's wife, the one who murdered his mistress. Oh, my gosh, the poor thing. It's terrible the way people talk about it behind her back. They're so insensitive.*

"Ken," she finally said without turning around to face him. "You're a pig and I feel nothing for you. If you want me to be angry, then I'm afraid you'll be disappointed. If you want me to feel sorry for you, then you'll have to get over it."

What could he say?

"I'm not stupid," she continued. "I know you've cheated on me for years. I made my peace with that long ago when I realized I didn't love you anyway. See, Ken, here's the thing: you can't hurt me anymore because I couldn't care less about you."

He stood, wilting, without a zinger in reserve to throw back at her.

"I would have left you long ago," she said, "but I knew you'd run to the press and demonize me for your own political salvation. I couldn't give you that satisfaction. Besides, you would've taken half my money to lavish on your whores.

"So, what will you say?" she continued. "Will you say it was *my* fault you cheated on me with that whore—that it was *my* fault you murdered her?" She finally turned around to face him. "Don't worry, you'll still be surrounded by the press. In fact, you'll be the hottest story in town, for a few months anyway. And then you'll only be a pathetic footnote in history. It'll be a footnote that gradually shrinks until you're nothing but the answer to a trivia question. And do you know what that trivia question will be, Kenneth?"

She waited. He wouldn't give her the satisfaction of a response.

"Well, do you, dear?" she asked.

He did not respond.

"Okay, then, I'll tell you what it'll be. 'Who was the most humiliated and pathetic politician in American history?'"

He just stared at her with Deadly wrath (the Deadlies were piling up!).

"But don't worry about me," she said. "I'll survive. Sure, I'll be pitied for a while, but in a few years, while you're still rotting away in prison, the only blemish on my name will be that I was once married to you."

Andy Bradshaw called Stew Franks to buy another day for Lawson to decide whether he'd voluntarily cooperate. Stew and the rest of the gang at the prosecutor's office respected Bradshaw. He didn't try his cases in the press like the rest of them, and he wasn't trying to land a talk show gig.

Unlike William Sperry, George Miles's high-profile attorney, Bradshaw hadn't discussed the fee with Lawson—not while his friend was on the ropes as he was. He'd given so much free legal advice over the years that he didn't have much to spare. His compassionate fee schedule would've surprised court watchers, who assumed Bradshaw was loaded. Personally, I don't think this made him virtuous, just broke. But I can be hard on people.

Lawson arrived in Philadelphia the next morning. Bradshaw's office was small and cramped. His desk was a squeaky, stainless-steel doozie dating back to the Golden Age of Radio. The client chairs were the stackable kind you find at Walmart. Open law books, manila files, and loose papers were scattered everywhere. There were no diplomas, awards, or self-congratulatory symbols. Not one. That wasn't Bradshaw's style. Pride wasn't his thing.

He lifted a stack of papers from a chair to give Ken a place to sit. Some might have been embarrassed to have such a famous figure like Senator Lawson see his humble office, but Bradshaw didn't give a shit.

"Ken, I've given this some thought. We could probably delay giving them the samples they want, but you gain nothing by that. I think we're better off to cooperate, at least with respect to the hair, fingerprints, and semen. It's not a felony to sleep with another woman. The publicity of your affair will damage your career, but it won't send you to prison."

"Andy, I didn't kill her. You know me. I would never have done such a thing."

"Okay."

"Can't we convince them of that before they make this a public witch hunt?"

"The prosecutor has the burden of proof. They've got to prove beyond a reasonable doubt that you killed her. You don't need to prove a damned thing. However, I wouldn't categorize the state's prosecution as a 'witch hunt,' especially if the fingerprints on the murder weapon are yours, too."

"The fingerprints on the murder weapon?" asked Lawson. "They say my fingerprints are on that shovel? Oh, my God, Andy."

Lawson agreed to cooperate. He and Bradshaw went to the designated lab where they took a few strands of hair (they'd been good not to pluck them from the crown in back where every hair mattered). They also fingerprinted him. And then the dreaded semen sample. It was dreadful, not because the process of delivery was unpleasant, but because he knew it would scientifically seal his fate as an adulterous hypocrite.

Lawson had piled on when Bill Clinton had shamelessly erred, and when every other morally corrupt Democrat had been caught with their hookers and thieves (he'd taken the "Let's-talk-about-the-important-issues-that-affect-the-American-people" route whenever it'd been a Republican). So, this was deliciously awkward.

Perhaps if this had been a less sensational crime, involving a less sensational killer, in a less sensational manner, the crime lab would've taken its own sweet time to complete their work on Lawson's samples. But, under the circumstances, they made it a speedy priority. The hair found in the bed was his, all right. So was the semen. And, worst of all, so was the partial thumbprint on the shovel's wooden handle.

Again, they met; Stew, Scott, Flygare, and Olson.

"Are we finally ready to move on this?" Stew asked.

"Mr. Franks, you have all the evidence we have. It's your call."

"What do you think, Scott?" Stew asked.

"We certainly have probable cause to arrest him. But there's something about this case that troubles me."

"What?" Stew tried to hide his impatience with all the hand wringing. He wanted Scott to grab a pom-pom for the pep rally. *Gimme a K! Gimme an E! Gimme an N! What's that spell? Ken! Ken! Siss boom bah!*

"I can't put my finger on it," Scott said (all this talk about fingerprints was catchy). "We've only got a partial thumbprint on a murder weapon covered with Javier Flores' prints. It just doesn't make sense."

"I think we can easily establish motive," said Flygare. "Chelsea threatens to expose the relationship. Says she's pregnant with his kid or something. If she does a tell all, she's famous overnight. She could parlay it into her own goddamned reality TV show."

"Okay," said Scott, "but what about the thumbprint?"

"What about it?"

"Well, there's just one."

"Yeah," said Flygare, "I'll admit that bothers me. But the fact that *any* of his prints are on the murder weapon is huge, along with the hair and semen match."

"So, do we have a go?" asked Stew.

"It's up to you guys," said Olson who looked to Flygare. Flygare nodded.

Stew called Andrew Bradshaw with the news that his client would be arrested for murder. He knew Lawson couldn't easily hide, so he agreed to give him a few hours to clean up any pressing emergencies before turning himself in. This would give Stew time to gussy up for his big show.

27

"CNN HAS JUST LEARNED that Senator Kenneth Lawson has been arrested in connection with the murder of Chelsea Miles." And so began the biggest criminal prosecution of their time. *"Sources inside the Philadelphia County Police Department report that the Republican senator from Pennsylvania has voluntarily turned himself over to authorities investigating the grisly murder. A formal statement is expected soon, sources tell CNN."*

Every channel on the dial had the "Breaking Story" running in print along the bottom of television screens at home and abroad.

Stew Franks removed his navy pinstripe suit from the dry cleaner plastic. He re-tied his tie three times until the knot was perfect, then stood before the bathroom mirror to rehearse his speech. Chelsea's innocent life had been barbarically snuffed out, and he would convict her killer! Yep, this was for Chelsea, and You-Know-Who would be her avenger.

He strode to the podium with purpose. The American flag hung limp behind him, and a smaller replica was pinned to his lapel (it didn't go with his tie, but he was a patriot who would've thrown the tea into the harbor if given the chance, so noble were his principles). The press was gathered, waiting eagerly on his remarks.

"Ladies and gentlemen. Kenneth Lawson was taken into custody this morning for the murder of Chelsea Miles." They gasped and looked at one another, mouths open, shutters clicking. Oh, it was perfect—just the way he'd dreamed it would be. "The evidence will show that Mr. Lawson was engaged in a relationship with Mrs. Miles and was the last one to see her on the afternoon of her murder. Evidence collected at the scene shows the crime was committed by Mr. Lawson, and we are confident of a conviction. We are mindful of the fact that Mr. Lawson is a well-known person and this trial will generate unusual publicity. However, it is neither our desire, nor our intention, to try the case through the media." Uh-huh. "Instead, we will rely on the appropriate channels within the judicial system."

"Mr. Franks!" a reporter shouted from the back. "Can you confirm their relationship was physical?"

"There is evidence to confirm that, yes."

The reporters were shouting down each other, holding up recorders, pens, notepads, and cameras. "Has Senator Lawson admitted his involvement?"

"Mr. Lawson has not made a public statement. However, the investigation has been thorough and we are confident that the case will result in a conviction."

More shouting. "Have you discussed the charges with the victim's husband, George Miles?"

"We have. He has expressed shock and disappointment and has pledged to support the prosecution in any way he can."

Scott Benjamin stood off to the side, watching (Stew wouldn't let him anywhere near his podium). This was the easy part—standing up in front of the cameras in a press room. Here there was no burden of proof, no opposition, and no cross examination—no other theories to shed the small amount of doubt necessary for an acquittal. This made him nervous because something didn't feel right. There was this gnawing anxiety, like a faceless beggar was tugging at his sleeve.

Scott was no dummy; he knew this case would catapult his career. He tried to tamp down his pride, but it swelled like a book left out in the rain. Every Tom, Dick, and Harry would critique his performance. This was theatre and he was stage left, about to get his fifteen minutes.

Andrew Bradshaw called his own press conference thirty minutes later. He swung to the podium, bent forward, joints over-oiled. He hadn't fretted over his rumpled outfit. He pulled a folded paper from the inside pocket of his sport coat and flattened it on the podium, then squinted at the writing while his reading glasses remained perched on top of his head.

"Ladies and gentlemen, I will be brief. My client, Senator Kenneth Lawson, did not kill Chelsea Miles. It is true that he had an improper relationship with her, and he apologizes for that poor judgment. He will resign his senate seat effective immediately." Shutters were clicking non-stop. "He will do so not because he is guilty of any crime, but because he does not want the citizens of Pennsylvania to be dragged through the sensationalism of this legal drama. There are important issues facing this country, and Senator Lawson wishes to minimize any distraction he might be. He has asked me to express his sincere apology for his misjudgment, but denies in the strongest possible terms that he had anything to do with Mrs. Miles's death. Thank you."

He lurched away while the reporters shouted questions at his back.

Ann Lee and the rest of Lawson's staff watched these televised news conferences in utter (serious utter) disbelief. That the senator could be guilty of an "improper relationship" with a woman was no shocker. But *this*? This was unimaginable, even to Lawson's fiercest critics who routinely accused him of horrible things. He had sex with a friend's wife and then brutally murdered her? With a *shovel*?

The phone was going bananas at the senator's office. Ann closed her door and pulled out her copy of the blackmail note. No wonder Lawson had been so edgy. What about her co-worker, Paul McDonald? He obviously knew about the blackmail. What else did he know? Was he involved in the crime somehow? She put the letter back in her drawer and walked down the hall to McDonald's office. She knocked on the door and opened it a crack. Paul was sitting at his desk staring blankly at some irrelevant papers.

"Not now, Ann."

"Hey, listen, I just wanted to talk. We've both been with him for a long time."

"And what are we going to do now?" he asked.

"I don't know," Ann said. "I can barely think. You were closer to him than I was. It's such a shock. Did you have any idea this was coming?"

"Of course not! Believe it or not, Ann, Lawson doesn't tell me who he sleeps with, or who he murders."

"Yeah. Of course. I just wondered if you had any idea that someone was on to him or anything."

"And what's that supposed to mean? Do you honestly think

I knew he was involved in something like this? Are you out of your mind? Give me a little credit for once."

"I wish I could, but I think you know more than you're saying."

Paul stood and glared at her. "What, exactly, are you saying? Because unless you have some proof, I suggest you get the hell out of my office."

"I know about the blackmail letters." She waited for him to say something. He was mute. "But, see, here's the thing, Paul. I didn't conspire to hide them like you did. And I didn't pay anyone off like you did. I took the information *I* had to the police."

"What information? What possible information could *you* have?"

"Oh, I have plenty," she said.

"So what, exactly, did you take to the police?"

"A copy of the latest blackmail letter. I'll admit, Paul, that's the only one I had, unlike you who knew everything and said absolutely nothing."

"You have no proof!"

"Oh, but I do."

Paul was in delirious agony, crashing in real time. He tried to say something, but couldn't.

"The detectives were quite interested in the copy of the letter I gave them. They asked how I got it. I told them that you and the Senator were acting very strange, especially where the mail was concerned. So, I grabbed the mail before you could get to it, opened the most suspicious looking one, copied it, and put it back in the stack so you could rush it into Senator Lawson. Other than that, I hardly told them anything."

Paul slumped to his chair. The next dropped shoe wouldn't command a live CNN feed, but it would be big news to Paul McDonald's Facebook friends. He'd lose his career and face criminal conspiracy charges, to say nothing of obstruction of justice and aggravated assault. No, it didn't look good for poor Paul.

"For the record, Ann, I only did what he asked me to do."

"Then it must feel awful knowing you were taking your orders from someone who might soon be on death row." She turned to leave, then stopped and turned to face him again. "I hate to rub salt in the wound, Paul, but it must gall you to know that at least Lawson got laid, whereas you just got screwed."

Rebecca went to her mother's house as soon as she heard about the arrest. Surely there'd been a ghastly mistake. She elbowed her way through the growing crowd of media already assembled on the front lawn, salivating like dogs over a sausage wagon. They shouted for her reaction. What did they want her to say? That she was bursting with pride? That she would've taken a shovel to the bitch, too? Susan let her in and quickly closed the door.

"There's no way dad killed that woman," Rebecca said with puffy eyes. This was a declaratory statement, one meant to establish his innocence once and for all. However, it was also part question, for she was imploring her mother to confirm the fact.

"I don't believe it either, but there are things about your father . . .."

"I know he cheated on you, mom. Okay? But that doesn't mean he's a murderer."

"Ken and I have not—"

"You mean dad."

"Very well. Your father and I have not been close for many years. He's had his mistresses, I'm not stupid. But the way he sleeps around . . . ."

"I know, he's wrong, but it doesn't mean he killed her. He's not a monster. Wouldn't we know it if he was?"

"Maybe she threatened him."

"So he *killed* her? Come on, mom, you don't believe that."

"No, I suppose I don't. But they say they have evidence that he was involved somehow."

"Evidence of what? That he slept with her? Okay, fine. I'm sure he's not proud of that. But that doesn't make him a criminal. I'm sorry, mom, but it doesn't."

Rebecca peeked out the living room window. It was sunny and crisp but she hoped it would start snowing, or that golf-ball sized hail stones would pelt the lepers camped out there. Give them all a wicked case of frostbite, because that's what they deserved.

"Look at them out there."

"The Eisenbergs next door have already called the police."

Rebecca left her mother's house and ran through the horde to her car. She caught her toe on a cable and stumbled. They surrounded her car, their cameras and faces aimed through the windows, mouths open, yelling. She was in tears as she inched backwards down the driveway, partially hoping to mow some of them down.

She called John on her cell. "It's a set-up, Becca," he said. "I just talked to dad and he swears he didn't do it and there's no way they can prove he did. It's a political set-up."

"So you talked to him?"

"Yeah, I called like three times and he finally picked up and said there's no way."

"But then why would they arrest him? I don't understand."

"Because they want to humiliate him."

"So it's true he was cheating on mom?"

"I guess that part's true. I mean, dad pretty much admitted that part to me."

"What did he say? Was he sorry?"

"He just said he made a stupid mistake and he's paying for it now."

"But was he sorry?"

"Yeah, I guess. You know dad."

"I thought I knew him."

"Listen, he's not a murderer, okay? There's no way. But those pricks always bash him for everything he tries to do." A lengthy pause. "It's bullshit!"

"You get on his case, too. I don't want you to get mad, but it seems like you're always taking the other side."

"Becca, come on. That's just politics. This is serious. He's our dad, okay? I don't agree with him, and he's a jerk for cheating on mom, but he's not a murderer. I don't care what they say."

"That's what I think, too."

"You know what pisses me off the most? Just knowing the Democrats are happy about this. Think about that. They're actually *happy*. It makes me want to puke."

28

DAN LEONARD SAT IN A BAR OPPOSITE a beautiful woman he'd met trolling South Beach. Even though he was a private detective, and probably should've known better, he didn't know she was a prostitute. He thought he'd lured her in with his charm and the way he'd hidden that soft paunch under the loose-fitting Tommy Bahama shirt. And, don't forget, *she's* the one who'd hit on *him*. Maybe that higher-priced hair gel really was the ticket. See, that's the way it is with men. They all think they're fighter pilots. I get a real kick out of it.

"Can I get you another drink?" he asked her.

"Sure." This lovely hooker had the uncomfortable suspicion that the guy sitting across from her, the frumpy middle-aged loser, actually thought she liked him. How awkward, she thought. She'd have another drink, and perhaps dinner on his dime, but after that he'd have to pony up.

"So, what do you do for a living?" Dan asked.

"Oh, I'm just a working girl," she forced herself to giggle. "I just do the best I can."

"Yeah, it's tough making a living out there."

"You have no idea."

"So what is it exactly that you do?" he asked again.

"Oh, I do some massage and some private modeling. Personal services—you know?"

"Yeah, I figured you were a model or something."

Was he *serious*? Did she have to hit him over the head with it? She was a professional, though, so she continued to be lovely, scanning the joint over his shoulder to see what else slithered in.

"*Holy shit!*" Dan nearly spit his rum and coke all over the Lovely Hooker, staring at the television screen mounted above the bar.

"What is it?" she asked.

Dan asked the bartender to turn up the volume.

"Earlier today, following the arrest of Senator Lawson, several of his staff members were still expressing shock." It was being covered everywhere, even on Fox—which allowed for the possibility that it was a witch hunt orchestrated by liberals, and that viewers shouldn't rush to judgment. Its producers also took the opportunity to remind its viewers of the many slimy things Democrats had done.

"What's the matter, Babe?" she asked, just as lovely as could be. She had to reel him back quickly because nothing, and I mean nothing, douses a good boner like an unexpected shovel murder.

"Uh, it's nothing. Well, yeah, actually it's sort of a big deal."

"You mean about that congress guy? What a douche bag."

"Yeah, I think I recently did some work for him."

"What? You work for the government or something? You're not a cop, are you?"

"Uh, no, no I'm not a cop," clearly he was distracted from her, which was something she wasn't used to—a guy watching TV (and not even a sporting event) when he ought to have been staring at her breasts (the plastic surgeon may have gone a bit overboard, for they were nearly ready to pop).

"Hey, I'm sorry, but I gotta go. Can I get your number? Maybe we can get together some other time."

"I understand. Call me anytime." Lovely Hooker handed him a business card. Dan barely looked at it, and not long enough to read the catchy slogan *"We'll escort you!"*.

Dan went back to his motel room and sat in front of the television. The job he'd done for this Paul McDonald guy was obviously connected to this scandal. He needed to go to the cops, pronto. He had photos of the blackmailers *and* the kidnappers; a bonanza of dirt. He checked out of his motel and caught a flight back to Philadelphia. McDonald might try to make him a co-conspirator, for Dan knew how men behave when they've been caught with their pants down. They'll say or do anything to save themselves.

Javier Flores scrounged around Juarez looking for work, and looking over his shoulder, too. His roommates back in Philadelphia knew where his family lived, and he knew the Policia had ways of making people talk. They'd threaten deportation, then deport the poor snitches anyway.

Javier's wife was happy to have him back, but he'd been edgy. He'd finally found work as a laborer on a road construction project. He didn't earn enough money to splurge, but after toiling a few days, he settled into a cantina for a cerveza. A black and white television with rabbit ears sat on a wobbly table in the corner of the bar, beneath an aging poster promoting a bullfight. No one was watching the fuzzy screen. However, Javier was sitting close enough that he heard the stern monotone of the thickly mustached news anchor.

"Un official de alto de los Estados Unidos ha sido acusando en la brutal asesinacion de su amante. El Sanador Kenneth Lawson de Pennsylvania fue arrestado ayer pore star involucrado en el asesinato de Chelsea Miles, una mujer que el tuvo una relacion my cercana por mucho tiempo."

Javier was stunned. He didn't know the gringo named Kenneth Lawson from Adam. All he knew was that he wouldn't be hauled back to Los Estados Unidos in handcuffs. His guilt or innocence was no longer relevant. *Muy bien!*

Dan Leonard drove straight to the local police station the moment he landed back in Philadelphia. Within an hour, he was sitting in a depressingly gray room that smelled of guilt, deceit, fear, and stale coffee. Everything about the room was hard—floor, ceilings, walls, desk, and chairs. A detective walked in with a Styrofoam cup of coffee and sat across from him. He pulled out a small notebook, Dragnet style, and nudged his glasses up with a crooked finger.

"Leonard, is it?"

"Yes."

"You're here voluntarily?"

"Yeah. I'm the one who called you."

Dan began telling his tale. After making a few notes, the cop closed the small notebook and slipped it into his shirt pocket. "Wait here," he said. He left the room and called Flygare, who worked out of a different precinct.

Dan sat in the room, staring at himself in the two-way mirror, until Flygare finally arrived.

"Tell us what you think we should know."

"Okay, here's the thing," Dan said. "I was hired to tail a few guys, which I did. The guy who hired me never told me his name or why I was supposed to follow them. I was just doing what he asked me to do. That's all." He then proceeded to barf up all he remembered in projectile fashion. He kept waiting for the detectives to smile. He kept waiting for them to show some goddamned *appreciation.*

"So how'd you make the connection between the person who hired you and Senator Lawson?"

Dan told them how he'd used his crackerjack investigative skills to trace the phone number and then connect the number to Paul McDonald, who he found on Facebook. He'd learned that McDonald worked on Senator Lawson's staff. So, when he heard the news about the arrest, he simply added it up. He hoped they'd be impressed—maybe hire him as a paid consultant on a few other unsolved murders.

"And you say you've got photos?"

"Oh yeah, I've got lots of photos. I don't have them on me, but I can get them to you." McDonald sat back, satisfied, on the cusp of receiving a Good Citizenship Award.

"We'll need the photos," said Flygare. "Have you had any communication with McDonald since you saw the abduction?"

"Yeah, I called him from the scene. See, I was there where the kid was being held in the storage shed. By then the cops were there and I told McDonald what was going on. That's when he told me to get the hell out of there, so I did. I went to Miami, but when I saw the story about Senator Lawson on the news, I figured I better tell you guys what I'd seen. I wanted to cooperate so there'd be no mistaking I had anything to do with any of this."

"So you saw this abduction, and then you went to Miami."

"Uh-huh."

"You didn't call the police."

"Well, I didn't know for sure, you know, if there was a crime or whatever. But I was definitely going to call them fairly soon." There went the Good Citizenship Award.

"Uh-huh."

Dan agreed to email the digital photos he'd taken. Based on the photos, the detectives identified Whitey as the guy in the hospital—the one with the big knot on his head. Whitey gave up Glen's identity quicker than Judas throwing Jesus under the bus, and without the thirty pieces of silver to show for it (he was still mad at Glen for leaving him alone in the van with that psycho kid in the beanie).

A few days later, Jesse and Slim were still in the county jail. They hadn't even *asked* for a lawyer. Even if they'd been constitutional scholars, they wouldn't have demanded a speedy trial. No way; they were safe in jail—safe from the kidnappers and whoever had hired them in the first place—probably that cold-hearted congress dude who'd taken the spade to the missus.

The boys were basking in their jailhouse fame. They'd broken one of the biggest stories in state history. "Tell 'em what you seen, Slim," said Garth, one of the articulate inmates at the county correctional facility. "You guys ain't gonna believe this shit. Go on, Slim, tell 'em." The inmates crowded around to hear Slim tell the story, again, for it became more salacious with each telling.

"Well, see, we were in this mansion," Slim began. "We busted in, ya know, 'cause we didn't think anybody was home. So, we snuck into the bathroom when all of a sudden we seen the hottest chick you ever saw, naked as a fuckin' jaybird, just ridin' that congress dude. Swear to God." He sighed and shook his head. "It was amazing."

"How far away were you?" Garth asked with unmitigated want. I used Garth to excite the other inmates, making them suffer in the process. Their envy levels spiked, as did their lust, and they couldn't do a danged thing about it. Hence the suffering.

"We had us front row seats, dude. We seen the congress guy, too. That's why he got busted, 'cause we seen him."

The inmates, none of whom had the perk of a conjugal visit, sat slack jawed. Slim's storytelling skills partially failed him, which was just as well, because the inmates had imaginations with billion-dollar production budgets. Therefore, the scene that played out in their minds was more vivid and rich in detail than what Slim had actually seen in the first place. They licked their lips and shifted in their seats. Garth's throat was so dry he could barely swallow. He would've traded Lawson places on death row to have been there. They didn't want to hear about Lawson, of course—the woman could've been with Abraham Lincoln for all they cared. They only wanted details about her. Did she have a nice ass? How big were her knockers? Slim gave deeply satisfying answers to each question, even when the answer was wholly a product of his lustful imagination.

A few days later, Jesse nearly soiled himself when a new inmate showed up. There was Whitey, head wrapped in gauze, standing in the cafeteria line with his tray. Jesse knew this fiend would knock his block off, and then make him his jailhouse bitch for the rest of eternity. He'd take all his commissary money, too. Whitey turned and looked at him. A tiny flicker of recognition appeared on his face but quickly passed because Jesse was not wearing his beanie, and Whitey was dimwitted. I can only do so much.

Paul McDonald's mother called the moment she heard the news. Surely there'd been a mistake. Senator Lawson, bless his heart, was a God-fearing man! He'd probably been framed by the same crooked bunch that condoned (and hid) Hillary's numerous lesbian affairs. Paul assured her that justice would prevail, but he knew better. He'd been shocked that Lawson had actually killed her. She must've done something very bad to upset him. And now the liberals would take this one measly, isolated incident and blow it totally out of proportion.

McDonald knew he'd be brought in for questioning. He'd paid The Interrogators off the books, but if they were caught (and talked) it would lead back to him. His zealous commitment to the greater good (keeping a man of righteous principles in power) had exposed him to great personal risk. But he'd done what he could to keep the balance of power in the hands of the Republicans, because God prefers working directly through them. He just does.

The police came for him the next day. Reporters, who'd been staking out Senator Lawson's office, recorded the scene for posterity. McDonald was bawling hysterically as he was led away in handcuffs. He saw Ann Lee watching from her high moral horse, all smug and self-righteous. Had she no remorse for taking down their boss? Where was her loyalty? Did she *want* the country to go down the tubes?

29

GEORGE MILES HAD MIXED FEELINGS about Lawson's arrest. He'd probably dodged the bullet for good, unless new evidence surfaced which pointed in his direction. At least he knew his fingerprints would never be found on the shovel. He was relieved that his peers would finally be more comfortable around him, because they'd wondered, of course they had. Did George really whack his wife? Could he be trusted with a gardening tool? He does act a bit fishy, doesn't he, like he's hiding something?

At the same time, George was disappointed that his investment in Ken Lawson had come to such a hasty end. Kiss the reliable chip in the Senate goodbye. He'd have preferred that the two kids who'd broken into his house had been arrested, or his Mexican landscaper. He also figured Lawson's well-paid defense team would try to pin the murder on him instead. Damned lawyers had no shame. No shame at all.

When the press hounded him for a reaction to the arrest of his friend, George said "no comment." People interpreted hostility in the response, but really it was apathy. He knew he couldn't publicly pout about the arrest of his wife's killer. It would be the height of insensitivity to mope around muttering the truth: "Here's the thing: I wasn't crazy about her, okay? Let's see you try living with someone who chews with her mouth open. It's not pretty, and you don't get used to it like I thought you would. And, let's be honest, she was costing me a fortune. Besides, I figured she was sleeping with my convenient buddy, Senator Lawson. Did I care? Sure, I cared. But, hey, I look like a toad, okay? I'm not stupid. I know she married me for my money. So, when I found out Lawson was having his way with her, I figured I could blackmail him into voting for my ammo company."

People didn't understand George. How many times over the years did they wonder out loud, *Why doesn't he just retire? When's enough enough?* They didn't understand that age hadn't changed his fundamental character. He was still passionate about business. This notion that he should retire to a contemplative state of being was patronizing. Not everyone thinks like Thoreau (I thought he was a slacker, myself. Slothful as they come).

There was one thing people close to George *did* know about him: this hard-charging billionaire had a combustible temper. He usually got what he wanted because he was so rich. And when he didn't, he'd erupt. In fact, those who'd been hired to ensure that he always got his way had nicknamed him The Eruption.

The tricky thing about The Eruption was the volcanic nature of his temper. His wrath was difficult to forecast (I could always see it coming, but that's just me). So, the peons crept with care in his presence, fully aware that the eccentric boss could blow for any reason, even something as insignificant as the way the maid ironed his boxer shorts (*Dammit, Rosalinda! The goddamned crease is off center again! How in the hell am I supposed to wear these!*).

His first wife had accused him of physical abuse. George adamantly denied this. Sure, he'd thrown the television remote in her "general direction" after a dinner party when she'd had too much to drink and blabbed about their finances to another couple. And there'd been the time he "might have pushed her, a little" after she threw out his quart of Haagen-Dazs because, according to her, he'd become "embarrassingly" fat. She'd been handsomely paid in the divorce to keep her opinions to herself.

George was surrounded by minions of admirers, but in moments of honest reflection, he knew it was the money they admired. Without it he'd be nothing but an old man who looked like an irritable toad. But, alas, he still had the dough, so these groupies laughed at his jokes, leaned in whenever he spoke, and plied him with compliments.

George was never guilty of sloth; I'll give him that. It was the only Deadly he'd avoided. He worked hard, but he'd never stooped to the level of mere domesticity. He could probably figure out how to make a cup of coffee, however it'd been forty years since he'd done it—forty years since he'd thrown a load in the wash. Your billionaires just don't do those things. And if you think he knew where the spare light bulbs were kept, you're crazy. He drove the nicest cars and drank the most expensive wines, but he'd convinced himself it hadn't been for show (uh-huh, right). When he donated to his alma mater, he didn't outright *demand* they name the new stadium after him. I barely put my pinky on the scales for that one. Oh, the pride.

George's second wife had given him his only heir, a boy he hadn't seen in many years. His son had been seduced by a misguided sense of entitlement—I could spot it from a mile away. George should've seen this coming. The little prince spent the first years of his life shuttled around in the family's private jet. When he was six-years-old, and had been forced to travel on a commercial flight, he'd leaned over to his mother and asked, "Who are all these people getting on our plane?"

George hated that second wife, and his disdain dribbled over to the product of her cold and heartless loin. When she moved to St. Croix, and wanted to take their son with her, George had relented. He still corresponded occasionally with his son, now forty years unemployed, but didn't respect him. I'd seen to that.

What George Miles wanted was someone who would kiss him without holding her breath, with the full recognition that he was a toad, and not because he could buy South Dakota. Unfortunately, those were women who looked like him. And, of course, he didn't want anything to do with one of *them*.

So, he kept slogging through the life of a billionaire, alone on his Gulfstream IV. His solitary pursuit of money had been a fraudulent illusion, and he knew it deep down. Lest he forget, I reminded him of it as often as I could.

30

NO SOONER HAD MAGGIE RESIGNED HERSELF to sharing potatoes with her communal brethren in Guatemala, that she heard the breathtaking news that her daughter's killer was the rich and famous Kenneth Lawson. Immediately, the potatoes became blander, the anti-capitalism rants more annoying, and the life of shared poverty more distressing. If Lawson had killed her precious Petunia, and if he was rich, there would be damages to pay.

Her fellow ex-pats were suspicious of Maggie's commitment to their cause, what with all the traveling to and fro to cash in on her daughter's murder. Therefore, the travel money was harder to come by this time. She'd finally wrenched the cash from a fellow hippy (a pleaser who couldn't say no to anybody, and hated herself for it).

"Jane, I'll tell you what; give me the money to fly to Philadelphia, and I'll pay you double when I come back."

"But, Maggie, how can you afford that?"

"I got myself a really good legal case there on account of Petunia's death."

"Petunia?"

"Yes, my daughter, Petunia. She got murdered."

"Oh, I'm so sorry, Maggie. I didn't know you had a daughter."

"Sure I do. Remember? I'm pretty sure I told you. The guy that killed her owes me damages for all I've been through."

"Oh, my goodness. You say she was *murdered*?"

"Yeah, someone hit her in the head with a shovel. I can't bear to think about it."

"That's the worst thing I've ever heard."

"Yeah, I'm pretty broken up about it. That's why I need the money—to get me a good lawyer so I can get paid for all I've been through."

"But what good would it do to get a bunch of money? It won't bring her back. We shouldn't care about the money, Maggie."

"I know. Money's corrupt. It enslaves poor workers around the world so corporate America can keep getting richer. Believe me, I know. That's why it's important to teach this rich killer a lesson. He needs to know that money causes heartache."

"But if money causes heartache, why would you—"

"My lawsuit will teach those rich people that you can't worship life and money at the same time."

"I'm not sure what you're talking about, Maggie."

"Trust me, Jane. I'll pay you back double. You can donate your money to a good cause. That's probably what I'll do with my share."

Maggie's logic was difficult to follow, even for me, but she was a communal sister in need. Besides, if Jane doubled her money, she'd have enough to hire her own lawyer to sue the ex-husband who'd pissed away their tax refund on that whore in Vegas. She loaned Maggie money, but not enough to get a direct flight.

Maggie hopped aboard a small plane that took off from a dirt runway, becoming airborne just in time to miss the terminal that was hardly bigger than a Tuff Shed. From there, she finagled her way on to other planes and buses, arriving in Philadelphia four days later.

She spent the first night on a cot next to her mother's bed in the crummy, low-budget nursing home. Grandma's caretakers were surprised when Maggie announced she was there to see her mother (they didn't know the senile old woman who slept with her Bible had a daughter). Maggie ingratiated herself with the nursing staff to weasel food for a few days while she combed through the phone book looking for personal injury lawyers.

The full-page color ad from Donald C. Harris & Associates was promising. Mr. Harris sat behind an impressive desk wearing a loud suit and menacing "Don't Fuck with Me" scowl. He was tanned and his veneers were white as snow. Behind him were rows of law books that hadn't been opened since the Eisenhower administration. The glossy ad promised that Mr. Harris would personally do all the work (and not some young associate). This had been a big selling point because he looked tough. Unfortunately, he was a bad lawyer who'd simply outspent other bad lawyers to get first dibs in the Yellow Pages. He spent his time creating cheesy marketing slogans and negotiating volume television ad rates.

Maggie's call was immediately passed to a young associate. Young Associate repeated, several times, that there would be no fee unless they won. Maggie didn't know that this youngster with his brand new diploma had never handled a wrongful death case in his life. She went to see him.

"So what's my case worth?" Maggie asked. "I've been through a lot, you know, losing my daughter and all."

"Did your daughter provide any financial support to you?"

"Not really, but I've suffered in other ways."

"I'm sure you have."

"So how much do you think we can go for?"

"Well, how close were the two of you? Did you spend a lot of time together?"

"We were very close," Maggie said.

"How often did you see each other?"

"Not that much. But, see, here's the thing; we didn't need to see each other because we expressed our love in other ways."

"I see. Tell me some of those other ways so we can build that into our case."

"Well," Maggie said, "we didn't need to show our love through talking and stuff. We just felt it. And we liked the same kind of music, and things like that."

Young Associate plumbed the depth of their close relationship before producing a retainer agreement. Maggie signed it, and slid it over to the lawyer.

"So, how much do you think we're looking at here?"

"It's difficult to say," said Young Associate. "I presume Senator Lawson may want to settle this, but he has a lot more pressing worries. If we're reasonable, he might just pay us quickly—just to get it out of the way."

"So, like, how much are we talking?"

"It's difficult to put a price tag on the loss of one's estranged daughter."

"But if we go the estranged daughter route then I should get even more because I was denied the chance to reconnect with her. See, I was going to start visiting and talking to her a lot more. That's what makes it so painful. So, what's that worth?"

"Well, it just depends on—"

"You think we oughta go for ten mil? Or is that too low? I know you'll go for a lot because you get your 30%."

"Actually, we get a third."

"Yeah, that's what I said; 30%."

"No, it's 33.3%. That's a third."

"Oh. Then we'll just go for a little more to make up the difference. So, tell me, what are we looking at?"

"I think somewhere in the neighborhood of $100,000."

Maggie was dumbfounded. Did she hear that right? "*That's it?* For my Petunia?"

"The damages are lower here because you didn't suffer any economic loss, and you rarely saw her. However, whatever you get will be tax free."

Maggie had never paid a dime of taxes in her life. She was still reeling from the paltry sum her own flesh and blood would fetch. It was hardly even worth the trip. A measly hundred grand? It beat hand-watering the marijuana plants in Guatemala, and swapping zucchinis for colonics. But a hundred grand? Outrageous.

"We'll make a settlement demand to Lawson within the next month or two. We'll probably demand $500,000 to give us some wiggle room to negotiate. You just never know. It's highly doubtful, but maybe he'll just pay it."

That's all Maggie heard. She was basically guaranteed $500,000, and she'd probably get it within two months, at the latest. This was top-of-the-line greed—a king-sized Deadly. Can you imagine how much fun I have?

31

"ALL RISE! THE FIRST JUDICIAL COURT in and for Philadelphia County and the Commonwealth of Pennsylvania is now in session, the Honorable Gustav Franco presiding. You may now be seated." This was the big moment and the bailiff spoke his one-liner with gravity, for the pews were crammed.

Myron, the bailiff, loved to wear his uniform and carry a gun that hadn't been fired in thirty years. At a pudgy 5'5", his roundness made his arms stick out like the hands of a clock, pointing to four and eight o'clock, respectively. He wasn't very menacing.

Today's arraignment offered no suspense. Everyone knew Lawson would plead not guilty. Even criminals who were guilty as sin pled not guilty to get bargaining leverage. I've seen it a million times. This is how it goes: "I'll tell you what," says the defense lawyer, "if you reduce the charges from Murder One to, say, shoplifting, we'll change our plea to guilty." The prosecutor reminds him that his client had been caught holding the switchblade still dripping with blood. "Yeah, I know. That's why he'll plead guilty to shoplifting, which he didn't even do, by the way. So, whaddya say? Deal?"

Ken Lawson was led into the courtroom. He was dressed in an orange jumpsuit—a snappy line from the Philadelphia County Casual Collection. "Corrections" was neatly stenciled across the back in a Century Gothic font. His hands were cuffed in front of him and linked to a chain around his waist. His ankles were also chained together. Lawson was accustomed to people looking at him when he entered a room, but he'd usually be wearing an Italian pin stripe instead of the orange one-piece. For a prideful man, this was hell.

Lawson would be allowed to upgrade to the Armani for the actual trial, because it would be highly prejudicial if the jury saw him like this. He just *looked* guilty, with a heart as ugly as the stone of a peach. Jurors would hold their breath in case the handcuffs failed (*Watch out, Regina! He's loose!*). But for now, without the jury present, he wore what all prisoners wore. Judge Franco didn't care if he was King Tut.

The courtroom could hold two-hundred people, and two-hundred-thirty of them were wedged into the wooden pews. These citizens would remind people at cocktail parties from that time forth that they'd been there. Susan had boycotted the proceeding as she would the remainder of the trial schedule. She refused to stand stoically by her man at the podium while he did the ol' Mea Culpa like all those other wives (that was so 1990's). Rebecca and John were too embarrassed to show up. Can you imagine the whispers? *I heard he damned near cut her head off with that shovel. For all we know, he probably had sex with her after he killed her. Shhhh! Here come his kids!*

Judge Gustav Franco was a decent man; flawed like the rest of you, but decent. I'd rank him somewhere between Solomon and Judge Judy. He'd been a football star in college but the ensuing years had made him fleshy. His large jowls looked like they stored an emergency cache of food—a portable pantry of sorts. There was so much skin hanging below his chin that a confused Tom turkey might try to court him. Thus, Judge Gus Franco was known as The Gobbler (behind his back, of course).

The Gobbler was a no-nonsense judge who performed his legal duty between Phillies games. I don't understand your obsession with sports. Yippee! The Dodgers won! Who cares? The Gobbler was rumored to wear a Mike Schmidt jersey under his judicial robe for good luck, and announced unnecessary recesses so he could sneak back to his chambers for score updates.

The jail was located in the basement of the courthouse. The defendants were brought up to the courtroom in a secure elevator for their arraignments. Typically, when the judge calls the defendant's name, the prosecutor fumbles through a stack of files. Once he finds the right one, he skims it to get the gist of the case. You see, prosecutors don't lose sleep mulling over Class B misdemeanors. They just don't. However, in this celebrated case, The Gobbler handled Senator Lawson's arraignment separately. This wasn't done out of courtesy to Lawson (Judge Franco was a Democrat). He only did it to accommodate the crush of media.

Franco ruled the proceedings would not be televised because he didn't want a circus. Lawson was relieved. He didn't want people to see him like this. Stew Franks, however, was disappointed. He'd already appealed to Franco to make it a public event.

"Your Honor," Stew had said. "It is incumbent upon this court to allow the media to broadcast these proceedings. This is a public courtroom and the citizens, who have expressed unusual interest in this case, should be allowed to watch it on television."

"I am aware, Mr. Franks, that this is a public courtroom. However, I will not allow this to become a public spectacle. The media will be present, but there will be no cameras."

"I don't want it to become a public spectacle, either," Stew lied. "But I am determined, Your Honor, to petition on their behalf for an open court process."

"Your petition is denied."

That had been a week earlier. Now the citizenry was seated, and The Gobbler began: "This is the time and place scheduled for the arraignment in the case of the Commonwealth of Pennsylvania vs. Kenneth Lawson. Are the parties ready to proceed?"

Stew Franks solemnly stood. "Yes, Your Honor, the state is ready to proceed."

Andrew Bradshaw unfolded himself and also stood. "Thank you, Your Honor, we are ready."

"Very well then, Mr. Bradshaw, will you and your client please stand."

They stood and approached the lonely podium in the center of the courtroom. Bradshaw walked slowly so as not to outpace his shuffling, shackled client. It was silent except for the jingling of chains.

"Mr. Lawson," said Judge Franco, "you have been charged with the first-degree murder of Chelsea Miles. How do you plead?"

"Not guilty," said Lawson too forcefully, as if this whole monkey business was outrageous.

"Very well. We will notice this case for a Pre-Trial." The judge leaned away from his microphone and asked his clerk for an open date approximately two months down the road.

Beth Cummings, the clerk, was stern and frigid. She had no sense of humor and hated all men. She clipped off a date to The Gobbler. There wasn't a male in the courtroom who didn't practically shudder whenever she spoke. Indeed, there was an instinctive longing to reach for their genitalia to protect it from the likes of Beth, whose mere voice would cause it to retract in shame, and fear.

"Has the State provided all its evidence to the defense?"

"We have, Your Honor." Stew was grateful for another speaking part.

The State was required to provide all evidence it had to the defense, even the stuff that didn't support its tidy theory that Lawson was guilty. The State couldn't hide anything, and if it did, it risked a dismissal, or at least a mistrial. If they got caught, that is. Sometimes the prosecutor "forgets" to provide the juicy ammo that might result in an acquittal (Oh, you mean you wanted *that*? Humph, I'll be darned). These naughty little oopsie daisies amuse me, but they upset judges.

"Is there anything further, counsel?"

"Yes, Your Honor," Bradshaw said as he leaned into the microphone at the podium (which worked about forty percent of the time). "We also filed a Motion for Bail to be set. I believe the State was provided a copy of our Motion."

"We were, Your Honor," said Stew, anxious to be heard again.

"What is the state's position, Mr. Franks?"

"Your Honor," Stew cleared his throat. "This is a grave and monstrous crime. We believe bail should be denied."

"Your Honor, if I may," said Bradshaw. "While the crime is indeed grave, the defendant adamantly denies his involvement. Senator Lawson has been an upstanding citizen with no criminal misconduct in his past. His roots are deep here in this state and no one, not even Mr. Franks, can seriously argue that he represents a flight risk. Bail is appropriate here so the Senator can help prepare for his defense."

"I will take the matter of bail under advisement," said Judge Franco. He was inclined to grant it, but he hated Lawson's politics and found his crime to be reprehensible. So, he'd let Lawson wallow in jail for a few days, mostly out of spite.

"If there is nothing further," The Gobbler continued, "we will see you gentlemen in court March 2nd for the final pre-trial in this case. I will ask my clerk (even the judge winced when he referred to her) to clear ten days on the calendar for the trial in late March. I assume that will be a sufficient amount of time?"

"I am optimistic," said Stew, "that we can satisfactorily conclude the presentation of the State's evidence within that ten-day period of time barring no unforeseen and unnecessary delays on the part of the defense in this proceeding blah blah blah . . ." he continued rambling, just for the sake of rambling.

"Is that a 'Yes'?" The Gobbler asked impatiently.

"Yes, it is," said Stew, restraining himself.

"Very well then, this court is in recess."

32

LAWSON HADN'T DARED TURN AROUND to face the throng of media in the courtroom, for his shame was too great. Besides that, he'd never looked particularly good in orange. However, he'd faced a dreadful dilemma. Should he look straightforward and allow the gallery to gaze upon his prominent bald spot? Or should he turn slightly to the right to show them his best side and risk offending the judge? He'd felt victimized either way.

After the short hearing, Lawson was led from the courtroom and down the elevator to jail in the basement. He thought the arraignment had been wholly unnecessary, and in his advanced stages of narcissism, he assumed it had been done simply to humiliate him. He was also furious that the judge hadn't immediately granted his motion to be released on bail. He knew it was because Gus Franco had been appointed to the bench by a Democratic Governor years earlier, and was therefore soft on crime (except where Lawson was concerned).

Lawson was segregated from the other inmates in a wing occupied by other celebrity lawbreakers (and child molesters) for their own safety. This did not reassure him. What was he, a United States Senator, doing locked up like a common criminal? He'd heard about "country club" prisons for affluent white-collar criminals. It was hogwash, because who was more white and affluent than he? And this place sucked. The meals were bland and served without wine. There wasn't much socializing, either. Jailbird neighbors knew he was some kind of government big-wig, but they didn't habitually read the *Congressional Record*, and the time they collectively spent watching CSPAN was negligible. These morons would've been hard pressed to name the current President, much less a United States Senator. It was galling to Lawson that two-bit losers on reality TV shows had more fame than he did. He wasn't even as famous as the Duck Dynasty guy.

Lawson's cell was smaller than his shoe closet. A desk was bolted to the floor and the twin bed had a thin, lumpy mattress with suspicious stains. The itchy wool blanket and ticking blue striped pillow (sans case) were further burdens for someone accustomed to high thread counts. A stainless-steel throne sat in the middle of the cell, and he had no privacy while using it.

There was the noise, too. Inmates talked to themselves, sung country western songs out of key, farted, belched, and bitched. They professed their innocence, and then bragged about their crimes. I just have to smile over this. The fuckin' system this, and the fuckin' system that. Insulting outbursts, racial epitaphs, bigotry, and screeching homophobia. It was like a symphony to me.

Ken was a New Fish—that's what they call the newbies. He was allowed into the common area a few hours each day where a television shrieked its juvenile nonsense (how can you stand it?).

He was everywhere—on every channel. Late night comedians were thrilled with the hypocrisy. And I was impressed with the sheer number of jokes that could be mined from the use of a simple gardening tool. Then there were all the people coming out of their holes to get their fifteen minutes. People Ken barely even knew stood in their front yards, gushing to their local television news reporters about how they'd been Lawson's best friend in high school and never saw this coming (although one fellow, who was apparently in Ken's 7th grade algebra class, remembered him as "a boiler waiting to blow").

Susan Lawson would not comment, other than to express her sympathy for the victim's family. However, as the weeks passed, she'd become more visible, showing up at feel-good charity events with her checkbook and practiced smile. I found this to be greedy in its own way. Chalk up another Deadly.

John and Rebecca were in free fall—horrified with news leaks that dribbled forth from Stew Franks' office (who'd promised not to try the case in the press, haha). Their dad had brutally murdered his mistress? *Their dad?* Inconceivable. They privately lamented that their days in first class were probably over.

This was to be Date Night for Scott and Theresa, a tradition relieving them of the joys of parenthood. But this night they'd taken the chaos with them, where the girls chucked saltine crackers and sippy cups at each other. The perimeter of the restaurant table looked like Dresden after all the good work I'd done with WWII. They returned home and put the girls to bed, but their conversation was interrupted from the other room. "Can I have another drink?" "When is it going to be Christmas?"

By the time the questions finally petered out, Scott and Theresa had enough energy to either have sex or talk, but not both. Scott would have normally opted for the former but that night he chose the latter. "This Lawson case is heating up."

"I know. It's all over the news."

"Stew didn't let me say anything today at the arraignment, but he promised I'd get some witnesses at trial."

"You really think it's going all the way to trial?"

"Probably. Lawson swears he didn't do it and won't plead to anything. So, unless he caves and pleads to second degree, or even voluntary manslaughter, I think this is going all the way."

"So what do *you* think? You think he really did it?"

"Yeah, I think he probably did."

"Probably?"

"No, I do. But there are some things that don't add up, and the defense will milk them for all their worth."

"Which witnesses will you get?"

"I think Stew will give me a few of the experts—maybe the blood spatter and fingerprint guy. I might get the State's Medical Examiner, too." Stew would do this because he knew their testimony could be dry and boring. He also knew Scott had a better grasp of the technical issues. Of course, Stew articulated the reasons a bit differently to Scott (*Why don't you go ahead and take the fingerprint expert because you could use more experience*).

Scott would also take a large role in the penalty phase of the trial (there are two phases in a capital murder trial—the guilt and penalty phases). If the jury found Lawson guilty, they'd reconvene a few days later to hear evidence about an appropriate penalty. It could be life in prison, or death. This one smelled like a death penalty case to me. And how I love a good lynching!

Paul McDonald would be a star witness in the penalty phase. They'd drag his carcass into court to tell the jury how he and his boss conspired to strong-arm the witnesses, even to the point of kidnapping and beating them. Hardly the stuff of a repentant sinner.

"It looks like a pretty strong case to me, at least from what I've heard," said Theresa.

"I just don't get why Lawson would kill her. He's a United States Senator for crying out loud, not some crazy half-cocked maniac."

"What? You don't think those egomaniacs commit crimes?"

"Yeah, I guess. But you'd think if they got into a fight or something, there'd be some evidence of it. They hadn't chucked anything at each other or anything like that—everything was in perfect order in that room. And she didn't have any defensive wounds or any other marks on her body. So, what, the ranking Republican Senator on the Defense Appropriations Committee just one day decides to up and *murder* somebody? With a shovel?"

"Well, if there wasn't a struggle," said Theresa, "then it was probably someone she knew."

"But a United States Senator?"

"I don't care if he's a senator. So what? The guy's a creep. He probably lost it when she said she was pregnant with his baby or something like that. I know it's a leap from an affair to murder, but the guy was a slime ball. I mean, *somebody* did it, right? So, why's it such a stretch to think it was the egomaniac pig she'd been having an affair with? He was right there."

"Yeah, okay, but how do you get around the fact that he used a shovel from outside to kill her? It makes no sense."

"Maybe they argued and he left and walked outside, but he was still steaming. He's really freaking out. He sees the shovel and goes back in."

"Sure, that's possible. But what, he first finds some gloves and puts them on before he touches the shovel? I mean, come on."

"Oh," she said, "I thought you said his fingerprints were on the shovel."

"Well, they are and they aren't. There's just one of his thumb prints on the shovel, but tons of other fingerprints that *don't* belong to him, probably the landscaper's."

"So there you have it. He did grab the shovel."

"And only left one partial thumb print?"

"Sure," she said, "after he murdered her he just wiped them off but missed a spot."

"But if he'd done that, which makes sense I guess, why are there so many other prints still on the shovel? Why weren't they also wiped off in the process?"

"Wasn't the landscape guy still there when Mr. Sleaze Bag sneaked away?"

"Yeah."

"So Sleaze Bag grabs the shovel, kills her, and wipes off the handle. Then the landscape guy uses the shovel again after that. What's the big mystery?"

Why hadn't he thought of that? Yeah, duh, that was it. But Scott didn't want the love of his life to think he was dense, so rather than salute her for cluing him in, he just said, "Yeah, I guess that's *possible*."

Ken suffered in jail for three long days before Judge Franco released him on bail. He set the bond at one million dollars. 3-D Bonding provided the bond for fifteen percent, or $150,000. Nonrefundable. There was money to be made up and down the chain of heartbreak. Chelsea gets clobbered by a shovel and before you know it, the money starts flowing to lawyers, bondsmen, experts, newspapers, and cable outlets. This was no tragedy; it was a bonanza!

Susan made it clear that Ken would not be allowed to return home (technically, she'd said he could, but only over her dead body, and he didn't need another one of those). Ken had no friends either, all of them scattering the way people do when someone vomits and they don't want to be splashed on. He still had his apartment in D.C., but the judge made it a condition of his bail that he couldn't leave the state. He took a few changes of clothes and rented a furnished apartment in Center City.

His new neighbors at the apartment complex had mixed feelings about the new tenant on the third floor. Some were thrilled to have the most famous face in America living there, even if he was a shovel wielding monster. *Omigosh! Have you seen who moved in to 3F? It's that Lawson guy who cold-cocked his mistress!* Others hated having the media camped out night and day in the parking lot. *I don't give a rat's ass if Babe Ruth moved in; I just wanna park my Buick in the goddamned carport!*

You like to say there's no such thing as bad publicity, but Lawson had his doubts. When he had to go to the grocery store (a place he'd rarely been), people nudged each other. He knew they weren't gossiping about the price of avocados.

Rebecca talked to her mom and brother as often as she could, hoping to find comfort, some reassurance that her father wasn't a monster. She was completely off kilter, like someone had taken her purse and turned it upside down, dumping everything onto the mud. She called John from her apartment.

"Have you talked to mom lately," Rebecca asked him.

"I just got off the line with her. It's the worst. Everybody stares and whispers behind her back. It would suck."

"It does suck."

"She can hardly leave the house anymore. They won't leave her alone. Like, what's she supposed to say?"

"She's been through a lot," Rebecca said.

"I just wish she'd come out and support dad's innocence."

"She said she thinks he's innocent."

"Yeah, but she only said it, like, once. She needs to let dad move back in and tell everyone he didn't do it. That'd go a long way, that's all I'm saying."

"Put yourself in her shoes," Rebecca said. "Dad's having sex with this total tramp the day she gets killed?"

"She wasn't a tramp."

"So now you're going to defend her?"

"No, but she wasn't a tramp," John said. "She wasn't doing anything dad wasn't."

"And now dad spends the rest of his life in prison because of her? You think that's fair?"

"Of course it's not fair," he said. "But she was murdered for God's sake. That's not too fair, either."

33

MAGGIE LAY ON THE COT next to grandma's bed in the low-cost nursing home, dreaming of a face-lift, lipo, and a new car—all the things she was rightfully entitled to because her daughter had been murdered. And because the harm had been egregious, she believed she was entitled to the bounty right away. So, she called her lawyer about getting a loan to tide her over until her ship had formally docked.

"I need some money to tide me over."

"Well," said Young Associate, "it's impermissible for our law firm to loan you any money."

"But you can just take it out of my winnings in a month or two."

"Unfortunately, the lawyer code of ethics doesn't allow for that sort of thing."

"Why on earth not?" she asked.

"Clients would just hire the lawyer that advanced them the most money."

"What's so bad about that?"

"You shouldn't choose a lawyer based on that."

"Why not?"

"You just shouldn't, that's why." Young Associate believed the better way to choose a lawyer was the pizzazz of his catchy jingle.

"But I have a good case. You promised me $500,000."

"Maggie, I said we would *demand* that much, but we'd be lucky to get $100,000."

"Okay, fine then, loan me against the hundred. I won't tell anybody."

Young Associate's hesitation cost him. "How much do you need?"

"Just a couple thousand. I need to get me a place. Once we get all the money then I'll buy me a nice house and car and make a bunch of other investments—like stocks and stuff." Maggie had been living in the commune too long.

Young Associate agreed to do something under the table for "humanitarian" reasons. Maggie rented an apartment near her lawyer's office to impatiently wait it out. She called Young Associate every day, exasperated that it was taking so cotton pickin' long. He was exasperated with her, too (*It's that Maggie lady again on line three. What should I tell her? Tell her I'm in court. Okay, but that's what I told her last time. Then tell her I'm at the dentist).* He took every third call, each time reminding her that these things take time. He promised to call her the very *instant* there was something to report. She'd call the next day anyway.

The settlement demand for $500,000 made its way to Ken Lawson via Andrew Bradshaw. He meant to talk to Lawson about it the next time they met, but he forgot (his focus was keeping his client out of the electric chair, and he had no idea how much Maggie yearned for the cosmetic lift). In the meantime, the deadline for responding to the offer was fast approaching. *Pay within thirty days or else!* Or else what?

When Lawson finally learned of the potential civil suit, he got wrathy in a hurry. "Can they *do* that?" Lawson asked. "Can this greedy bitch really sue me for money?"

"That has been a central component of our legal system for a long time, Senator." Bradshaw normally called him "Ken," but made the formal reference to demonstrate that someone in Lawson's position should have known better.

"That's bullshit! I've always favored tort reform, and now I know why."

"I am a criminal lawyer, Ken. Civil law is not my specialty, but I can have someone look into this if you'd like."

"So how much do you think I'll have to pay this gold digger to get her off my back?"

"I don't know how much you'll have to pay this mother for her daughter's murder." Bradshaw believed that a mother who sued her child's murderer shouldn't automatically be labeled a gold digger. Of course, Bradshaw didn't know Chelsea's mother.

"Maybe we ought to just pay her something to go away."

"That's a possibility," Bradshaw said. "But paying her now implies you're responsible for Chelsea's death. And that's not the message we want to send to anyone, including the media and all those potential jurors out there."

"We just blow her off then?" asked Lawson.

"Let me think on that for a bit," said Bradshaw. "I'll let the attorney know we're considering our options. That will buy us some time. I don't want to become distracted by this."

Bradshaw called Young Associate to inform him they'd think about it, but wouldn't formally respond for a few months. Young

Associate blustered about the humongous verdict they'd get, blah blah blah, but that's about it. The civil case would have to wait.

Maggie was incensed. "So you're going to just sit there and take that baloney? I need me a lawyer who'll fight!"

"I am fighting," he said.

"Well, if they think they can bully me around like this, they have another thing coming!" You see, Maggie had an unwavering belief in the righteousness of her own tantrum.

Maggie used the next loan (Young Associate had caved in yet again) to buy a computer and spent her days surfing for exotic cruise destinations. When she wasn't browsing her wish list, she'd while away the hours forwarding those annoying kitten and puppy photos, and cheesy *Love Is So Beautiful* passages to her contact list. She also sent those ridiculous chain messages where your entire future is predicated on whether or not you forward it on to ten additional people. Ugh, how do you stand it?

She called her attorney nearly every day to give him a little boost. Young Associate resented his client from hell: Maggie Tucker. This resentment caused him to accumulate a Deadly résumé. He also resented his boss, Donald C. Harris, the egotistical star of his own TV commercials (*Prideful jerk*), because he hogged most of the attorney fees (*Greedy jerk).* He didn't do any of the work, either (*Slothful jerk).* He was a fat pig, too (*Gluttonous jerk*), and got the hottest secretary (*Lustful jerk*). There was no justice in it. So, Young Associate was filled with Wrath. His boss just got lucky, that's all. And for that, Young Associate was Envious. Hence, it was a clean sweep of the Deadlies—all seven of 'em.

34

SCOTT BENJAMIN WAS GEARING UP for the biggest trial in decades, but I've noticed there's no pause button with two kids and a pregnant wife. Therefore, he brought his work home, lying in bed until two in the morning, reading about fingerprint analysis. Theresa lay next to him with ear plugs and sleep mask, asking every ten minutes how much longer he was going to keep the light on.

Andrew Bradshaw had been involved in high profile cases before, but never one like this—a murder saga everyone and their dog was glued to. Most of them were rooting for the death penalty. It's not like they had anything against Lawson, personally; they just thought a death sentence would be a lot more exciting. It's always been that way. You and your so-called civilized nature. Unfortunately, Bradshaw also had other cases to worry about; orange-clad clients pacing in the pokey, demanding that their case be top priority. You think they cared about Lawson?

Bradshaw had broached the possibility of a plea bargain, but Lawson would have nothing of it. He wouldn't plead guilty to a danged thing. Besides, Stew Franks wouldn't agree to a lesser charge anyway, itching as he was to try this case to a jury (and the media—the whole world, really).

On March 2nd, the day of the Pre-Trial, Scott awoke to the last snowstorm of the year (the snow had been pretty for a few days in December, but by now everyone agreed it was ugly). He turned up his coat collar, blew on his hands, and kicked a clump of dirty snow off the front tire. Rush hour traffic was snarled due to the storm. Everyone thought everyone else was a selfishly bad driver. Scott finally arrived at the courthouse and parked in the underground garage reserved for judges and lawyers. He took the elevator to the fourth floor where Judge Franco's courtroom was located. Members of the press who couldn't squeeze into the packed courtroom patrolled the corridor looking for someone, anyone, to interview. They mauled Scott when they saw him, but he pushed past them and into the courtroom.

The courtroom looked like the dining room of the Titanic. It was paneled in dark mahogany and chandeliers hung from a raised ceiling rimmed with elaborately carved gilded scrollwork. The walls were adorned with large oil paintings depicting important scenes from Pennsylvania's history (signing of the Declaration of Independence, white settlers subduing the Indians, etc.). The early birds who'd set their alarms to squeeze into the pews would be disappointed, because this was only a routine preliminary hearing. There would be no witnesses, or photos of Chelsea's naked, bludgeoned body. Myron, the bailiff, was busy imposing his authority like an armed usher at a nephew's gaudy bar mitzvah.

Scott caught the eye of Beth Cummings, the frigid clerk, who stared him down until he took his seat next to Stew Franks. Their table sat next to the jury box where twelve upholstered chairs were the only empty seats in the house. Soon they would be filled with ordinary citizens, charged with deciding the fate of the ranking member of the Senate Defense Appropriation Committee.

Andrew Bradshaw sat at the other counsel table, next to ex-Senator Lawson who wore a suit and tie, without accessory shackles. Bradshaw had picked him up at his apartment in his twelve-year-old Volvo, and driven into the underground parking lot to avoid the media. But the press and paparazzi found them anyway, swirling around like a Biblical plague of locust.

Beth's phone buzzed and she cuffed it to her ear. She hung up and told the attorneys the judge wanted to see them in his chambers. The three of them stood and followed her (at a safe distance), leaving Lawson alone at the counsel table where he fidgeted under Myron's watchful eye. There would be no funny business; not in his courtroom.

The attorneys were ushered through a doorway hidden behind the judge's elevated bench into a hallway which led to the judge's chambers. Judge Gustav Franco, aka The Gobbler, was seated behind his desk. Everything was rich brown, including the leather chairs with tarnished gold rivets. It smelled musty from legal tomes with outdated legal precedent that filled the sagging bookshelves. No one read the books, of course, but they looked good and made The Gobbler look smart.

"Welcome, Gentlemen. Please make yourselves comfortable. I believe you've met my clerk."

The lawyers awkwardly said hello to Beth, mindful not to make unnecessary eye contact with her.

"As you undoubtedly know, the media is here in force," the judge said. "Are there any matters we need to discuss here in chambers before we retire to the courtroom?"

"Yes, Your Honor," said Stew. "We would like to renew our Motion to have the trial televised. Perhaps the court will reconsider its position in view of the public interest this case has generated."

"Counsel, I see no reason for that. We can conduct the trial efficiently and fairly without cameras. I don't want anyone preening for the cameras." His gaze rested longer on Stew than anyone else.

"So, are you going to deny our Motion?"

"Yes, I believe I've made my position clear. No cameras. Now, is there anything else?"

There was nothing, so the lawyers returned to the courtroom. Judge Franco hung back a few moments to make his courtroom entrance special. He lifted his robe from the hook on the back of his door and pulled it over his head. The sheen of his wingtips was a bit dull, so he lifted each shoe, buffing it on the back of his pant leg. He looked at the reflection of his framed diploma and straightened his hair. He was ready to go. When everyone had settled into the courtroom, a signal was given to Myron, who puffed out his chest and belted out the announcement: "This Court is now in session, the Honorable Gustav Franco presiding." Judge Franco walked in through the hidden door behind his perch, then up a few steps, and sat down heavily. The seat cushion exhaled a hiss of air. "You may now be seated," Myron announced to the crowd, most of who had already begun sitting, beating him to the punch. This always bugged him—this modest act of civil disobedience.

"We are here," the judge began, "for the Pre-Trial hearing in the case of The Commonwealth of Pennsylvania vs. Kenneth Lawson. Are the parties ready to proceed?"

"Yes, Your Honor," Stew and Bradshaw both stood and said in unison.

"Very well. I see that you have provided the court with a list of your witnesses and exhibits. It appears to me that this case can be tried in five or six days, instead of the ten we had previously set aside. We will seat the jury on March 16th." Judge Franco then reviewed other important deadlines for filing Motions, questions for the prospective jury panel, and submitting the legal instructions to the jury. When he finished, he asked the attorneys if there were any other matters that needed to be addressed.

"Your Honor," Stew stood with solemnity. "I would like to renew our Motion to have these proceedings televised because of the enormous public interest this case has generated. I understand the court has previously denied that motion in chambers, but I simply wanted to make a formal record of that ruling for the benefit of the court reporter."

"Counsel, will you please approach the bench," Judge Franco said. I was impressed with his poker face when I knew he was about to unload his wrath, projectile style. I was reminded of a cartoon character with steam coming out of his ears.

The three attorneys stood huddled in front of the judge's bench. Judge Franco put his hand over the microphone and turned on Stew.

"Mr. Franks," he hissed, "If it is your intention to insult this court, then you have succeeded. However, I assure you this is no way to curry my favor. If you say one more thing about televising this trial, I will hold you in contempt and you will not be permitted another word in my courtroom. Have I made myself clear?"

"Yes, Your Honor."

"Are you absolutely sure you understand? Because I thought I'd made myself quite clear before you tried to embarrass the court and give the media reason to criticize the way we're going to proceed here."

"Yes, Your Honor."

The Gobbler stared him down for another five, painfully long, seconds before ordering the attorneys to return to their tables.

Both sides huddled after the hearing. Scott was upset with Stew over the fool he'd made of himself with Judge Franco. This was no way to begin. He felt better after they reviewed the evidence. No case was ironclad (well, there was the OJ case), but this case had hardly any weaknesses.

They could establish motive. After all, who had a better motive to silence the only person on earth who could expose his scandalous affair than the senator himself? And the fact that she'd been pregnant? Even better.

They could establish opportunity. Lawson was the last person to see her alive. They'd been fornicating like mad—just inches from where she was murdered, and where his semen wound up. Who had a better opportunity than that?

They had the murder weapon with Lawson's thumbprint on it. The landscaper's prints were also on the shovel because he'd used it during the normal routine of his job, presumably both before and after the murder. But there was zero evidence he'd ever set foot in the house.

And George? Surely he had motive. Who wouldn't be upset to learn his wife had been in their bed doing the no-no with another man? He'd come home within the window of time that Chelsea had been murdered. But if he'd done it, why was *Lawson's* thumb print on the murder weapon and not George's? And why would he have put the shovel back outside where it'd been easily found by the police? (It baffled the cops that either man, both with high school diplomas, hadn't washed the damned thing off).

Scott was confident they had their man. Lawson's guilt quadrupled with the evidence that he'd hired thugs to kidnap and assault witnesses to his crime.

Rebecca sat at the kitchen table in her mother's house, pushing the last few wilted leaves of romaine around with her fork, the remnants of a salad that a friend had dropped off. Susan commented on this friend's loyalty—the way she'd courageously butted through the lecherous media (she'd done so wearing sunglasses, hat, scarf, and baggy coat with the collar turned up, hurrying to the front door with her hands covering her face, but still).

"And they call themselves journalists," Susan said. "Pathetic."

"Mom, I know you're upset with dad, but don't you think you should *say* something?"

"There's nothing to say."

"But they're saying he must be guilty because you won't come out and say he's innocent."

"Because I don't know if he is."

"Come on, mom. You know he didn't kill her."

"And tell me, Rebecca, just how do I know that?"

"Gol, mom, it sounds like you think he did it."

"I don't know what to think."

The two of them sat, Rebecca absently playing with the fork and Susan staring blankly at the closed curtain.

"How's he doing?" asked Rebecca.

"How should I know? I suppose he's surrounded by his high-priced legal team."

"Don't you even care, mom?"

"Of course I care. But there isn't much I can do at this point, now is there?"

"Have the lawyers said you need to testify?"

"No, nobody tells me anything."

"That's probably because dad thinks you're still mad at him."

"Mad at him? *Mad at him?* Now why on earth would I be mad at him? He was sleeping with his best friend's wife and then probably killed her. So, why, darling, would that possibly upset me?"

"Come on, mom. He screwed up, okay? Get divorced if you want to. But don't you think you should try to keep him out of prison?"

"Maybe that's where he belongs."

"You don't mean that, mom."

"I don't know what I mean, Rebecca. I'm a pariah. I'm pitied and gossiped about. Even my friends won't have anything to do with me. You saw how Gail dropped off that salad. She left before I could even tell her we're not murderers. What have I done to deserve any of this?"

"You haven't done anything, mom."

"No I haven't. So why should I rush in like all those other pitiful wives who stand next to their cheating husbands while everyone watching knows damned good and well he's guilty. It's pathetic and I won't do it, Rebecca. I won't."

35

JAVIER ASSUMED THE COAST WAS CLEAR now that there'd been an arrest. His wife hated to see him go, but he could make double the dinero in El Norte, especially now that it was springtime. There would be plenty of landscape work to do in Philadelphia.

The night before he left, Javier told his children stories about America; the huge houses and heated swimming pools. He promised to return with something special for each of them, including the new baby now marinating in the womb for seven and a half months. The next morning, he simply walked across the leaky border. There'd been no need to burrow under a fence, or swim the Rio Grande by moonlight.

"Are you going to the trial, mom?"

"No, John, I'm not. I won't be an object for the media. I won't be *that* woman, and I won't be pitied."

"Has dad asked you to go?"

"No. It's the one decent thing your father has done. He knows I still have my pride."

"So, you're just going to stay here, hiding inside until it's over?"

"I refuse to sit here for the rest of my life while the self-righteous media camps outside my door like vultures."

"Where will you go?"

"I've already booked a trip to Bermuda."

"You're going on a *vacation* while dad's on trial for murder?"

"I'm not going on a vacation, John. I'm getting away from this circus. Somewhere out of the country, and I don't want the paparazzi following me there. I trust you won't tell them where I've gone. It's none of their business."

"Does dad know?"

"No, and I don't want you to tell him either."

"So when are you coming home?"

"When it's over. When this whole public nightmare is over."

It was now a week before the trial and Ken was scared. Really scared. He might spend the rest of his life in a cold, cement cell with lousy sheets, sans duvet; sheets he'd have to wash himself in the prison laundry, constantly looking over his shoulder, waiting to be raped by gangs. Don't kid yourself; he'd seen the movies. Or he'd be lashed to a gurney with canvas straps when they stuck a needle in his arm.

He recalled the feeling on election night—the butterflies. He'd give anything now; even agree to go completely bald, in exchange for the worries that now stewed low in his gut. There was no way to control the events, nothing he could do. I suppose he could root for Chelsea's immediate resurrection, but let's face it; his faith in God, when it came right down to it, was erratic.

Susan had been aloof, pretending not to care. But the truth is she did care. She'd be tuned to CNN in the privacy of her Bermudan suite. She didn't know if Ken would be convicted, but, gun to her head, she assumed he would, along with most legal analysts, psychics, and bookies. If Ken had asked her to testify on his behalf, about what a good and decent husband he'd been, she might have swallowed her pride and done it. But he hadn't even asked.

Ken didn't expect any support from Susan, and he couldn't blame her. How long would he have clung like a barnacle to the Good Ship Susan if it'd started taking on water? John and Rebecca, his disgraced kids, would be the only ones in the crowd hoping for something other than the noose. And, by the way, you know that's what everyone was rooting for, whether he was guilty or not. You're pretty much all the same. I may be the virus, but you're the host.

George hadn't decided if he would attend the entire trial, or not. His desire to sit through the brutal murder trial of his wife was unappetizing. However, it might look calloused if he didn't—they'd all look over at him during the sad parts and expect to see him weeping. The prosecution would have him testify that he'd come home to retrieve some papers and left a few moments later (he'd perjure himself silly by not admitting he'd had a heated row that afternoon with the treasonous slut). He would describe the depth of their romance, hanky in hand, and what a soul mate she'd been (the extracurricular was heartbreaking and very much out of her character).

The defense would suggest *he* was the killer. Their cross examination would focus on his humiliating motive. He'd been smack dab in the house shortly after his loving wife had toweled away the excitement of another man. And that couldn't have been pretty. But, alas, his fingerprints weren't on the shovel and Lawson's were. George would've had to go to the garage to yank on a pair of gardening gloves (if he could find them, because he'd never worn a pair), grab a shovel (if he could find it, because he'd never dug a hole), and then murder his wife in the heat of passion. It was all quite illogical.

The Governor of Pennsylvania had long coveted Lawson's senate seat. He was also a Republican, but a moderate one, so he and Lawson had their philosophical differences on God, gays, Mexicans, guns, women, black people, yellow people, red people, Georgetown prostitutes, and the environment. However, as fellow statewide office holders from the same political party, they were usually praiseworthy of each other. It was only in private that they said things like "right-wing fruitcake" or "he acts like a goddamned Democrat."

When Lawson resigned "for the good of the country," the Governor appointed a crony of his to be the interim senator until a special election could be held the following year. The crony made an under-the-table promise that he wouldn't run for re-election, paving the way for the Governor to finally scratch that itch. This interim-senator was a welterweight, at best, so he needed a strong transition team. There was no one more qualified for Chief of Staff than Ann Lee. When word of Ann's promotion trickled down the gutter to Paul McDonald, who was out on bail but desperately unemployable, he'd hated her for it.

Meanwhile, Maggie continued to pester Young Associate.

"Yeah, say, any word?"

"No. Like I keep telling you, we won't hear anything for weeks, at a minimum."

"So a week, huh?"

"No, Maggie. I said weeks."

"What am I supposed to do in the meantime? Just sit here like a bump on a log? Don't they know I lost everything when he took my Petunia? Now I can't even pay my bills."

"They're focused on the criminal case for now and we won't hear anything for a few months. I'll call you as soon as I hear anything."

"I thought you just said a week. And now it's another month?"

"No, I said a *few* months."

"Humph. Okay, I'll give you a shout tomorrow to see if we've heard anything."

Jesse and Slim were still in jail. They'd met with the prosecutors in preparation for their testimony where they'd been told to tell the truth, the whole truth, and nothing but the truth. This would be tricky because they'd embellished the details so often they couldn't remember what was fact and what had only been a product of their lustful imagination.

The lawyers were gearing up. Stew was shopping for a new suit and Scott was cramming for his cross examination of the fingerprint expert. Bradshaw was racking his brain for an alternative explanation for the murder, one that didn't have his client swinging the shovel at Chelsea's head. His only hope might lie with Javier Flores. If Javier testified that he hadn't touched the shovel after 3:30 p.m., Bradshaw could cast doubt on the prosecution's theory that Javier's fingerprints were still on the handle because he'd reused it after the killing. Other than that, Bradshaw's only hope was that the burglar who'd entered through the basement window would come forward in a fit of conscience, Jean Valjean style, to demand that he, and not Lawson, be executed. *Spare this innocent man! It was me!*

The prosecution had been trying to find Javier for months with no success. Now with the trial a few days away, they'd given up on him. But Bradshaw kept looking. He told his Hispanic private detective to keep checking with Javier's ex-roommates, the ones who'd bought his pickup. Bribe them with tequila, or serenade them with a mariachi band, but, dammit, find him!

36

DAY ONE. MONDAY, MARCH 16TH.

"ALL RISE! The First Judicial Court, in and for the Commonwealth of Pennsylvania is now in session, the Honorable Gustav Franco presiding. You may now be seated." Myron was pleased that it'd come out perfectly. Thus, began the biggest trial the city had ever seen.

The courtroom was crammed beyond the fire marshal's recommended range, and the citizenry who couldn't get in milled about in the courtyard, shivering in the cold. They were hoping for a bombshell *(This just in! Lawson admits to other gardening tool murders!).*

Reporters spilled from the courtyard on to Filbert Street—former journalism majors checked their hair and makeup, adjusted their ties, and took sips of bottled water, hoping for the sensational. Media trucks were parked everywhere. It looked like the manager of a KOA had gone AWOL, leaving drunk RV'ers to park at their whimsy.

Inside the courtroom, extra bailiffs were on alert in case someone went berserk. Lawson wore a custom navy twill and sat next to the empty jury box. He stared straight ahead, expressionless. Bradshaw sat next to him, the only attorney not wearing a dark blue suit. His out-of-style blazer with patches of leather on the elbows complemented his superstitious pair of unmatched socks. He'd arrived early to snag the table nearest to the jury. Rebecca, who was sitting next to John on the third row of pews, mouthed the words, *I love you.*

At the counsel table to their left, Stew and Scott fussed with papers and exhibits. Stew looked magnificent in his new haircut and suit, I'll give him that. He'd walked slowly up the courthouse steps, pausing to speak into any microphone shoved in his direction; reminding viewers that he was The Chosen One called upon to bring justice to this abhorrent crime.

"Gentlemen," Judge Franco said, "are we ready to proceed?"

"Yes, Your Honor," said both Stew and Bradshaw, simultaneously.

"Very well," he said. Then to Myron: "Please bring in the prospective jury panel."

Myron opened a door next to the jury box and seventy wide-eyed citizens filed in. The first dozen took upholstered seats in the box and the remainder was seated in reserved, roped off pews, like they do for the family at a funeral. Fifty-eight of them would be sent home after having been grilled, sniffed, prodded, and ultimately rejected. The twelve who survived the gauntlet would brag at cocktail parties for years to come.

The attorneys had been given a list of these seventy jurors, and they'd spent the past few days snooping through their backgrounds. Therefore, they already knew the highlights (and lowlights) of the jurors' pitiful lives (not as much as I did, of course, but still they knew plenty).

"Ladies and Gentlemen," said The Gobbler, his double chin jiggling like lemon Jello before it fully sets. "You have been randomly asked to serve as jurors in this case. Twelve of you will be selected to hear the evidence and render a verdict. This case has generated enormous publicity and I assume you've all heard something about it. However, nothing you have heard is evidence.

"You are obligated to disregard anything you have previously heard or read and consider only the evidence that is formally introduced in this trial. Please raise your hand if you cannot comply that important duty?" None of the jurors raised their hands (they were all shameless liars because, really, how were they supposed to disregard everything they'd heard on television?).

"Some of you may have voted for the defendant in the past. How you voted will remain confidential. However, is there anyone of you that cannot judge the facts of this case fairly, regardless of your political persuasion?" The jurors sneaked peeks at each other trying to guess who'd voted for him, but none of them raised their hands.

"Very well, we will now begin Voir Dire." Lawyers love all that legal gobbledygook because they think it makes them look smart. *Voir Dire? Was this the French Revolution?* They ought to just call it "the part where they quiz the jurors." But Voir Dire's shorter, I guess. Judge Franco had a standard list of background questions and went through each one. For example, did any of them have a problem taking off two weeks to attend the trial? Duh, of course they did. Who wouldn't? But they all chickened out and no one raised their hand (besides, this trial promised to be a doozie). He next asked if any of them could not be fair. Who's going to raise their hand on that one? *Uh, judge, listen, I'm just an unfair person, okay?*

The jury selection process lasted five hours. A few of the jurors were dismissed for medical reasons (who wants a narcoleptic snoozer, or someone with Turret Syndrome blurting out obscenities?). Other hard-core law and order types were dismissed because they believed anyone who committed a crime, even a misdemeanor, ought to be strung up by the neck, no questions asked. Then there were a few self-righteous Democrats who believed all Republicans were guilty of *something*. The judge kicked them off for being, uh, unfair. The list had now shrunk to forty-seven. He then allowed each side six "peremptory challenges," meaning they could kick six people off the jury panel at their whim.

Myron hitched up his leather holster, waddled over to Stew Franks, and handed him a typewritten list of the forty-seven names, in order. The holster hadn't been broken in and it squeaked when he walked. Otherwise the room was silent. Stew would now use one of his six peremptory challenges to cross a name off the list. He crossed off a woman on the front row who looked quite smitten by Senator Lawson and would've voted him People Magazine's Sexist Man of the Year. Myron then walked over to the table where Bradshaw and Lawson sat huddled, gossiping about each juror. They crossed off the guy on the second row who wore a mullet and thought the system was too soft on crime. Myron took the list back to Stew who nixed the guy who said he'd once been framed by the cops and thought they were all crooks. Bradshaw then axed the morally superior feminist on the back row who donated to Planned Parenthood and hated men like Lawson for wanting to boss her uterus around.

Around and around it went with Myron doing all that waddling back and forth until each side had crossed off its share of names. The first twelve jurors on the list who'd survived the cut would comprise the jury. The other jurors were dismissed with an offer of immunity if they'd been given a parking ticket. Beth administered an oath to the twelve jurors who now stood in the jury box, right arms raised (the seven male jurors appreciated the barricade that separated them from her). The judge called a brief recess so they could use the bathroom and call their families and employers. When they returned, the trial began.

Stew Franks took a final sip of water and strode gravely to the podium in the middle of courtroom as if the weight of Chelsea Miles's ghost, and every law-abiding citizen in Pennsylvania, was on his rounded shoulders. This was his moment. He wasn't a method actor and had no flare for the theatre, but he knew how it felt to have the spotlight upon him. And never had the light shown so brightly.

"Ladies and Gentlemen of the jury," he began. "We are here today to gain some measure of justice for Chelsea Miles, a beautiful young woman who was brutally murdered without reason or provocation, other than to hide the ugly truth about her killer.

"Most of you know the public persona of Senator Kenneth Lawson. Perhaps at one time you respected him. You knew him as a law abiding, faithful husband and servant of this great Commonwealth. But that was all a façade. The evidence you will hear over the next several days will reveal the *real* Kenneth Lawson, the one who sits before you today."

Unlike a closing argument, Stew would not be allowed to "argue" the case in his opening remarks. For example, he couldn't say, "So, as you can plainly see, he was a maniacal killer who damned near beheaded this angelic girl after copious amounts of unwelcomed sex." He was only allowed to outline the prosecution's evidence.

Stew stood behind the podium, describing the illicit fornicating on that fateful Tuesday afternoon (well, he didn't actually *describe* it describe it. Jesse and Slim would do that when they took the stand). He took the jury through George's anticipated testimony, the adoring husband who'd been decimated by the murder of his wife (hey, just because she cheated on him didn't mean she didn't love him, or his money). He also outlined the testimony of the detectives and the expert witnesses, including the fingerprint, hair, and blood spatter specialists. He told the jury they would also hear from the medical examiner concerning the cause of death, murder weapon, and the approximate time of death.

"After you have heard all the evidence, I am confident you will agree that Kenneth Lawson was guilty of this despicable and cowardly act. He had the motive and the opportunity to kill her. And his fingerprints were on the murder weapon. All this can lead to only one conclusion beyond any reasonable doubt; the cold-blooded killer sits before you today. Thank you."

As Stew walked to his chair he made a point to stare at Lawson, a death stare to let him know his time was up.

Bradshaw walked quickly, long arms swinging, and stood in front of the jury like he couldn't *wait* to speak on behalf of the honorable man who'd been unfairly accused of this terrible crime. He pushed the podium off to the side—he wanted nothing between him and his jurors. No scribbled notes on a legal pad, or a teleprompter.

"My client is imperfect. His behavior that afternoon is enough evidence of that. He had no reason to be with Chelsea Miles that afternoon except to have an inappropriate sexual relationship with her. That was wrong. It was immoral and dishonorable. The prosecution will hammer home that point, again and again, to make you think that because he behaved badly he must have also been a murderer. But as indecent as his sexual behavior was, that is not what he's charged with.

"The crime he is charged with is not sexual impropriety, but murder. And what concrete evidence is there of that? Will the prosecution call any eyewitnesses? No. The only evidence that relates to the crime of murder is one small thumb print on the shovel handle, a handle that is full of other fingerprints as well. Will they offer the testimony of the owner of those other fingerprints on the murder weapon? They will not.

"The prosecution has a heavy burden. It must prove beyond a reasonable doubt that Ken Lawson was the killer. It's not enough that they prove he was a wandering husband, or that he used bad judgment. It is not enough that they prove he *might* have been the killer, or that he *could* have been the killer.

"Ken Lawson isn't required to prove anything. We aren't obligated to prove he *didn't* commit this crime, nor are we obligated to prove who did. The law that you have sworn to uphold requires us to prove nothing. Thank you."

37

DAY TWO. TUESDAY, MARCH 17TH.

"ALL RISE! The First Judicial Court, in and for the Commonwealth of Pennsylvania is now in session, the Honorable Gustav Franco presiding. You may now be seated."

"Welcome back ladies and gentlemen of the jury," the judge began. "You will now hear the evidence, beginning with the prosecution's case. You are to give it the weight you believe is appropriate. Counsel, you may call your first witness."

Stew stood in his second favorite suit. "The Commonwealth calls Jesse Samuelson."

Jesse was summoned from the hallway outside the courtroom where he'd been pacing. He thumbed his shirttail into his pants and ran his fingers through his hair. He spit his gum into his hand but didn't know where to put it, and the bailiff was staring at him so he didn't dare litter. All heads turned to watch him enter from the back double doors, clutching the gum in his hand. His stomach was a churning mess and he wished they'd allowed him to snort something that morning in jail.

He was hardly recognizable without his trademark beanie and smart new haircut. He wore slacks (with a *belt*) and a button-up shirt. The belt was a worthless accessory because his pants still hung awfully low, like mid-hip. It was obvious he didn't dress up much, or have regular church-going clothes. His discomfort was plainly evident.

"Mr. Samuelson," said Stew. "I understand you are currently under arrest for breaking and entering the home of George and Chelsea Miles."

"Yeah, I am." Jesse had never been called Mr. Samuelson. He sat up a little straighter in the witness chair and pulled at his collar. Gum still clutched in his other hand.

"What was the date that you broke into their home?"

"I think it was like November 28th, or whenever the lady who lived there got killed."

"Yes, that is indeed the date Chelsea Miles was murdered."

"Yeah, that's what I thought." He slipped his hand under the seat and stuck the gum there.

"How do you know you were there the day she was murdered?"

"Because the next day we were watching the news and it came on about how they found her dead in her bedroom. And we were, like, 'No way! That's the lady who lives there!'"

"We?"

"Yeah, me and Slim."

"Are you referring to Leslie Monson?"

"No, it was a guy name Slim Monson."

"Mr. Samuelson, I believe his correct legal name is Leslie, but his nickname is Slim."

"*Leslie?* No way. Really? I didn't know that, but yeah, that's the guy I was with, I guess." Poor Slim would hear about this later that day from Jesse (actually, he'd hear about it for months).

"How did you gain access to the home?"

"Whaddya mean?"

"How did you get into the house?"

"Oh. Well, I was there doing a bathroom remodel job a few weeks earlier and I left a basement window open a little bit so I could get in later if I needed to."

"Why would you need to get into their home?"

"Can I say? Like, am I supposed to say the real reason?"

"Yes, Mr. Samuelson, you are under oath to tell the truth."

"Okay then, I left it open so I could come back later to steal some stuff."

"Is that why you returned on November 28th? To steal something?"

"Uh-huh." Some of the jurors put their heads down, and covered their mouths. Jesse took a sideways peek at the judge, hoping he hadn't just compounded his crime, under oath.

"What time of day were you in the home?" asked Stew.

"I'd say about 2:30."

"How long were you inside?"

"Just long enough to take some stuff from the bathroom and see the lady and the guy."

"You wanted to steal something from the bathroom?"

"Yeah."

"What was it in the bathroom that you wanted to steal?"

"Some pills."

"What sort of pills?"

"Pain pills, mostly."

"Did you go into the den in the home?"

"What's the den?"

"Did you go anywhere other than the bathroom?"

"No."

"Did you go into any other room and steal anything?"

"Like what?"

"Mr. Samuelson, you tell me. Did you steal anything else from the home?"

"Not that I can think of. Maybe I took some booze once, but it wasn't their best stuff." He glanced again at the judge to be sure he got that last part. "That was a few weeks before when we were doing the remodel job."

"You stole some liquor?"

"No, just some vodka."

"Did you ever steal a laptop computer?"

"No."

"Did you ever steal any jewelry?"

"No."

"Are you certain of that?"

"Yeah."

"You testified you were there just long enough to steal the pills and to 'see the lady and the guy' I believe you said."

"Yeah."

"Where were you when you saw the lady and the guy?"

"In the master bathroom."

"And where were they?"

"In the bedroom. It's right next to the bathroom."

"How then did you see them?"

Jesse paused, a bit confused. "I just looked at them with my eyes." The jurors looked down at their laps again.

"I meant, how were you able to see them? Was the door opened?"

"Oh, I see what you mean. Yeah, the door was open about three inches and that's when I saw them."

"Tell the jury, Mr. Samuelson, what you saw."

"Is now when you want me to say what they were doing?"

"Yes, Mr. Samuelson, now is the time."

"So, like, do you want me to say what position they were doing it?"

"Mr. Samuelson, I just want you to tell us what they were doing?"

"They were having sex."

"Are you sure it was Chelsea Miles?"

"Well, yeah. I know this isn't good to admit, but I was staring right at her the whole time."

"Who was the man that you saw that day."

"It was him." Jesse pointed to Ken Lawson who shrunk in his chair.

Stew led Jesse through the remainder of his testimony, including the silver Mercedes that was parked down the street, Slim's re-entry into the house, and how they'd discovered it was Senator Lawson that had been there.

"And when did you come forward with this evidence?"

"I think it was about two months ago. I'd say a few weeks after the murder."

"Why did you come forward at that time?"

"Because we got caught."

"Because you got caught doing what?" Stew asked.

"We got caught trying to blackmail him."

"Blackmail who?"

"Him." He pointed again at Lawson.

"How did you do that?"

"We just sent him a letter asking him to pay us some ransom money or we'd tell the cops what we saw."

Stew didn't want to quibble with the ransom business, because there'd been no evidence of kidnapping, and he figured the jury knew what Jesse was talking about. He finished up and turned Jesse over to Bradshaw for cross examination.

"Jesse," began Bradshaw, "you didn't see Mr. Lawson harm Chelsea Miles in any way, did you?"

"No."

"They weren't fighting?"

"Uh, no, they weren't fighting, that's for sure."

"Did Chelsea Miles seem to be in any distress, or seem to be acting in any way against her will?"

"It didn't look like it to me."

"Did she appear to be acting voluntarily?"

"Yeah, I'd say so. If anything, she was the one on top of him."

Stew's next witness was Leslie "Slim" Monson, who was ushered in and sworn to tell the truth. He'd also been given a makeover. His shirt was smartly tucked into khakis (that were obviously brand new—there was the original vertical crease, and the horizontal one too, about mid-thigh). Aunt Eloise wanted to attend the trial (proud as she was of Slim's fame), but she was afraid to leave Uncle Wayne in charge of the house.

Slim answered Stew's preliminary questions, much the same as Jesse had.

"Please tell the jury, Leslie, what you saw then when you returned to the home."

"You can just call me Slim. I don't really go by Leslie anymore."

"Alright, Slim. What did you see when you returned to the house?"

"Okay, so we were there to steal some pills, that's all. Jesse goes in and then comes back out all excited like. He told me what he saw and I'm thinking maybe I should go in there to cobrate his story."

"So you went back in to corroborate Jesse's story?"

"Uh-huh."

"Did you steal anything?"

"No, sir."

"You didn't steal any pills?"

"No, that was Jesse." Slim felt guilty for having thrown Jesse under the bus like this, but he was under oath.

"Did you take a laptop computer?"

"No."

"How about any jewelry?"

"No. Like I said, I just went in to make sure what Jesse said was true, you know, coberate it all up."

"How did you get into the house?"

"From the basement window that Jesse left open."

"And where did you go once you were inside?"

"Straight to the master bathroom, and I sorta hurried because I didn't want to miss it." Slim looked up at the judge. "I'm just telling the truth because I'm under oath."

"What did you see when you entered the master bathroom?"

"I seen it all."

"And what was that?"

"Well, I seen them doing intercourse." Slim was determined to use the correct words, figuring it would make him seem smarter than if he'd said they were *"fuckin' like rabbits,"* which is what he normally would've said.

"And who, specifically, was having sexual intercourse?"

"You mean the lady and Lawson?"

"My question is, who was in the bedroom?"

"Yeah, the lady and Lawson."

"I am asking you the names of the two people. Did you say one of them was Mr. Lawson?"

"Yeah, that's what I keep saying."

"And who was the other person."

"The lady."

"And was that woman Chelsea Miles?"

"Yeah, the lady that lived there."

"Uh-huh," Stew nodded, hoping Slim would offer more. He didn't. Stew moved on to the testimony concerning their blackmail scheme. He wasn't allowed to ask the boys about the subsequent kidnap and assault, because that wasn't technically relevant to the crime of murder. However, Stew could quiz him about the blackmailing because that was related to the boys' motivation for coming forward to testify. Slim told the jurors all about the cut-out pasted letters, the ten grand, and the threat that they had photos (which, he acknowledged, they didn't have, and he apologized to the court for the fib).

Bradshaw's cross examination of Slim was similar, too.

"I'll call you Slim if you prefer."

"Yeah, that's what everybody calls me."

"Slim, did Chelsea Miles appear to be in any danger when you saw her?"

"I wouldn't say she was in danger. But maybe she could've pulled a muscle or something."

"Excuse me?"

"They were moving around a lot and maybe she could've pulled something."

"No, Slim, I meant to ask if Mr. Lawson appeared to threaten her with any harm. Did she appear to act willingly?"

"I'd say she was willing, if you was to ask me. He wasn't saying anything, but she sure was."

"You heard her speaking?"

"Sort of."

"What did she say?"

"Well, see . . . they weren't really like words. It was more, like, you know . . . howling."

"*Howling?*"

"Yeah, I guess that's what you'd call it. She was a leaning back making these noises."

"Noises?"

"Yeah, pretty loud ones, too."

"And those noises were what?"

"Howling's the best way I could put it. They weren't real words."

"No further questions."

"Uh, wait," Slim said. "I think I said something at the first that wasn't true and I just remembered it." He looked sideways up at the judge. "So, should I say it now?"

Bradshaw looked at Stew, who looked at Judge Franco. They appeared to shrug their shoulders as if to say, go for it. "Ok, Slim," Bradshaw said, "tell us what you'd forgotten to say."

"See, the other lawyer asked me if I stole anything and I said I didn't. But I just remembered I stole some pickles."

"You stole some *pickles*? From the Miles home?"

"Yeah, I stole a bottle of pickles from their fridge when I was leaving, and I don't want to purge myself."

"Thank you, Slim. It is important that you not perjure yourself. Is there anything else we've missed?"

"No, just that I'm sorry. Me and Jesse both feel real bad about the whole thing."

After a short recess, the trial resumed with the testimony of George Miles. George looked comfortable in his tailored suit. Unlike the two previous witnesses, his pants were properly cinched around his waist, per the original design. He was well spoken and appropriately somber, as befitting the husband of a murdered wife.

Stew led him through his background and marriage to Chelsea St. Claire, the love of his life. He'd been deeply hurt to learn his wife was having an affair with Senator Lawson, whom he'd once considered a good friend. He refused to look at Lawson, whose head was bowed, because Ken, for all his many flaws, realized he'd done something shamefully wrong.

"When is the last time you saw your wife alive?"

"Early in the morning of November 28th, a Tuesday I believe," George lied. "The day she died."

"What did you do that day?"

"I spent the morning at my office downtown. I was scheduled to be in Chicago that afternoon and had intended to leave directly from my office. The trip was to be a short one—one night—and I planned to return the next morning. However, I realized I'd forgotten some papers at my home, in my office there. So, I returned Tuesday afternoon to retrieve them on my way out of town."

"Do you recall what time it was when you went home that afternoon?"

"Yes, I do. It was approximately 3:30."

"Was anyone at the home when you arrived?"

"I didn't think so. I was in and out very quickly, perhaps five or ten minutes, and didn't see Chelsea." He was such a liar. "I assumed she was out."

"Where did you go in your house when you went home?"

"I came in through the garage and went straight to my office which is located on the opposite side of my home from our bedroom. My home is quite large and I called out to see if anyone was home but no one answered. I assumed Chelsea wasn't home."

"You mentioned you came in through the garage. Did you notice whether Chelsea's car was there?"

"It may seem a bit ostentatious, but as I said, our home is rather large and we actually have two garages. I parked in the east-side garage and Chelsea ordinarily parks in the set of garages on the south side of our home."

"What time did you leave your home?"

"Perhaps five or ten minutes later. I would estimate 3:40. I believe the flight log shows I arrived at my hanger at approximately 4:10, and it's a half hour drive from my home."

George testified he'd had a lonely night in Chicago watching television. He did so with a straight face. I was impressed he could lie with such conviction. Nary a word about the pricey escort. He testified he'd tried to call Chelsea to say goodnight, but she hadn't answered. Oh, he'd called her all right, to say he wanted a divorce. He then described how he'd returned the following afternoon and discovered her body. Like any good, innocent citizen, he'd cooperated in the investigation.

"Mr. Miles, we understand Chelsea was pregnant."

George put his head down. Stew allowed the poignant moment of misinterpreted emotion to marinate within the silence of the courtroom.

"Did you know about the pregnancy?"

"Yes." This was another choice bit of perjury, for he hadn't a clue. "Chelsea had told me a few days earlier."

"How did you feel about it?"

Again, George put his head down and removed his glasses. He took a tissue from the box sitting between him and the frigid clerk who actually appeared to show compassion. "I was thrilled, of course. We both were." A few more moments of quiet. "When you get to be my age, and are told you will be a father . . . a child to love . . .." He dropped his head again and wiped his eyes with the tissue. Stew wanted to end the testimony on this highlight, but George wasn't finished. "The thing that is so painful to me now is wondering if the child was even mine." One more head bow, and one more orchestrated moment where the only sound was the palpable heartache of this decent man, himself a victim of Lawson's treachery.

"We are sorry for your loss." I thought Stew was going to cry, too. "No more questions, Your Honor."

Bradshaw was careful with his cross examination. He intended to be respectfully brief.

"Mr. Miles, I understand you have known Senator Lawson for many years."

"Yes, I have."

"Have you ever seen him act violently in all those years?"

"No."

"Doesn't the brutal act of striking a woman to death with the blade of a shovel seem contrary to the Senator's temperament?"

"It does," George said. "At least the temperament I was exposed to."

"So—"

"But I can also tell you that I didn't think he would sleep with my wife, either."

This cross examination was a boner, and Bradshaw knew it. He berated himself, for he knew effective cross only allows for a simple "yes" or "no" answer (and preferably a painfully embarrassing one).

"Mr. Miles, isn't it true there were items stolen from your home on the day Chelsea was murdered?"

"I cannot be certain of that."

"But didn't you immediately report to the detectives that jewelry and a laptop had been stolen?"

"Yes, I did. However, I wasn't certain of it."

"You weren't certain about whether your laptop was missing?"

"That's correct."

"So was it missing, or wasn't it?"

"It was."

"And it's still missing?"

"It is."

"And you told the detectives it had been stolen that day?"

"I thought that was possible, yes."

"Possible?"

"I cannot be certain it'd been stolen."

"But you reported it missing to the police within an hour of the time the body was discovered."

"Yes."

"And you also reported the theft of some expensive jewelry."

"Well, on that I can't be as certain."

"But you did report it."

"Yes, I told them I thought it'd been stolen, yes, but I wasn't sure."

"Now, Mr. Miles, you don't honestly believe that Senator Lawson stole your wife's jewelry, do you?"

"I don't know."

"And you really don't believe Senator Lawson stole your laptop either, do you?"

"I don't know."

"What are the odds, Mr. Miles, that Senator Lawson stole Chelsea's jewelry and a laptop computer from your home office?"

"Objection!" said Stew Franks. "That calls for speculation."

"Indeed it may, Your Honor," said Bradshaw. "I'll withdraw the question. I have nothing further from this witness."

Testimony from the detectives, Flygare and Olson, was exhaustive (overkill, if you ask me). They meticulously described everything that was done from the time they were first notified, to the time of the arrest. There was a labeled baggie for this and a labeled baggie for that. And there were more photographs of the scene than of a couple's first child. They identified each one, nearly one hundred in all, and entered them into evidence as exhibits. Some of them were gruesome.

The exhibits were all placed on a table at the front of the courtroom. The table was crowded with a shovel, alarm clock, bed sheets, books, and picture frames spotted with blood drops. It looked like a picked over yard sale. By the time they had completed their testimony it was time to close for the day.

Reporters hurried from the courtroom to file their reports before the six o'clock evening news. It was cold and windy outside and the reporters' hair blew and swirled in their faces as they fought for space in front of the marble steps to breathlessly report all the incriminating evidence against Senator Lawson. And, indeed, it was incriminating, for Lawson's behavior had been raunchy.

Bradshaw and Lawson waited in a vacant conference room for the media to give up and leave. Lawson was nearly inconsolable. The evidence had systematically slain him. They had no other suspects. Lawson had the motive and the opportunity, and he'd been made to look like a complete slime ball to boot. George, his old friend, had said it best. He didn't think Senator Lawson would have done this terrible thing, but he didn't think he would have slept with his wife either.

Stew was counting his chickens; just as tickled pink as he could be. He hadn't stumbled (there were the awkward exchanges with those two numbskulls, Jesse and Slim, but still) and he looked dashing in his new suit. He left the courthouse quickly lest the media tire of waiting for him. The Conscience of the People stepped out to the courthouse steps, holding forth in front of the cameras, radiating confidence!

It was premature, this chicken counting business, but Stew heard the faint hum, the clarion call, to higher office. The special election for Lawson's senate seat was less than eighteen months away.

38

ERIC LOEBOWITZ WAS CRUEL, even as a kid. His was a casual form of cruelty; if other kids teased him about his red hair and freckles, he'd simply beat the shit out of them. He now sat in jail the second day of the Lawson trial. He'd been no stranger to jails—the government had given him room and board several times.

His cellmate was an inmate named Turd (a nickname his birth mother wasn't fond of at all). Turd was a big talker. He'd started yammering that morning, boasting about his sins. He was a small-time thief, but listening to him you'd think his record of misdeeds began with Butch Cassidy. He wouldn't shut up and poor Loebowitz could take it no longer.

"Shut the fuck up," he said. "You ain't done shit."

"Hey," said Turd. "I've taken down more shit than you've ever dreamed about."

Loebowitz should have let it go, but I egged him on. "How many people you killed?" This seemed like a perfectly sensible question to Loebowitz.

"Damned near killed some guy a few months ago," Turd boasted. "Busted up his nose pretty good. You?"

"You don't wanna know."

"Yeah, you talk real tough, man. You're just a killin' machine ain't you, big boy."

"Just shut the fuck up," Loebowitz said.

"Name me one, tough guy."

"Fuck off."

"How'd you get in here, anyway? Steal a six pack, did ya? Snuck it out under your shirt?"

"I said fuck off, and I meant it." The steam was rising. I hardly needed to nudge him, but I did anyway. *Don't let this loser talk to you like that. You're Eric Loebowitz, for Pete's sake.* Loebowitz had serious wrath issues, and I know wrath when I see it. In fact, he was in jail because he'd beaten a man to death with a tire iron. I saw the whole thing, and it wasn't pretty.

"I'll shut up soon as you tell me somebody you messed up."

"You really wanna know?"

"Yeah, because I'm guessin' all you did was sell some weed on the side. What, you got caught with more than an ounce? Ouch, dude, you're bad."

Loebowitz was tempted to simply break Turd's neck, for that's what he normally would've done (this guy had no diplomacy skills whatsoever). But I appealed to his pride. "How about the lady that was married to that billionaire? Does that count, you fuckin' moron?"

"What lady?" Turd was not a habitual news watcher. "You mean the one who got killed by the senator guy?"

"Yeah."

"You're a fuckin' idiot. Guy's on trial right now. Where have you been, you fire-crotch moron? You ever seen a TV? Nice try though, tough guy."

"He didn't kill her," Loebowitz said. He sat on his bunk and cracked his knuckles, one at a time. "And you call me a fire-crotch again and I'll kill you. Swear to God."

"You're full of shit. Dude's gonna get the chair."

Loebowitz stood from his bunk and took a step toward Turd who tried to look back at him, all tough like. But he knew this redheaded freak was serious, and it scared the crap out of him.

When Turd met bail later that day, he called his lawyer, Nick Lowe, a public defender. He told him about the conversation he'd had with Eric Loebowitz.

"I believe this crazy motherfucker," said Turd. "Maybe I could get something outta this from the DA." The scent of opportunity wafted about like a lingering fart.

"I know one of the lawyers on that case," Lowe said. "I'll call him, but he probably won't make a deal now. They're already halfway through the trial and it looks like Lawson did it."

"I'm tellin' ya, he did it, and I want a deal. They owe me." Turd was big on justice.

Lowe reached Scott Benjamin on his cell about seven o'clock that evening. "Hey, Scott, it's Nick Lowe."

"Yeah, Nick, what's up?"

"Listen, I know you're in the middle of trial, but that's why I'm calling you. I've got a client who says there's a guy sitting at County who claims he killed Chelsea Miles."

"Is this a joke? Who told you that?"

"A new client who just posted bail on a theft charge. Claims this guy swears he killed her. He might be blowing smoke to get a better deal, but he sounds pretty serious."

"What's the guy's name?" Scott asked. It was a typical scenario—tough talk in jail. Some snitch knows who killed JFK, knows the guy on the grassy knoll, and wants a deal out of it.

"This probably won't pan out, but if it does, I'll want a deal for my guy."

"Shit, Nick, I'm so swamped right now I don't have time to even check this out."

"You might want to make time for this. I'll get you his name. Give me an hour. At least talk to him."

Lowe left a message on Scott's cell an hour later. The guy's name was Eric Loebowitz.

Scott's office was a block from the courthouse, and the jail. He'd made a call and learned that Loebowitz had been arrested two days earlier. An eyewitness had seen him beat a man to death with a tire iron at a junk yard. Loebowitz didn't have an attorney yet, so Scott was technically allowed to talk to him. He decided to swing by the jail on his way home.

Eric Loebowitz wasn't surprised when Scott Benjamin, some deputy prosecutor, came asking him about the Chelsea Miles case.

"Here's the thing," said Scott. "I can probably help you on the charge you're facing if you cooperate. What was it, a Capital One? You murdered someone with a tire iron, was it? That's not good, Loebowitz. You're looking at the death penalty. So, if you have anything to say, you'd better say it fast, because once this Lawson case goes to verdict, you're screwed. We'll fry you."

"So you're telling me that if I give you something on the rich lady's case you'll give me a deal?" asked Loebowitz.

"Depends what you've got. But I don't have time for games, so if you're playing us, I'll see to it that you get the needle. Count on it."

"Okay, so what do you wanna know?"

"I want to know if you had anything to do with Chelsea Miles's murder."

"And if I say yes?"

"Then I want to know what you know, and how you know it."

"Maybe I was there."

"Are you telling me you killed her?"

"Maybe."

"You need a lawyer. I want to do this right. If you've got something legit, and want to strike a deal, I want you to have a lawyer. I don't want anybody saying I coerced you."

Scott didn't want to believe Eric Loebowitz was anything but a crazy redheaded freak. Guys spouted off in jail all the time. Loebowitz was a cold-blooded murderer with nothing to lose. But Scott had to be sure, so he called the public defender's office and the wheels were greased to get Loebowitz an attorney, post haste.

It was after eight o'clock when Scott arrived home. The girls were already in bed.

"I saw you on TV," Theresa said. "You looked pretty good."

"Really? What was I doing?"

"You were standing on the steps next to Stew while he was lecturing on his trial strategy. To be honest, you looked like you wanted him to shut up so you could go inside and get out of the cold."

"Well, then the camera didn't lie."

"That Lawson's a sick creep. I can't believe I voted for him."

"Was there anything else on the news about me?" If there was one person Scott could be semi-honest with (let's face it, no one's *totally* honest) it was Theresa.

"It showed you walking in and out of the courthouse, but that's about it."

"Is it true what they say, the whole bit about the camera adding ten pounds?"

"No, you looked good." Slight pause. "You looked great. Swear."

"Really?"

"Of course. But maybe we need to get you a new suit. That one seems a little tight."

"I look *fat*?"

"No, no, of course not. That's not what I'm saying at all." Liar. "It's just getting older and maybe doesn't hang as well." Pants on fire. "But, no, you don't look heavy in it at all." Hanging from a telephone wire.

Scott sneaked into the bathroom to see how tight his suit fit. The button did pull a bit. He swore he'd start running again as soon as the trial ended. Uh-huh. He settled into his folding metal chair in the third bedroom that served as his home office, and called Stew on his cell, bringing him up to speed on the call from his buddy at the Public Defender's office who represented the snitch.

"Yeah, and lemme guess," said Stew. "This Loebowitz freak is going to say he killed Chelsea Miles. Am I right?"

"Well, yeah, that's what he says. But I cut him off before he gave me any details. I figured we needed to be completely above board so it won't look like we coerced a confession."

"Listen, Scott, I hate to burst your bubble, but you won't need to coerce anything out of this guy. He'll tell you whatever you want to hear. What was he arrested for? Murder, was it? Obviously, he's going to say whatever he can to get a deal."

"He sounded pretty convincing to me. I think we need to check it out."

"Scott, we're in the middle of a huge murder trial. We've got our guy. Okay? No two-bit punk murdered Chelsea Miles for no reason. We're going to convict Lawson. The guy did it. Everybody knows that."

"But don't you think we have a duty to tell the defense about this?" Every attorney in the country, even those who went to night school, knows this is the state's sacrosanct obligation—to disclose any credible exculpatory evidence to the defense.

"Scott, listen, we're obligated to disclose all *credible* evidence. This isn't credible, okay? We don't have a duty to go running around worrying about every jailhouse snitch. We'd never get any work done. So, no, we don't need to tell them about this, and we can't afford to spend any more time on it. It's a wild goose chase. To be honest, I'm surprised we haven't had more crazies coming out of the woodwork saying they killed her. We'll probably have a few more before we're finished."

Scott thought Stew was a bit cavalier over the legal duty to disclose this information to the defense, but he had to admit this was probably an untimely diversion.

39

ANDREW BRADSHAW WAS RESTLESS. The trial wasn't going well and there wasn't much he could do about it. It was late in the evening. His housekeeper hadn't come and his place was a mess. Three days of dishes were in the sink and the bed hadn't been made in a week. A newspaper was lying on the coffee table; a lousy photo of Senator Lawson stared back. *Senator Lawson's murder case underway.* Every day a new story graced the cover. *Arrest stuns Senate.* The next day it might read: *Washington on edge as murder trial begins.*

Bradshaw threw a Hot Pocket in the microwave and turned on the television, hoping to take a break from the trial. He sat on the sofa, clicking past Seinfeld reruns and commercials promising a spectacular end to erectile dysfunction. He stopped on Geraldo Rivera and his panel of trial experts. He should've turned it off, should've gone to bed, but they were debating his trial skills and he couldn't resist.

It was easy for them to nitpick, sitting as they were in the comfort of the studio where everything was scripted and there was only token opposition. *I agree with my distinguished colleague on your panel, Geraldo, but I think blah blah blah.* It was like watching a panel of ex-ballplayers dissecting the New York Yankees coach's moves. *Well, geez, Lewis, I think he shoulda pulled Martinez in the 8th before he gave up the homer.*

The former prosecutor looked like a freshly scrubbed Boy Scout and the defense attorney looked like Willie Nelson. They were debating whether Bradshaw ought to call Lawson to the witness stand.

"It would be a terrible mistake to let Lawson testify," said Boy Scout. "Stew Franks would be licking his chops to have a shot at him on cross."

"Well," said Willie, "as a former defense attorney, I know Andrew Bradshaw (he did?) and he's a real gambler (he was?). I'll bet he puts Lawson on the stand because he's got nothing to lose at this point. It's his only shot. We're getting to the Hail Mary point in this trial (we were?) and he needs to take a big risk."

Bradshaw had considered calling Lawson to testify in his own defense. He knew it was risky because it would open the door for Stew to bring up all the unsavory things Lawson had ever said, or done, making him look like an untrustworthy schmuck. If he didn't testify (the 5th Amendment gave him the right to keep his big mouth shut), the prosecution couldn't dredge up his past transgressions and parade them in front of the jury.

But if Lawson didn't deny he killed her? If he just sat there, never opening his mouth throughout the whole trial? What ya trying to hide? Bradshaw would remind the jury, again and again, that Lawson didn't need to prove squat. That sounded good, on paper, but jurors are less concerned with legal theory than they are with the simple truth. If he didn't do it then, by golly, he oughta say so! They should've called me to the stand. I could've told them every detail of the crime, for I saw it all. Go ahead; put me under oath.

"I'll say this," said Boy Scout, "Lawson is a well-trained speaker. He's been in so many debates that he probably wouldn't get rattled by a good cross examination."

"I agree, to a point," said Willie Nelson. "Lawson has been through enough bruising political campaigns that the buried skeletons would have surfaced by now."

"That's a good point," said Boy Scout, "but putting him on the stand will just give Stew Franks the chance to ridicule him for his hypocrisy. He slept with his best friend's wife, after all."

"But Franks will do that anyway. He's been doing it the entire trial."

Geraldo wanted air time. "How did you both feel about Andrew Bradshaw's cross examination of the eyewitnesses?"

"I thought he missed a golden opportunity to remind the jury that these young men didn't actually see the crime, and didn't see her in any distress whatsoever."

"I agree. I think he made a big mistake there."

Bradshaw almost threw his shoe at the television, because that's *exactly* what he'd emphasized in the cross exam. He turned it off.

Fortunately, the jury would not be watching this program, or any other newscast. The Gobbler had sequestered them in a hotel not far from the courthouse where they wouldn't be tainted by any television news. They watched Dancing with the Stars instead, under the watchful eye of courtroom personnel who had pizza brought in.

40

DAY THREE. WEDNESDAY, MARCH 18TH.

This was Scott's big day, handling the direct examination of the prosecution's expert witnesses. Direct exam was challenging because there were restrictions on what Scott could ask, and how. He couldn't "lead" his witnesses down the merry path. For example, he couldn't ask: "Isn't it true the hair on the pillow belonged to that balding Lawson creep?" Instead, he'd have to ask: "Whose hair was on the pillow?" The drama occurs in cross examination where lawyers tear into witnesses to make them look stupid, or guilty. Even though all this evidence about blood, semen, and fingerprints was crucial, it wasn't really opposed by the defense. After all, Lawson had already admitted that he'd been in that danged bed with Mrs. Miles, and had plopped his seed in her bushel.

"Our first witness today, Your Honor, is Dr. William Carlisle." Carlisle was the state's Medical Examiner, an old pro who had performed numerous autopsies and testified in dozens of murder cases.

Scott led him through his impressive credentials, and then got to the point. "Based upon your experience in forensic pathology, did you determine the cause of Chelsea Miles's death?"

"Yes. She died as a result of a forceful blow to the left side of her head by a blunt object, presumably the shovel that had remnants of her blood and tissue on the blade."

He testified that Chelsea's death occurred quickly given the massive damage done to the temporal and parietal lobes of her brain. He further testified the time of death could have been anytime on the afternoon of November 28th, but most likely between 3:00 and 5:00 p.m.

Scott's next witness was the hair expert. Dr. Joy Matthews explained to the jury that most of the hair samples found in the bedroom belonged to Chelsea and her husband George. However, there were also hairs on the bed, pillows, sheets, and even mattress that belonged to neither of them (Oh my, Lawson had been busy!). She'd chemically compared them to samples taken from Ken Lawson's scalp and they were an exact match.

Dr. Matthews was excited about her subject and assumed most of the jurors were, too. And they were, to a point, but her enthusiasm exceeded that of the jurors, especially when she waxed on with long-winded explanations about chemical compounds. Scott tried to reel her in, but this was a big moment for her, too, and she wanted to cash in. So, she carried on. *Just one more thing I'd like to add about the chemical composition of keratin in the medulla and cortex of the human hair that . . .* Bor-r-ing.

Bradshaw's short cross examination revealed something of interest.

"Dr. Matthews, you mentioned you found evidence of crystalline tropane alkaloid in the hair samples belonging to Mrs. Miles. What is that?"

"Crystalline tropane alkaloid is a serotonin-dopamine reuptake inhibitor," she said, as if any numbskull on earth should know what that was.

Bradshaw was no mere numbskull. "For those of us who don't know chemistry, can you tell us what that is, in plain English?"

"Cocaine."

Bradshaw paused for a moment to let it register.

"Are you saying Chelsea Miles had been using cocaine?"

"It appears in her system, yes."

Bradshaw knew this had nothing to do with Lawson's guilt or innocence, and he had to be careful lest the jurors think he was disparaging poor Chelsea's chaste memory (that cheating slut). But he was fighting for his client's life.

Judge Franco called a lunch recess. There were several places to eat near the courthouse, but the attorneys ordered in, and so did the jury. They didn't want to battle the crush of media that wouldn't show an ounce of restraint. Only Stew ventured outside to be rewarded with the cameras and microphones.

While Stew was busy providing the citizenry with an update on Ken Lawson's guilt, Scott was cramming for his next witness. He also checked his messages. Still nothing from the public defender's office, even though he'd emphasized that he wanted to speak to Eric Loebowitz's appointed attorney as soon as possible.

Scott's first witness after lunch was the state's fingerprint expert. Dr. Cynthia Davenport looked like an academician, in an unbecoming way. It was this very look that gave her instant credibility—she looked too rumpled to be anything but smart.

She lectured the jurors on Complicated 101. This, too, for some reason, gave her ultimate opinion more oomph (*Jeepers! All those big words—she must be one smart cookie!*). And that ultimate opinion was this: the thumb print on the shovel belonged to Kenneth Lawson.

"Fingerprints are traces of an impression from the 'friction ridges' or raised portions of the skin. Humans have epidermal ridges that were given to us (she didn't say who'd doled them out) to amplify vibrations triggered when our fingertips brush across an uneven surface. Those imperceptible, subtle vibrations transmit signals to the delicate sensory nerves involved in our fine texture perception. These ridges also help us grip rough surfaces, as well as smooth or wet surfaces, too."

"How can a fingerprint identify a specific individual?" asked Scott.

"The flexibility of these friction ridges ensures that no two fingerprints are ever exactly alike in every detail. Even identical twins have different prints."

"How long do fingerprints last on an object?"

"It depends on the object, but there are examples of fingerprints lasting decades, or more. It also depends, of course, on the environment. But," she helpfully added for the prosecution who was shelling out $375 per hour for her time, "they would remain on the shovel's handle for several days, at least."

Bradshaw tried to rattle her on his cross examination. However, all the rattling backfired.

"Ms. Davenport, (he intentionally dropped the whole "Dr." bit—I mean, come on, she couldn't even give a flu shot) will you admit that you cannot be 100% certain the thumb print belonged to my client?"

"Of course I cannot be 100% certain." She paused briefly for effect. "There is always the possibility that it belonged to someone else. I would estimate that possibility to be in the range of approximately one in four billion."

Touché.

The final witness for the day was the prosecution's blood expert. Dr. Ben Stanley was handsome with brown wavy hair and a cleft chin. He was tall and lean and wore a slightly wrinkled cotton shirt and khakis, the same outfit he wore every day. Stanley was down to earth, but the jurors could tell he was very smart. He appeared even smarter because he *didn't* use big words all the time; he just sprinkled them in here and there to demonstrate he *could* use them if he wanted to. The two younger female jurors on the front row briefly considered applying for jobs in the state's forensic lab where he worked.

Stanley testified that the blood found on the shovel's blade belonged to Chelsea. This fact was uncontested because it didn't shed any light as to Lawson's guilt. It was the shovel's *wielder* that was in doubt (at least according to the defense).

Stanley was also an expert on blood spatter. Using a fancy blend of chemistry, math, and physics, he could determine Chelsea's movements while shedding her blood and the direction the blood was travelling when it hit the wall. He'd brought poster-sized photographs of the bedroom wall that had been sprayed with blood. It was actually quite morbid when you think about it. He showed the jury the direction the blood was traveling by pointing out the feathered edges of the blood drops when they'd hit the wall. The jurors nodded to let him know they were with him so far. The two younger female jurors sat forward in their seats, nodding with slightly more vigor.

"You mentioned earlier, Dr. Stanley, that this was a 'medium velocity impact spatter.' How did you determine the velocity of the blow?"

"We break the velocity, or speed, the blood is travelling into three broad categories; low, medium, and high. These three categories are based mostly upon the size of the blood drops."

"The low velocity impact spatter produces the largest drops of blood?"

"Correct."

"Can you give us an example of something that would produce a low velocity impact spatter?"

"Maybe if the person had a bloody nose and it dripped. In other words, there is no significant force propelling the blood away from its original source."

"By its origin, you mean the nose?" Scott immediately felt less smart for asking this.

"Yes."

"So we'd see smaller drops of blood with a medium velocity impact?"

"That's correct. The drops of blood in a medium velocity case would be smaller than in a low velocity case—perhaps one to three millimeters in size."

"Can you give us an example of something that would produce a medium velocity spatter?"

"We often see medium velocity spatter patterns when a victim has been beaten. There is more force, so the blood leaves its original source at a higher velocity."

"And, finally, I believe you said there is high velocity impact spatter."

"Yes. A high velocity impact produces still smaller droplets of blood, almost like a mist. We would usually see this from, say, a bullet, or an explosion."

"And you believe this case involves a medium velocity impact?"

"Yes, that is correct."

"Would that be consistent with being hit by a swinging shovel?"

"Yes, I believe it would."

Stanley testified that Chelsea was standing near the foot of the bed, facing the door. She was struck on the left side of her head, causing her head and body to rotate clockwise as she fell to the floor.

"How are you able to determine that, Dr. Stanley?"

"We can tell the angle of impact by measuring the relationship between the lengths of the major and minor axis of the blood spatter. Through simple math and physics we can graph the angle of impact by measuring the lengths of each droplet of blood."

Stanley could see he'd lost the jurors. They couldn't mask the look—not even the two young females, who desperately wanted to show him they understood. However, Stanley just compounded their inferiority complexes by stepping down from the witness stand and writing the lengthy mathematical equation he'd used on a whiteboard next to the jury box, like he was Albert Einstein. The jurors had no idea what the hell he was talking about, but the younger females nodded anyway. *Gotcha. Uh-huh, now it makes total sense.*

Bradshaw, who actually *did* understand the physics, wisely chose to keep his cross examination short. He saw the lusty look on the faces of the female jurors and wanted Dr. Stanley off the stand before one of them raised their hand to ask him his favorite date movie. Besides, none of his testimony proved Lawson was the shovel wielding fiend.

The trial ended for the day. Scott would call their semen expert the next day and the prosecution would rest. He felt good about the progress of the trial. Their evidence had come in without any surprises or glitches, and he was confident of a guilty verdict. But still there was the nagging question of Eric Loebowitz.

His cell phone rang on the way home. "This is Scott."

"Hi Scott. Veronica Arnold here. I've got the defense in the Loebowitz case."

"Oh, yeah, Veronica. Thanks for calling." He wished it had been assigned to anyone else, for Veronica had a well-deserved reputation of dubious integrity—she was, quite simply, a sneaky little bitch. No one at the prosecutor's office trusted her. Me, I liked her.

"So, here's the deal," she said. "I've talked to him, and he's got quite a story to tell. But you can't have it unless we work something out. He's looking at a Murder One for killing some guy with a tire iron. I told him if he cooperates there's a good chance we can get that reduced."

"Listen, Veronica, obviously I'd like to hear what he has to say. But I can't promise anything until I know what he's got. And it has to pan out. We're only a few days away from a verdict and I think we've already got our man."

"You won't if my guy talks. He sounds credible. Give him a deal and he'll cooperate. And, just so we're clear, I want a deal for both the tire iron case *and* the Miles case. We'd consider voluntary manslaughter."

"I doubt we could do that, even if he's legit. But I'll see what I can do and get back to you tomorrow."

Scott thought they should probably disclose Loebowitz to the defense. However, he'd been seduced into believing Lawson was the guilty man (I wonder who seduced him?). He decided to sleep on it another night before approaching Stew again.

Bradshaw was ecstatic. His private detective had finally found Javier Flores. This was huge for the defense. Maybe. The bi-lingual private detective had pestered Javier's old roommates for weeks. On a whim, he'd driven to the apartment to try one more time, and guess who opened the door? *Lo siento, Javier!* Javier was tempted to flee again, but he'd been handed a subpoena requiring him to cooperate (it wasn't clear why this simple piece of paper would be so compelling when the INS was not).

Bradshaw sped over to Javier's apartment before Javier had a chance to *vamanos rapido*. The cramped apartment smelled like refried beans and there were empty sleeping bags on the dirty shag carpet of the living room. There was hardly any furniture and nothing on the walls. Silent Mexican shadows appeared briefly in doorways and in the hallway.

Bradshaw found Javier to be a soft-spoken, handsome, middle-aged man. A front tooth was half silver. This man, who smelled like cheap aftershave, had been born on the wrong side of a critical latitudinal line. The private detective translated for Bradshaw.

"Matar el Senorita Miles?"

"No. I no kill anybody."

"Fuiste en su casa ese dia?"

"No, I not go in house all the day."

"Alguna vez ha tenido sexo con ella?"

Javier looked at the private detective, then at Bradshaw, and then back at the translator. Did he ever have *sex* with her? Were they *serious*? "No."

"Has visto alguien entrar o salir de la casa por la tarde?"

"No, I no see people go in the house that afternoon. Esperar, he visto el marido de la senora llegar a casa y luego irse."

"What did he just say?" asked Bradshaw.

"He says he saw the lady's husband come home that afternoon and then left shortly thereafter."

"Y el parecia tener prisa."

"And he seemed to be in a hurry."

Javier told Bradshaw he'd used the shovel that morning to dig up the annuals in the flower beds on the south side of the house. Later that afternoon, he'd moved to the other side of the house to trim the privet hedge. They were so tall he'd needed a ladder to reach the top and it had taken him all afternoon. He paid no attention to the comings and goings of the house.

Javier didn't recall using the shovel that afternoon and would've had no reason to do so. Aside from a confession of murder, which would have been lovely, this was what Bradshaw had hoped to hear. If Lawson had used the shovel to kill Chelsea, and then wiped off the handle (leaving his lone thumbprint like a complete bozo), why were Javier's prints still on it? The prosecution's convenient explanation was that Javier had simply used it again later that afternoon. But, aha! he hadn't.

This didn't exculpate Lawson (that pesky print was still there), but it messed with the prosecution's tidy theory. Bradshaw would fling it up on the wall like a wet dirt clod and hope it stuck.

41

DAY FOUR. THURSDAY, MARCH 19TH.

Scott knew he had to duke it out with Stew over the Eric Loebowitz dilemma. However, he had another witness that morning and he didn't want to be distracted with the annoying issue of duty and guilt. Not with the world watching.

"The prosecution calls Dr. John DePaulis."

DePaulis was led into the courtroom where all eyes followed him to the witness stand. He was of ordinary height and weight with no unusual characteristics, except that he was as hairy as an ape everywhere but on the top of his head. DePaulis was the kid who'd flaunted dense pubic hair in the sixth grade, but, unfortunately, the rich blessings of testosterone that had made him a hero to other six-grade boys had become a curse as he aged. By the time he was a sophomore in college, that quirky hormone had robbed him of his mane on top, replacing it with a scalp so shiny it looked wet.

Dr. DePaulis testified about his vast laboratory experience testing semen and sperm. The jurors maturely listened to this testimony without giggling, but they had to wonder how he'd come to specialize in this area.

"Genetic material present in sperm can be analyzed and used as a genetic fingerprint to identify a specific male," testified Dr. DePaulis.

"So," asked Scott, "can you identify the owner of the semen if it's outside the lab?" The *owner*? Was it something you owned? And do you lose legal title to it upon discharge?

"It can be challenging to identify sperm inside a woman, or on clothing, if it's old and decomposed."

"You mean if the sperm is old?"

"Yes. However, we can still detect the presence of enzyme acid phosphatase, which is at least circumstantial evidence of the existence of semen or sperm. Remember, there are a quarter billion sperm released in a single ejaculate of semen. Surely they can't all hide." He smiled at his clever quip, but no one else did. Which was awkward.

"Were you able to identify the owner of the semen found in Chelsea Miles and at the scene of the murder?" This "owner" business just sounded wrong, but he didn't know how else to rephrase it.

"Yes."

"Who did it belong to?"

"Kenneth Lawson."

"Are you certain of that?"

"I can state that opinion with complete certainty, yes."

"I have no further questions for this witness, Your Honor."

There was no spellbinding cross examination. Bradshaw couldn't dispute that his client had known Chelsea in Biblical fashion. However, that didn't mean he'd killed her. Unless, of course, the prosecution could make the unconventional argument that Lawson's ejaculate of semen was so robust that it measured in the "high velocity impact" category; a ferocious blast of semen that'd killed her. So, yes, it had been wrong to ejaculate in her direction, but it hadn't been injurious to her health, and it hadn't been a crime.

Stew solemnly stood and announced to the court that the prosecution rested their case.

"Ladies and Gentlemen of the jury," the judge said after they'd resumed following lunch, "you will now hear from the defense. Mr. Bradshaw, you may proceed."

"Thank you, Your Honor. The defense calls Javier Flores to the stand."

"Objection!" Stew sprung up like an angry jack-in-the-box, spittle flying. "We were not told about this witness!"

"Counsel, please approach the bench," said The Gobbler, jowls jiggling.

Stew nearly sprinted to the front of the courtroom while Bradshaw lagged behind; the rhythm of his long swinging arms and legs completely out of sync, reading glasses still perched on the top of his head.

"Your Honor," Stew screeched at a high volume whisper, "we are not familiar with this witness! We have no idea what he will say."

"With all due respect," Bradshaw said, "the prosecution has already interviewed this witness. The court may recall that Mr. Flores was the primary suspect. They would have called him in their case if they'd been able to find him. Both sides have been trying to locate him for months. We finally found him last night. I can assure the court that he won't confess to killing Mrs. Miles. In fact, we believe he wasn't involved."

"Then why is his testimony relevant?" asked The Gobbler.

"Yeah, why?" asked Stew. The Gobbler looked at Stew, annoyed.

"Because he doesn't recall using the shovel that afternoon," said Bradshaw. "His testimony is directly relevant to the issue of fingerprints the prosecution relies upon."

"I'll allow it," said the judge.

"But that is highly prejudicial and—"

"I've made my ruling, Mr. Franks."

The jurors didn't know what'd been discussed at the bench, but they knew Stew had lost the argument by the way he walked back to his seat, shaking his head, like a baseball batter who'd just struck out on a called third strike.

Javier was escorted from the hallway into the courtroom. He was dressed like a Mexican landscaper. His hair was matted down and he turned a sweat-stained baseball cap around and around in his hands.

Beth first put the interpreter under oath (those oaths don't work, you know—you still lie if you can get away with it). She then administered the oath to Javier with the interpreter repeating everything from English to Spanish, and back to English again. This made for stilted testimony. Javier described his employment with Señor and Señora Miles. No, he never go in their house. Si, he work the day Señora Miles was murdered. No, he no kill Señora Miles. No, he not know who did. No, he no see people come to the house that afternoon except Señor Miles. He no see much because the garage was on other side. And si, the property was muy grande.

Bradshaw led Javier through the days following the murder and how the detectives had interviewed him in laborious detail.

He stole a disappointed glance back at Stew as if to say, "Shame on you. You've known about this witness all along, and yet you tried to hide him from this honest jury."

Javier testified that he'd tried to pull the annuals up by hand in the garden on the south side of the house, but the ground was frozen in late November and he'd required the shovel to dig them up. He recalled propping the shovel against the house, next to the door, when he was done. He spent the rest of the afternoon on the tall privet hedge on the other side of the property.

"Mr. Flores, did you ever return to the south side of the house where you'd put the shovel?"

"No, I already do work there."

"Did you ever use the shovel again that afternoon?"

"No, I no think so. I forget I leave shovel there. So I no put in garage. If I use again I remember to put in garage when I go home."

"Are you sure about that?"

"Si."

If Bradshaw could persuade the jury through his next witness that the fingerprint was not Lawson's, then maybe, just maybe, he had a chance.

"The defense calls Dr. Brent Kelly as its next witness." Kelly was a fingerprint expert who was commonly called by the defense in criminal cases. He knew where his bread was buttered and could be counted on to deliver favorable testimony, for a fee. His greed was scarcely hidden.

Kelly testified the thumb print on the shovel handle was too small to rely on. Also, it slightly overlapped another fingerprint from a different individual. This presented an inevitable source of error as compared to fingerprints taken under controlled conditions.

"For example," Kelly continued "the thumb and fingerprints taken from the clock on the bedside table are definitive and clearly belong to Mr. Lawson, but the partial print on the wooden handle of the shovel, well; it's just too fraught with uncertainty for me to be able to testify with scientific credibility."

Stew despised Kelly. He had battled him in court before and believed Kelly would say whatever he was paid to say—a hired whore for the criminally guilty.

"Mr. Kelly," Stew began with his cross examination, "we have met several times in the past, have we not?"

"Yes, Mr. Franks, I believe we have."

"And each time, you've testified that fingerprints belonging to a criminal don't actually belong to that criminal."

"Objection!" It was Bradshaw's turn to be pissed. "That question is blatantly improper and assumes facts not in evidence."

"Sustained. Mr. Franks, please rephrase your question."

"Isn't it true, Mr. Kelly, that you *always* testify for the defense?"

"That is who usually hires me, yes."

"Usually? Can you tell me a single time when you have testified for the prosecution?"

"Not off the top of my head."

"Of course not. Have you *ever* testified in court that fingerprints left at the scene of a crime matched those of the defendant who hired you to testify?"

"I don't recall, Mr. Franks. I have testified many times throughout the years." Kelly was beginning to squirm uncomfortably. The phony smile was just pasted on his face.

"Well, Mr. Kelly, as a matter of fact, I actually *do* know the answer to that question," Stew said. "I have combed through your previous trial appearances carefully. I can report that you have testified in court 108 times. And *every single time* you testified *under oath* that the fingerprints did not necessarily belong to the accused defendant. Every single time. What a remarkable coincidence."

"Is there a question in that speech, Your Honor?" Bradshaw was desperate to derail this line of inquiry.

Stew made the judge's ruling unnecessary. "I have no more questions for this witness," he sneered. I particularly enjoyed the way he'd pronounced the word "witness," like he was sucking on a ripe lemon.

Dr. Kelly slithered from the witness box under the suspicious eyes of the jurors who wondered if he was going to present a copy of his bill to Bradshaw and demand payment before exiting those miniature swinging saloon doors behind the lawyer tables.

Scott got another call that night from Veronica Arnold, Loebowitz's publicly appointed attorney. The Loebowitz mess hung on him like the heavy vest the dentist puts on your chest to x-ray your teeth—this nagging uneasiness at a time when he should've been prancing in the spotlight. A small-time snitch named Turd and a creep like Loebowitz had soiled his moment by getting into a jail-pissing contest. And the case had been assigned to Veronica We Hate Her Guts Arnold, arch enemy Numero Uno of the prosecutor's office.

"Hey, Veronica," he said. "I've been so swamped in trial I haven't been able to discuss this with Franks. Let me give him a call now. It looks like the trial will stretch at least until Monday, so we have a little breathing room."

"Listen, Scott," she lectured, "I don't want to tell you how to do your job, but this deal won't last. I could always go to Bradshaw directly."

"Yeah, I suppose you could," said Scott, "but the last time I checked, Bradshaw couldn't make deals on behalf of the prosecutor's office. So, I don't want to tell you how to do your job either, but you might want to mention that to your client. Tell him he should confess to a murder and get nothing in return. Oh, and then prepare for your disciplinary hearing with the bar."

Scott hung up the phone. Ugh, she was exasperating. He drew a breath, and dialed Stew's number.

"Scott, my boy!" Such optimism in his voice! Such joy! And why not? He'd just made the defense's fingerprint expert look like a fraud, and the defense was out of arrows. They probably had only one more witness: Ken Lawson himself. Then he could stand before the jury in another new suit (he'd been saving a handsome charcoal-gray pinstripe) and confidently tell them he'd proved all he'd promised: Ken Lawson murdered Chelsea Miles in cold blood. Simple as pie.

"Listen, Stew, we need to talk about this Eric Loebowitz issue."

"Who? Oh, shit, Scott, don't tell me you're still hung up on that. I thought we'd already decided we had no duty to disclose him." His tone was still semi-jovial. "Let it go."

"No, Stew, *you* said we didn't need to disclose him. I still think we should."

"That's bullshit!"

"It's not bullshit, Stew. We have a guy in jail who claims

he killed Chelsea. How can we not disclose that? Sure, maybe it is bullshit, but that's not our call to make."

"The hell it isn't! We don't need to disclose every Tom, Dick, and Harry who's on death row and claims it was he who shot Abraham Lincoln! Of *course* this thug is going to claim responsibility. Is he doing it out of the goodness of his heart? Of course not! He's doing it because he wants a deal. It's the oldest trick in the book. So this Lemwhiskey guy, or whatever the hell his name is, now claims he did it. Well, whaddya know! This guy's a cold-blooded killer, Scott. He's about to get life in prison or the chair, and so now he coincidentally confesses to the biggest crime of the century? Where there is no other evidence to implicate him? *Not one shred of evidence?* Why do you think he's doing this, Scott? Huh? To serve justice? It's to get a fucking deal!"

"But, Stew, his lawyer thinks he's credible. She thinks he's got a story to tell."

"Yeah, I'll bet she does. And who, pray tell, is this psychic lawyer of his who wants to cut a deal for him?"

"Veronica Arnold." Scott held his breath.

"You're joking." Stew did not freak. Not yet, for he thought Scott was teasing him.

"I'm not."

"There is *NO FUCKING WAY!* No way! You hear me! That bitch will do anything. You've *got* to be kidding me. So, we have a cold-blooded murderer who gets caught with his hand in the cookie jar and now wants a deal? And his lawyer is Veronica Arnold who's as crooked as they come? Are you *serious*? No way in hell, Scott! No way."

"But, hang on, Stew. Let's think this through. If Bradshaw

finds out about this, he'll throw a fit that we didn't disclose a potential witness."

"First of all, Scott," (the patronizing was in full swing) "I have been doing this for a long time. Forgive me here, but you're still wet behind the ears. This shit goes on all the time. You hear me? All the time. Bradshaw won't find out about it. And do you know why he won't? Because Veronica and her perfect upstanding client can get nothing from him. Not a thing. This piece of shit will only confess to a murder he didn't commit if he can get an *ad-van-tage*." He spoke the word slowly, as if he were teaching a preschooler to pronounce it for the first time.

"But, Stew, it's called a legal *du-ty*."

"Let me tell you something, Scott. If we disclose this crap to the defense they'll jump all over it to cast doubt on Lawson's guilt. There's no merit to it."

"They'll use that information to cast doubt? Listen to yourself, Stew! Need I remind you that is *the entire point!*"

"No," said Stew. "Not when it's bullshit and everybody knows it."

"Then we can argue that on cross examination. If it's such apparent bullshit, as you say, then the jury will recognize it, too. But at least we will have done our legal duty to disclose all witnesses who may have knowledge or information about the crime."

"I hate to beat a dead horse," said Stew as he was about it to beat it again and didn't appear to hate doing it, "but we have no duty in this case where there is no other corroborating evidence to support some bullshit contention that this Eric Loeberstein, or whatever his name is, did it."

They could have gone around and around on this issue for

days. Stew would not concede the point, blinded by his naked ambition to convict Senator Lawson at all costs. He was inflexible when it would have been wise to show a little flexibility. I can do good work with guys like Stew.

42

DAY FIVE. FRIDAY, MARCH 20TH.

The Gobbler had informed everyone the night before that the trial would not resume until ten o'clock the next morning because he had some other pressing legal work to tend to. By ten-thirty, everyone in the courtroom was antsy and bored. All, that is, except Ken Lawson who hadn't been comfortable enough to be bored in several months. The butterflies were spazzing out in his gut because a decision had been made that he would testify in his own defense.

Stew pulled rank, proclaiming he would conduct Lawson's cross-examination. He and Scott had been civil to each other that morning, neither one broaching the subject of Loebowitz. But the elephant roamed around their conversations, large and clumsy, bumping into them with its tail and trunk, unable to get comfortable in the cramped quarters of the courtroom.

"The defense calls Kenneth Lawson," Bradshaw said. He knew that legal pundits around the nation would have a field day with this move. Indeed, the decision to call Lawson to the stand had been a toughie. However, he felt he had no choice. The jury needed this former public servant to look them straight in the eye and tell them he did not kill Chelsea Miles, even if it meant he might get roughed up on cross examination.

Ken walked to the witness stand like a man to the gallows. He was good on his feet, but the fear of being convicted of first degree murder was terrifying. Of course, he knew that Stew Franks would attack him as a shameful pig on cross examination, but it beat the needle, or the noose.

"Please state your name for the record."

"My name is Kenneth Lawson," he'd found the strength to sit up straight and look them in the eye. He hadn't become a terrific politician for nothing.

Bradshaw led him through a series of preliminary questions, asking about his children and career (studiously skipping over his marital vows). Lawson's voice was clear and strong.

"Did you have an improper sexual relationship with the deceased, Chelsea Miles?"

"Yes, I'm ashamed to admit it, but I did. It was a one-time mistake and I have otherwise been faithful in my marriage. I have a strong belief in the sanctity of marriage, so this is something I'm ashamed about—the knowledge that I've hurt the people closest to me."

Bradshaw asked him about the length, duration, and frequency of the affair. Bradshaw's strategy had been to hit it head on—get it out on the table and get it over with—hopefully taking the steam out of the cross examination. In preparation for trial, Bradshaw had peppered Ken with questions about other improper relationships. Ken had refused to admit to any.

The preparation for his testimony had been exhaustive and thorough. "I've got to know Ken; have you been with any other women?"

"No, Andy," Lawson had said. "What do you think I am?"

"I'm just telling you, Ken, that if there's anything out there and the prosecution gets wind of it, they'll crucify you for lying about that, too."

"Don't worry, Andy. There's nothing."

"You're sure?"

"Of course I'm sure. Wouldn't I know about it?"

"Okay, that's all I'm saying. Speak now or forever hold your peace."

Lawson had remained firm in his denials; there'd been no other women. Period. Bradshaw could only hope there weren't more skeletons in the closet that would be loosed at the worst possible time.

After going through the events of that fateful day, they finally reached the crux of his testimony.

"Mr. Lawson, did you kill Chelsea Miles?"

"Absolutely not."

"At the time you left her home, had she been harmed in any way?"

"Absolutely not."

"Was there a fight or a disagreement between the two of you that day?"

"Absolutely not."

"Did she threaten to expose your improper relationship?"

"No, she did not."

"Will you swear to this jury that you had nothing to do with her death?"

Ken turned to face the jury. "I can absolutely tell you that I had nothing to do with her death. I swear it on my life." Ken was sincere and commanding. He didn't blink. He didn't lift his eyes to the sky. He didn't bite his fingernails, or put his head down when he said it. He looked at the jurors with all the polished sincerity he could. "I did not kill Chelsea. I swear it. And I have no idea who did."

"Thank you, Mr. Lawson. That is all I have for this witness, Your Honor." Bradshaw then turned his back and swung to his table. Suddenly he stopped and turned around to face Ken.

"Oh," he said as if he'd had a sudden thought that hadn't been choreographed (even though it had). "Just one more thing, if I may," he said, deliberately pausing again. "I was just wondering, Mr. Lawson. Are you able to have children?"

"Not anymore."

"And why is that?"

"I had a vasectomy eight years ago."

"Thank you. That is all."

Stew Franks rose from his chair and approached the podium for the cross examination. Once he arrived at the podium, he just stared at Lawson. Five seconds. Ten seconds. Twenty. It felt like a year. The courtroom was hushed. Finally, there appeared a trace of the tiniest smile on Stew's face.

"Mr. Lawson, do you know a woman by the name of Cammy Stillman?" And with that one god-awful question, Bradshaw knew he'd made a dreadful mistake in calling Ken to the stand.

"Uh, I'm not, uh, I'm not sure. The name rings a bell," said Lawson.

"Oh, I'll bet it does, Mr. Lawson. How about a woman by the name of Angela Kidman?"

"Um, yes, I believe I know who that is." Lawson had lost all his strength. Absent was the humble swagger. All his lustful mistakes were coming home to roost in front of his international audience.

"And how about a woman by the name of Janet Bergstrom? I presume you also know her?"

"Well, yes, I am familiar with her. Yes, I . . . well, yes, I think I know who she is."

"Yes," said Stew "I'm sure you do. In fact, I imagine you know her quite well. Shall I continue?"

Lawson said nothing.

"Mr. Lawson, those are but three of the women you have slept with in the past year alone. Isn't that true?"

Lawson was silent. Stew didn't care whether Lawson answered out loud, or not.

"Tell me, Mr. Lawson, how many more have there been? Or was it just the three? Or, wait, I suppose it would be just the four if we count Chelsea Miles."

Lawson was looking down at his lap and did not answer.

"Just this year." Stew shuffled some notes on the podium. "That we know about."

Lawson kept looking down.

"Do you even know their names?"

Still no answer.

"Mr. Lawson, isn't it true that, despite your claim to virtue, you have an uncanny ability to lie?"

Lawson looked out into the crowd of people. They were disgusted with their public servant, but also had pity for him at the moment.

"So your previous testimony, under oath, all this phony

business about the sanctity of marriage and that your affair with Mrs. Miles was a one-time mistake, that was just another lie wasn't it?"

Lawson did not answer. He just sat there, humiliated to the marrow. I've seen it so many times, but rarely on a public scale like this.

"Isn't it true, Mr. Lawson, that Chelsea meant nothing to you, that she was just another beautiful woman you used for your selfish pleasure?"

"No, that is not true." His voice was barely above a whisper. "I cared a great deal about her."

"Oh, did you? Well then, Mr. Lawson, who did you care about the most? Was it Chelsea or Cammy or Angela or Janet or *your wife*, or all the other women out there who you slept with? Would you care to rank them for us, in order?"

Lawson said nothing.

"Chelsea was the wife of your *friend*." This time Stew waited until Lawson responded. He had to wait for several seconds in the hushed courtroom when, finally, Lawson spoke so softly he was barely heard.

"Yes."

"You became enraged with her when she threatened to expose your affair."

"No, that's not true."

"You grabbed the shovel and struck her in the head to silence her."

"No, that isn't true."

Stew paused for effect and then said, as if he was genuinely saddened to do so, "But your fingerprints were on the shovel."

Bradshaw stood for re-direct. He needed to ask *something*

so the final words spoken by Stew Franks weren't the last thing the jurors heard.

"Mr. Lawson, your conduct with other women; is that something you are proud of?"

"Of course not."

"But, as you know, you are not on trial for your infidelity. You are charged with the first degree murder of Chelsea Miles. So, I will ask you again, Mr. Lawson. Did you kill her?"

"Absolutely not. I swear it on my life."

The court adjourned for a recess. Bradshaw said nothing to Lawson—completely ignored him. He couldn't bring himself to say something reassuring like: *Oh, that? Hey, no biggee. You just made me look like a complete jack-ass and probably sent yourself to prison for life. But, hey, it's not pathetic that you can't even remember their names. Don't worry about it. You were super!*

Stew was radiant when trial was adjourned for the weekend. He had thoroughly destroyed the ex-senator, dousing whatever remained of his reputation like a full bucket of water on a match. He was anxious to get out to the steps, between the pillars, where the eager media awaited him. He commanded Scott to stay and meet with Bradshaw and The Gobbler to work on the jury instructions.

Jury instructions are a series of written directions for the jury. For example, they are told not to surrender their honest convictions just to be popular (you all want to look good, I understand). Bradshaw insisted on an instruction that the state must prove its case, and that Lawson didn't need to prove a dang thing. He also insisted on an instruction that the jurors should have no doubt in their minds. Scott made sure that the jurors knew they could have *some* doubt and still convict him (the state wasn't required to prove its case beyond a shadow of a doubt—only beyond a *reasonable* doubt).

After Stew's humble sermon about his masterful performance for the Eye-Witness News at 10:00, and Scott and Bradshaw had completed their mundane toil hammering out the jury instructions, Scott went back to the office. It was late Friday evening when he called Veronica.

"Veronica, we'll give Loebowitz a deal if he's legit."

"What kind of deal?"

"I can't promise that we'll go to voluntary manslaughter, but if he testifies that he murdered Chelsea, and he can prove it, we'll cut him a deal."

"I can live with that," Veronica said.

"Let me call Bradshaw to disclose this new witness," said Scott. "I'll ask him to contact you directly. You can tell him that we've spoken and have an agreement."

"Okay, I'll look forward to his call."

"And, Veronica, one more thing. Stew Franks doesn't agree that we need to disclose this witness. So if this blows up on me, I'll be out of a job. You better not deliver Loebowitz unless this is totally legit. Because if it's not, and he's playing us, this office will never work with you again. Ever. And I'm serious."

Scott hung up with Veronica and dialed Bradshaw, who didn't pick up. Scott left him a message to call his cell. He believed he was doing the right thing, but he knew there would be hell to pay. Now that he'd made his decision, he felt some relief. Give the evidence to the jury and let them sort it out, because juries always do the right thing. Uh-huh, sure they do.

Scott's cell phone rang an hour later.

"Hello?"

"Yeah, Scott? This is Andy Bradshaw calling you back. You said it was urgent."

"Andy. Thanks for getting back to me. I just learned about a witness that may interest you. As much as it pains me, I felt it was my ethical duty to disclose him to you."

"Who is it? What's it regarding?" He tried to hide the excitement in his voice. He knew what he was about to hear would influence the outcome of the case, and maybe in a big way, but not yet comprehending how.

"Just call Veronica Arnold who's representing a guy named Loebowitz. She's expecting your call. And, Andy, I'm doing this without Stew's support. He doesn't know I'm making this call. I trust you will use good judgment in how you respond to the prosecutor's office."

"Scott?"

"Yeah?"

"Thank you."

43

DAY SIX. MONDAY, MARCH 23RD.

"Counsel, are we ready to proceed?"

"Yes, Your Honor," both lawyers stood and spoke, each quite confident for reasons of their own.

"Very well," said The Gobbler. "I believe the defense was going to rest. Is that true, Mr. Bradshaw?"

"No, Your Honor," Bradshaw said. "We have a final witness." Stew jerked his head in Bradshaw's direction. He had a look of panic.

"Very well, you may proceed," said the judge.

"The defense calls Eric Loebowitz to the stand."

There was a moment of silence, and then all hell broke loose.

"*OBJECTION!*" A few specks of Stew's spit nearly reached the podium in the center of the courtroom. He was on his feet, his face already blue with rage. "This witness was not disclosed and should not be permitted to testify!"

The Gobbler banged his gavel, his jowls jiggling like watered-down pudding. The hammocks of fat under his arms swayed in rhythm. Jurors and those in the gallery looked at each other. "This court will be in recess. I want to see counsel in my chambers. *Now!*" The jurors realized someone had done something terribly wrong to cause the flap to swing so much.

This was the moment Scott had dreaded. On their way back to the judge's chambers, Stew glared at him with a look that would have caused an ordinary junior associate to wilt like a carrot left too long in the fridge. "How *dare* you!" he hissed. Scott stayed at arm's length and kept his mouth shut.

When they were in chambers, with the door closed, Judge Franco began. "What in the hell is going on? Who's this new witness?"

"His name is Eric Loebowitz," Bradshaw said.

"I know his name, counsel. Who *is* he?" The judge was on center stage, too, and didn't want any shenanigans in his courtroom at this late hour in the trial.

"Mr. Loebowitz will confess to killing Chelsea Miles."

"*Excuse me?*" said the judge.

"This is bullshit!" screeched Stew.

"Counsel! That will be enough, and I won't warn you again!" Then turning on Bradshaw he said, "Tell me what the hell is going on."

"We just learned about his identity over the weekend, Your Honor. He is currently incarcerated following his arrest last week in connection with another murder. While in jail, he confessed to killing Mrs. Miles."

"And why would he do that?" Judge Franco asked. "Was he given a deal by the prosecutor's office?" The judge looked at Stew for confirmation, who looked with fury at Scott.

"Yes," said Scott. "I learned of his identity and thought it was appropriate that I disclose him to the defense. I don't know the full extent of his testimony, other than he claims to have murdered Mrs. Miles."

Stew stared at Scott with venomous intent. This was classic wrath, a priceless example of my good work with the Deadlies. The Gobbler saw the look and put two and two together. "I presume you were unaware of this witness, Mr. Franks?"

"Well," Stew was now in a very difficult position, "I was vaguely aware of a claim made by an inmate with a long criminal record who is coming out of the woodwork to get a deal. But I didn't believe then, nor do I now, that his testimony is the least bit credible. So, after careful deliberation, we concluded this was a diversion that would add nothing and cause an undue burden on the court."

"But counsel," asked The Gobbler, his flap swinging like a backyard hammock, "how can you say that it's not credible testimony if you don't even know what it is?"

"Well, I just figured . . .."

"I can tell you, Your Honor," Bradshaw broke in, "that Loebowitz's story is credible. The prosecution knew about him, so they can't claim surprise. Indeed, they were the ones who told us about him." He nodded in Scott's direction. "It is alarming that they didn't immediately disclose his identity the moment they discovered it." This time he stared exclusively at Stew.

"I am inclined to let him to testify," said The Gobbler. "Mr. Franks, I will give you every reasonable opportunity to conduct a thorough cross examination. If his story lacks credibility, I am confident your trial skills will make that clear."

They filed back into the courtroom. The jury watched them closely, trying to divine what had happened to cause such a racket.

Stew's face was the color of an over-ripe Roma tomato, so they figured he'd been the sore loser.

The Gobbler sat heavily in his cushioned leather chair. There was the whoosh of air in the otherwise silent courtroom. "Please bring Mr. Loebowitz forward to be sworn."

The rear door opened and two armed guards ushered in Eric Loebowitz. He wore the orange jumpsuit which complimented his red hair nicely. He was handcuffed and his legs were shackled. There was no expression on his face. The guard removed the shackles from his ankles so he could climb the two stairs to the witness stand. Beth asked him to raise his right hand to take the oath, but he could only raise it chest-high because the handcuffs were fastened to a chain around his waist. The only sound in the courtroom was the clinking of chains as he tried to raise his hand.

I wish they still used the Bible to swear witnesses. Maybe I'm just old fashioned, but now you can't even have the Number-One-Bestseller-Of-All-Time in your courtrooms? It's a downright shame, that's what it is. What's wrong with a little discrimination every now and then, huh? You all take these things so seriously.

"Please state your name," Bradshaw began.

"Eric Loebowitz."

"Where do you live?"

"I'm in jail."

"Where do you live when you're not in jail?"

"North Philly."

"Why are you in jail?"

"I got arrested last week."

"What was the charge?"

"Murder," Loebowitz said, as if he were stating his college major.

"Have you entered a plea in that case?"

"Not yet. I'm still waiting on my lady lawyer."

"Have you been offered a deal or some consideration for your testimony today?"

"Yeah, she says if I tell the truth about what happened they'll help me when I get sentenced. But I don't know what that'll be."

Bradshaw led him through the preliminary background information and up to the date of Chelsea's murder.

"Where were you on the afternoon of November 28th?"

"I was sitting in my car down the street from where the lady lived."

"And by the lady, you are referring to Chelsea Miles, the one that was killed?"

"Yeah."

"Why were you there?"

"Because I was going to kill her." Loebowitz said this so matter of factly that it somehow seemed less outrageous than it really was.

"What time did you arrive and park down the street?"

"Probably about 3:00, 3:30. Might've even been 3:45. I can't remember exactly."

"Were there any other cars parked down the street from the home when you arrived?"

"Yeah."

"Can you describe the vehicle?"

"It was silver."

"And what type of vehicle?"

"A car."

"Yes, I understand. Can you describe the make or model of the vehicle?"

"I think it was a Mercedes."

"What did you do once you parked there?"

"I waited a bit and then saw him leave in the silver Mercedes, if that's what it was."

"Him?"

"Yeah, him," and he pointed to Ken Lawson.

"Then what did you do?"

"I waited a few minutes I guess, then I got out of my car and was going to go inside. But then I seen the lady's husband drive up in a black car. Not sure what kind it was."

"Then what did you do?"

"I got back in my car and thought I'd wait for a while to see if he'd leave."

"Did he?"

"Yeah, about fifteen minutes later he finally drove away."

"So then what did you do?"

"I got out of my car and walked across the yard to the side of the house."

"Was there anyone else on the property that you could see?"

"Yeah, there was some Mexican guy cutting some bushes on the other side of the yard. He was standing on a ladder."

"Did he see you?"

"How am I supposed to know?"

"Well, did you see him look in your direction?"

"No, he was looking at the bushes."

"Okay, then what did you do?"

"I went in the door on the side of the house."

"Why?"

"Because I was going to kill her, why else would I go in?" As if this was the most natural thing he would say, or do.

"How were you planning to kill her?"

"I had a gun, a nine millimeter. But then I saw the Mexican guy and I was worried he'd hear the shot. So when I was going in the back door there was this shovel leaning up against the house next to the door. I just grabbed it and went inside. The door wasn't locked or anything. It was the same door the other guy left out of." Loebowitz nodded to Lawson who sat slack jawed listening to this testimony. "Course I was wearing gloves so I wasn't worried about fingerprints or anything."

"Then what did you do?"

"I found her bedroom and walked in. She was just standing by the end of the bed. She goes 'Who are you?' I didn't say anything to her, I just swung the shovel and hit her in the head and she was dead."

"Did you know Chelsea Miles?"

"Whaddya mean?"

"Did you know her before you swung the shovel at her?"

"No."

"Then why did you kill her?"

"Because I got paid."

"Are you saying you were *hired* to kill her?"

"Yeah."

"And who was it that hired you?"

"Uh, I think I'm gonna take the fifth on that."

"Excuse me?"

"Yeah, I'm not saying anything else until I talk to my lady lawyer again."

Bradshaw looked at the judge who looked at Stew Franks. There was a momentary stalemate when finally Judge Franco said, "Counsel, approach the bench."

Stew stood on wobbly legs, his potential senate campaign

stalling before the exploratory committee had even met. Scott also stood and made a movement to attend the bench conference with Stew and Bradshaw, but Stew awkwardly cut him off. Scott began to sit back down and then changed his mind and hurried to join the other two. To hell with Stew Franks.

Those in the gallery were dumbfounded. They wanted to bolt from the courtroom to call their studios. *Holy shit, Morris! You're not gonna believe this!* But they dared not miss what would happen next, so they waited for the attorneys huddled at the bench to finish their hush-hush conference.

"The witness has invoked the privilege, gentlemen," whispered The Gobbler. "I don't see how we can proceed further at this point."

"But he's already admitted to the crime, Your Honor," said Bradshaw. "He wouldn't further incriminate himself. He'd only be incriminating the person who presumably hired him."

"This is an outrageous distraction," said Stew, because he could think of nothing else to say.

"I'm going to call a recess until this afternoon," said Franco. "That will allow him to meet with his lawyer. I presume his attorney will be in touch with you," he said in Stew and Scott's direction.

44

SCOTT WAS BACK AT HIS DESK in the prosecutor's office, a block from the courthouse, when Veronica called. He put her on hold and walked down to Stew's office so he could participate in the conference call. "Stew, Veronica's on line three and she's ready to talk," said Scott. "I told her I'd grab you so we could conference her in."

"Oh, I see," said Stew. "*Now* you want to involve me."

"Stew, that's bullshit and you know it. I told you about Loebowitz and you refused to disclose him. As you can plainly see, that would've been a big mistake. So let's deal with it now."

"No, Scott. *You* can deal with the national mess you've made. I told you once before, but let me say it again nice and slow for you: I will not talk to that bitch. How's that? Is that clear enough for you, or do I need to say it slower? And, for the record, this is complete bullshit. This coldblooded murderer and his lawyer have played you like a fucking fiddle. You're bringing the reputation of the entire prosecutor's office down with you and there will be hell to pay when this is over."

"So, let me get this straight," Scott said, "just so we're perfectly clear. You won't even talk to the attorney of the witness who testified he murdered Chelsea Miles, and is about to tell us who hired him to do it? Is that right? I just want to be completely clear about this."

"You're goddamned right I won't!" Stew spit. "That murderer will say anything to get a better deal. Look how he's humiliated us so far. You've already given him a deal on the murder of an innocent man he killed with a fucking tire iron! And now his lawyer has you on the line like a carp, and will work you for an even better deal. If it weren't so outrageous it would be funny. But this isn't funny, Scott. You have completely overstepped your authority and it goes without saying that you'll be fired as soon as this case is over. That may be obvious, but I just want to be perfectly clear that you understand."

Scott returned to his office and closed the door. He picked up the line where Veronica was parked.

"Okay, Scott, here's the deal," she said. "My client won't say anything more unless you reduce the charge in the tire-iron murder to voluntary manslaughter. And we've got to have the same deal on the Miles case. Voluntary manslaughter for both of them."

"Come on, Veronica. I'm hanging out here alone on this one."

"That's non-negotiable, Scott. You want him to talk then you have to agree to the deal. Franco is pissed. In fact, he just called me again to see if we've worked something out. Just give my guy the deal and he's back in court this afternoon where he'll serve it up on a silver platter."

"Veronica, this is bullshit and you know it."

"Please don't lecture me. Do we have a deal, or not?"

"We have a deal," said Scott. "But let me be clear; if this blows up and we find out Loebowitz has been playing us, I will see to it that he never sees the light of day. And if I find out you knew this was bullshit, I will make it my life's work to see that you never practice law again. That, too, is non-negotiable."

45

MAGGIE HAD BEEN GLUED TO THE TELEVISION news, rooting for a conviction so she could finally get her just rewards. But the reporters were now saying the case against Ken Lawson might be in doubt. There was a new witness or something, which was causing a delay. What? This was an outrage! She wanted someone wealthy to be convicted already (and preferably someone who already had her settlement demand to avoid further delay).

She made her daily call to Young Associate and didn't like what he told her one bit.

"So, hold it," she said. "You're saying that if this Lawson gets off the hook because of some technicality you'd have to *drop my case?*"

"Well, if by technicality you mean he's innocent, then yes."

"But that isn't fair," she said.

"If it turns out a dead beat criminal committed the crime, we won't be able to collect the money."

"Why on earth not?"

"We can only collect from the person who actually committed the crime."

"So let me get this straight. You're now saying if somebody without money murdered my Petunia I'd get *nothing*?"

"I'm afraid so. And I've told you that all along. We could get a judgment against the guy, but how would we collect if he doesn't have any money? You can't squeeze blood out of a turnip."

"Then the government should pay it."

"Why should the government pay it?"

"Why shouldn't they?"

"The government didn't murder your daughter, that's why."

"But it's their fault I'm suffering."

"Why?"

"Because if this Lawson gets off on some technicality then it means they arrested the wrong man. And now I'm the one holding the bag."

"But you wouldn't have received any money if they'd arrested the guilty man in the first place."

"You just tell the government I'm not going away. You hear me? Not until I get my hundred thousand."

"But, the government—"

"Don't you 'but' me. You're just like all those other lawyers, trying to make a quick buck on the system. Just a bunch of ambulance chasers. You twist my arm into filing suit, and then you screw me over."

"But you're the one who came to—"

"Don't try to weasel your way out of this one, Buster. I'll report you."

"Listen, Maggie, Lawson may still be convicted. Let's just wait and see what happens."

"He sure better be because I won't be pushed around. You hear me?"

John and Rebecca were ecstatic. There was a witness who admitted he'd done it! Their father had been vindicated! His reputation was in the crapper, what with all the Cammy's, Janet's, and Angela's out there, but at least he wouldn't get the needle. Who knows, maybe their parents might even patch things up so holidays wouldn't be so complicated.

46

THEY RESUMED THE TRIAL AT THREE O'CLOCK that afternoon. Loebowitz was brought back into the courtroom, orange-clad and shackled, to resume his testimony.

"Mr. Loebowitz, I will remind you that you are still under oath. Do you understand that?" asked Judge Franco.

"Yeah."

"This morning, your testimony was interrupted because you claimed a constitutional privilege. The trial has been in recess to allow you time to speak with your counsel, as you requested. I understand you have now had an opportunity to consult with your attorney. Is that correct?"

"Yeah."

"And do you now wish to proceed?"

"Yeah."

"Very well. Mr. Bradshaw, you may resume your questions on direct."

Bradshaw stood and lurched to the podium. He had no idea what Loebowitz would say. For all he knew, Loebowitz might testify that his client had hired him. But he doubted it.

"Mr. Loebowitz, this morning you admitted in your sworn testimony that you killed Chelsea Miles."

"Yeah."

"You testified that you went to her house with the express purpose of killing her."

"Okay, yeah."

"You testified that you entered her home from the side door and intended to shoot her with a nine-millimeter gun you'd taken to the house."

"Uh-huh."

"But there was a Mexican landscaper on the other side of the house standing on a ladder trimming some bushes and you didn't want him to hear the shot, so you grabbed a shovel that was leaning against the house by the door, and entered her house."

"Yeah, that's what I said."

"Tell us, again, what you did when you entered her house with the shovel."

"Like I already said, I walked through the house until I found her room and I seen her standing there by the end of the bed with hardly nothing on. She said something like, 'Hey, what are you doing in my house?' or something like that, and I just swung the shovel and hit her in the head and she dropped. I figured she was dead, but I bent down to check, just to be sure, ya know."

"And she was dead?"

"Yeah."

"Then what did you do?"

"I walked back to her kitchen."

"What did you do with the shovel?"

"Took it with me."

"You took the shovel to the kitchen?"

"Yeah."

"Why did you do that?"

"Because I needed to transfer the print."

"Transfer the print?"

"Yeah, the fingerprint. It was really a thumb print."

"You transferred the thumb print?"

"Yeah, I had a one of his coffee mugs."

"One of *whose* coffee mugs?"

"His." Loebowitz pointed to Lawson.

"You had one of Mr. Lawson's coffee mugs?"

"Yeah."

"Where did you get one of his coffee mugs?"

"The guy's wife."

"What guy's wife?"

"That guy's wife," and pointed again to Lawson.

There was an audible gasp in the courtroom. Stew wanted to object but could not speak, and wouldn't have known what to say anyway.

"Are you saying Mr. Lawson's wife gave you a coffee mug that belonged to him?"

"Yeah."

"Why?"

"She's the one who hired me and I needed something with his fingerprints on it."

Bradshaw waited. The media wanted to bolt from the courtroom, to be the first to break this, but they didn't want to miss the rest.

"Are you saying that Mrs. Lawson hired you to kill Chelsea Miles?"

"Uh-huh. She told me her husband would probably be over there that afternoon. She wanted me to follow him and then wait for him to leave. When he left I was supposed to kill the lady, but make it look like he did it. You know what I mean? So that's what I was doing with the coffee mug. I was transferring one of his prints from the coffee mug to put it on the handle of the shovel."

"How did you do that?"

"Whaddya mean?"

"How did you transfer the print from the mug to the shovel?"

"Oh, I just went and ground down some graphite from a pencil and then dusted it over the print on the mug. Then I just used some clear tape and lifted it and transferred it to the shovel handle."

"Then what did you do?"

"I just left the way I came in and put the shovel back where I found it. I figured the cops would see the blood and get the print off it."

Loebowitz testified that Mrs. Lawson paid him $20,000 in cash and that he'd never heard from her again. In fact, he never spoke to her at all after the murder, the money had just been sent to a post office box a few days after the murder was discovered.

Stew Franks asked for a thirty-minute recess to gather his thoughts for the cross examination. There was a stampede for the door as every journalist ran to their cameramen, flushed and breathless.

John and Rebecca sat in the near empty courtroom. Their *mom*? How could that possibly be? He said their mom had paid him to kill her? No way. They weren't stupid; they knew their parents didn't have the greatest marriage, but they'd rarely heard them fight (too much apathy for that), not even over an accusation about leaving the kitchen light on all night, or fiddling with the thermostat. John and Rebecca went from hope to despair in the time it took this red-headed monster to speak their mother's name.

"It's not true," Rebecca finally said. It was barely a whisper. "It's not true."

By the time court resumed, Stew had regained about forty percent of his composure. The vacant senate seat was at stake, and so was his legal career. He'd spent all his money on those new suits and now was on the verge of being embarrassed in front of the back-stabbing-second-guessing-disloyal-lamestream media that he'd spent the previous month making love to. And it was all because of this red-headed freak who was stealing his dream. So he attacked with vengeance on cross-exam.

"You murdered a man in cold blood last week."

"Yeah."

"You beat him to death with a tire iron."

"Yeah. I got paid to do it." You've got to hand it to him; he was nothing if he wasn't a capitalist.

"In fact, he was so badly bludgeoned to death that he wasn't even recognizable."

"If you say so."

"Isn't that true?"

"Yeah, I guess."

"And now you've been told that if you testify in this case, and take the fall for this murder, then you'll be given a break on the other murder case, too."

"Yeah, that's what my lady lawyer said. Why else would I confess to it?"

"So you want us to believe that you killed Chelsea Miles

so that you'd get a break on *both* of the murders. Do I have that right?"

"Yeah, I guess that's how it works. I'm not a lawyer or anything but that's what she said."

"And 'she' is your lawyer?"

"Yeah."

"So, just so we're clear on this, your plan was that if you say you killed her, you would actually get *less time for both of them combined* than you'd get for the tire-iron bludgeoning in the first place—the murder you actually committed in front of witnesses. Did I get that right? I just want to be sure."

"I guess. At least I hope so."

"You savagely murder *two* innocent people and you are punished *less* than if you'd just savagely beaten one to death."

"Okay, yeah."

"So if you *say* you killed Chelsea Miles you actually get a windfall."

"What does that mean?"

"If you *say* you killed her you're actually better off than if you said nothing."

"I guess."

"Doesn't that strike you as convenient? Especially when you have nothing to lose?"

"I don't know."

"While you're at it, care to confess to any other murders? Maybe get away with all of them combined with a simple slap on the wrist?"

Loebowitz said nothing. Stew stared cold at the red-head in the orange jumpsuit and chains.

"You've been arrested, what, twenty times?"

"I can't remember, but yeah, probably."

"You don't strike me as the most trustworthy guy in town."

"I'm just telling you what I did. I wouldn't lie about it."

"Oh, no, of course you wouldn't."

Loebowitz glared back at Stew from the witness stand. He lifted his hand to scratch his nose and the chains jiggled. Otherwise is was deathly quiet. He didn't take his eyes off Stew. This was a Mexican staring contest for the ages.

"And you want us to believe you, because *if* we believe you then you get away with minimal punishment for beating a man to death with a tire iron *and* nearly decapitating an innocent woman with a shovel. Is that it?"

"Well, I wouldn't tell you that I killed somebody if I didn't."

Stew shuffled a few papers on the podium. "Have you seen the investigative report on this case?"

"I can't remember."

"You can't *remember*?"

"No."

"Nobody's shown that to you?"

"I can't really remember what I saw."

"Did anybody tell you what the evidence against the defendant was?" asked Stew.

"No."

"Didn't you meet with Mr. Bradshaw, the defendant's lawyer?"

"Yeah."

"And he showed you the file, didn't he?"

"He showed me some stuff I think."

"Have you seen any of the photos of the murder scene?"

"I don't think so."

"You don't *think* so?"

"Maybe I did, I can't remember."

"So you *did* see them?"

"It seems like he showed me some stuff."

"Some stuff?"

"Yeah, he just showed me some papers and stuff, but I can't remember any photos."

"So you've seen the report, the investigative report?"

"I'm not sure what it was."

Stew wanted the jury see that Bradshaw had coached Loebowitz on the details of the slaying so that his tale was more believable.

"You didn't really kill Chelsea Miles, did you?"

"Yeah, I did. And if you don't believe me I can tell you another thing I just remembered."

"No, I think you've said enough," Stew said with as much disgust as he could. And with that, he sat down.

Bradshaw stood and took a few steps in Loebowitz's direction for re-direct. "You remembered something else about the murder. What is that?"

"Well, the guy's wife, him I mean," Loebowitz pointed to Lawson, "gave me something else besides the mug."

"What else did she give you?"

"Well, I thought it was pretty weird, but she gave me a flower."

"She gave you a *flower*?"

"Yeah."

"Why did she do that?"

"How am I supposed to know? She just told me to leave it in the house after I killed her."

"She gave you a flower and wanted you to leave it in Chelsea's house?"

"Yeah. I didn't ask her why—figured it was none of my business."

"What kind of flower was it?"

"I think it was one of those petunia ones."

"And where did you leave it?"

"I just put it on the dresser before I left."

The two lawyers frantically grabbed their duplicate sets of the crime scene photographs, flipping through them, looking for a shot that showed the dresser.

And there it was, in the lower right-hand side of one of the photos. On top of the bedroom dresser, if you looked closely, there was a single pink petunia.

47

"THIS COURT IS IN RECESS. The attorneys will convene in my chambers," said The Gobbler with his poker face. He was no dummy—he knew the jury would take their cue from him. He was human though, and many times throughout his career he'd rolled his eyes, grunted, or chuckled at the absurdity of a liar's lie (but his nose for liars wasn't infallible—he believed his wife had been at Bunco one of those nights years ago).

When they'd settled in the judge's chambers (none of them were actually very settled), The Gobbler turned to Stew, who looked like he'd just been kicked smack dab in his nether regions.

"How do you wish to proceed, Mr. Franks?"

Stew believed Loebowitz was a foil. But that final little show with the petunia left a hickey. "Your Honor, this testimony was . . . unexpected. However, there is absolutely no corroborating evidence that places Loebowitz at the scene. Nothing. No finger-prints, no fluids, no foot prints, nothing. The *only* evidence of his guilt is his own self-serving testimony. And yet, there remains a mountain of evidence proving Lawson's guilt."

"Your Honor," Bradshaw spoke up, "the testimony of Loebowitz was credible. We aren't the ones who gave him a deal. That was Mr. Franks' office. This creates ample evidence of doubt, well beyond a reasonable doubt. I trust the state will reconsider, and dismiss the charges against my client."

"No way," said Stew. He knew the jury might not believe Loebowitz (that lying piece of crap) and still convict Lawson, like they should.

"Well," said the judge, "I won't dismiss the charges, but I urge the prosecution to carefully consider doing so. But, it's your case, Mr. Franks, and if you want to proceed you may certainly do so."

"That's our intention, Your Honor," said Stew. "We don't anticipate any more rebuttal evidence. I think all the evidence is in and we'll be ready to give our closing argument at the court's discretion."

"Where is Mrs. Lawson?" the judge asked. No one answered. He studied each of them, like they were supposed to know these things. "Well, where in the hell is she?"

The attorneys looked at each other, as if the other should know.

"You don't *know*?"

"We obviously didn't expect this, Your Honor."

"I'd advise you, Mr. Franks, to find her. We'll reconvene at nine o'clock tomorrow morning for closing arguments. In the meantime, I urge both of you to come to some agreement for the resolution of this case."

"Your Honor," said Bradshaw, "if you're suggesting a lesser plea of some kind, it will not be forthcoming. We are confident of an acquittal."

"Don't worry, Andy, we won't be offering a reduced charge,"

said Stew. "We believe Lawson was guilty and we won't accept a plea to anything less than first degree."

"Well then," said The Gobbler, "I suppose I'll see you all tomorrow morning for closing arguments."

Back in the courtroom, Ken sat is shock. Susan had hired a hit man to kill Chelsea? And she'd done it to frame him for murder? The murderous bitch had been willing to ruin him, to make him suffer a life in prison, or a lethal injection. And for what? Because he had an *affair*? Because he had rough sex with her during an inconvenient STD outbreak? Unbelievable.

The press had run for the steps and marble pillars to herald the news that Susan Lawson had hired a hit man to kill Chelsea Miles. The collision of anger, surprise, and relief demolished Ken's emotions. I would've declared them to be a total loss with a high deductible.

He turned to see his children in the gallery. I nudged a shameless reporter to get a statement from them. *Now would be a perfect time to get their reaction to mom killing one of dad's lovers. Get the feel-good family story of the year!* Lawson shouted at the reporter to leave them alone. The bailiffs made a move to Ken, fearing he'd gone berserk, but they didn't touch him. In fact, they allowed him to walk through the small saloon-swinging doors to comfort his children on the first row, then stood as a barrier to give them some privacy—but it wasn't much, and it didn't last long.

The bailiffs took Ken away. John and Rebecca retreated to the hallway on wobbly legs and found a quiet corner next to a utility closet. Rebecca punched Susan's number into her phone.

"Wait," John said. "Maybe we shouldn't call her?"

"Why not? This is *mom* we're talking about." She was on the verge of hysteria. "That lying scum is blaming *mom!*"

"But, maybe . . .."

"Oh no, don't even say it. You said so yourself, it's dad's enemies who are trying to destroy us. It's not mom."

She hit send and waited. There was no answer.

Susan returned to her suite from the spa at the exclusive hotel in Bermuda, walking gingerly; the small pieces of foam separating her toes. She'd spent the past few months in isolation, leaving only to be seen at public charities she cared nothing about—all these poor single mothers with their hands out. *Gimme a break. Here's an idea: get a job already.* She was ready to move on. She was tired of pretending she wasn't special.

It was early evening at the Fairmont Bermuda. She poured herself a glass of Le Montrachet and settled in to hear the latest developments from the trial. The television's audio came on briefly before the video and she thought she'd heard her name. She flinched. A reporter was standing in front of the courthouse.

"In a shocking development in the murder trial of Senator Kenneth Lawson, CNN is now reporting that a witness has confessed to the killing."

Please tell me this is not happening.

"This witness, a man by the name of Eric Loebowitz, has just testified that he was hired to kill Chelsea Miles by Susan Lawson, the senator's wife."

Mother of God, please no.

"Judge Gustav Franco has announced a recess in the trial until tomorrow morning. It is unknown at this time whether the prosecution will dismiss the charges against the former Senator from

Pennsylvania, or whether charges will be brought against Mrs. Susan Lawson who has not made an appearance at her husband's trial, and has not been reached for comment."

There was a knock at the door. Susan jumped. The knock came again. She pulled herself from the bed and walked across the suite. So this is how it would end, she thought. She opened the door. A uniformed hotel maid smiled at her. "Would you like us to turn down your bed for the evening?"

Susan collapsed onto the bed. She stared up at the ceiling; the thick crown molding and the heavy drapes. Too ostentatious, she thought. She looked at her phone; five missed calls from Rebecca, and several others she didn't recognize. She put the phone down and poured another glass of wine.

Talking heads on every channel were dizzy with joy. Any lawyer that had handled even a misdemeanor loitering charge was asked to comment on the significance of this development. Some thought the "persecutor's" office should dismiss the charges against the senator. Others thought his guilt was confirmed the moment he told all those bald-faced lies on the stand. There was still plenty of evidence to support a conviction. The jury was still sequestered, so they heard nothing of the maelstrom.

Stew Franks tried not to panic. After meeting with his team, he'd dared to believe that they could still convict Lawson. The peppy pep talks to the choir outlined all the evidence they had against him. Stew kept emphasizing that there was nothing to corroborate Loebowitz's story, and he shouldn't be so richly rewarded for his treacherous lies.

48

DAY SEVEN. TUESDAY, MARCH 24TH.

Court watchers were anxious. Would the prosecution demand a conviction, or would they dismiss the case? Many, including the RNC, wanted it over so they could resume fundraising for their pro-family agenda without this black eye staring at their donor list like a malevolent Cyclops. Once the trial ended the welt would go from black to blue, then to yellow, and then, mercifully, disappear like all good welts do. Of course, the DNC wanted it to linger until the Second Coming.

Stew would make a spirited closing argument, and look dashing when he did so in his new gray pinstripe. If Lawson was wrongly convicted, he'd console himself in knowing he'd simply done his job, for it was the jury's responsibility to fetter out the truth. Ahh, the truth.

Beth led the attorneys back to the judge's chambers where Stew announced they would proceed on behalf of the people! It was a nice little speech. However, in his zest for speech-making he'd forgotten that his audience was simply the judge, and not the press.

They returned to the courtroom to give their closing arguments and let a jury of Lawson's peers decide his fate. This "peers" business was rich. Peers? Of *Lawson's*? Ha! None of the jurors were multi-millionaire United States Senators. There wasn't even a Den Mother on the panel.

"ALL RISE! The First Judicial Court, in and for the Commonwealth of Pennsylvania is now in session, the Honorable Gustav Franco presiding. You may now be seated." Myron was into his fourteenth minute of fame, and it was the recognition of this fact that caused him to belt it with gusto.

The Gobbler had registered high levels of pride in the limelight (and so had his chubby wife, who wouldn't shut up around the ladies at the country club, all of whom were sick of it, but envious, too). He'd stayed up late to watch the Know-It-All's on cable television scrutinize his rulings. They nitpicked like they always do.

The judge told the jurors they'd be given the case for their deliberations. However, first they'd hear the attorney's closing summations. "Consider what they say, but remember that you are the exclusive judges of the evidence. Because the prosecution has the burden to prove its case, Mr. Franks will speak first. He will also be allowed a short rebuttal. Mr. Franks, you may now proceed."

Stew looked snappy in the new charcoal gray. He'd tried on several ties, finally settling on a solid red, having read somewhere that red is the power color. Now he walked to the center of the pit, bowed his head as if in prayer, and began.

"Ladies and Gentlemen of the jury, I humbly stand before you as an officer of this court, charged with the grave responsibility of seeing that justice is done for this brutal murder. I do so with confidence that you will also discharge your sacred duty to evaluate the reasonable, credible, and *corroborated* evidence, and find the defendant guilty of this horrific act of violence.

"And what is that evidence? Is it enough that the defendant appears to have no moral compass, no rudder of decency in his life? For surely there is plenty evidence of that. Is it enough that he was engaged in an illicit affair with the wife of a good friend? For surely there is plenty evidence of that. Is it enough that the exposure of that tawdry affair would spoil his reputation? Is it enough that he, and he alone, was with her the afternoon that she died? Or that his hair was at the scene, in her bed, and on her pillow? Or that his semen was the last ounce of selfish lust he could offer before killing her?

"The defendant does not tell the truth. He will lie to his friends. He will lie to his wife. He will lie to all the other women that he uses. He will lie to the voters. And, most importantly, he will lie to you. And he will do so under oath. Why? To preserve this carefully crafted façade that has been polished to an ugly shine. Because it is his reputation, as phony as it may be, that he will preserve at all costs. So, he will silence anyone who might expose the real person that he is.

"Chelsea Miles made the fatal mistake of getting close to him, so close that she could unmask him. She paid for that with a beastly blow to her head, one so vicious and calculating that he silenced her forever.

"Until today, when she can speak to you from the grave and beg you to give her justice.

"Now, the defense will stand up here and tell you that we need to prove his guilt beyond a doubt. Even though we believe the doubt is slim, at best, it is definitely *not* our legal duty, nor is it yours, to find he is guilty beyond doubt. The law allows for there to be doubt. But is it *reasonable* doubt? Is it reasonable to doubt that he was alone with her moments before she died? Absolutely not. Is it reasonable to doubt that he alone had a motive to kill her? Absolutely not. Is it reasonable to doubt that he had the means and opportunity to kill her? Absolutely not. Is it reasonable to doubt that he held that shovel in his hand? Absolutely not."

Stew reviewed the testimony of his expert witnesses and their stellar credentials. He reminded the jurors that the blood, hair, semen, and medical examiner evidence all pointed to Lawson, and Lawson alone.

"And what about the fingerprint experts? Dr. Davenport testified there was absolutely no doubt in her mind that the thumb print belonged to the defendant. It was not sufficiently smudged or 'overlapped' or anything else to cause her to believe it belonged to anyone else. And this business from that wretched liar, Loebowitz, about making a finger print with a pencil and some scotch tape? Ridiculous. Do you honestly think Dr. Davenport, the premier fingerprint expert in the country, would be fooled by some convicted felon who, in a few seconds, taped a thumb print onto the shovel? Be serious for a moment. Do you honestly think she'd be fooled by that preposterous fraud using the microscope in her lab? It's a farce. It's a farce made up by a vicious killer trying to escape punishment for beating an innocent man to death with a tire iron.

"And the defense's fingerprint expert? He would testify that the earth is flat if he was paid to. You heard his testimony. Out of the 108 times he has testified, he has never found that the fingerprints matched the criminal who'd been charged. Not a single time. Imagine that. It's insulting.

"But that is what the defense has done. They will parade anyone up here on the stand and throw as much mud against the wall as they possibly can, hoping some of it, just enough of it, will stick to cause you to doubt. But don't be fooled. These desperate acts of contrived 'evidence' don't change the fundamental facts. And those facts are these: Ken Lawson was in the room where Chelsea Miles was murdered moments before her life was snuffed out to hide the ugly truth that he will say or do *anything* to maintain his place of power and prestige.

"The defense makes these arguments that are woven together with mud, arguments that don't survive the scrutiny of logic and reason. But what else have they got? Nothing. Nothing that is reasonable or compelling—only the stench of diversion.

"You see; the defendant thinks he's above the need to act morally. He'll cheat on his wife with the wife of his best friend. He'll sleep with other woman whose names he doesn't even bother to know, and then lie about it under oath. He thinks he's above the law. But he's not. His murderous rage will be repaid by your thoughtful sense of justice and duty."

Andrew Bradshaw had seen it all in his career (and so have I). He'd seen guilty men go free over silly technicalities, and innocent men convicted of crimes they didn't commit. So, when he stood to give his final argument, he did so with a sense of urgency. His client, he honestly believed, was innocent.

"Mr. Franks gives a fine speech. He's done a good job of showing that Ken Lawson is guilty of sin and moral weakness. But, with all due respect to Mr. Franks, that wouldn't be too difficult in this case. Ken Lawson *is* guilty of moral weakness, and he *is* guilty of selfish, offensive conduct. But it is not illegal conduct. And it is not murder.

"If this trial were about whether my client slept with Chelsea Miles on the day of her murder, we would have pled guilty. If this trial were about whether my client did his wife wrong, we would have pled guilty. If this trial were about hair, semen, and blood, we would have pled guilty. But it isn't about any of those things.

"Mr. Franks wants you to believe that we threw a bunch of mud against the wall, hoping it'd stick. But it seems to me that's what the prosecution did. They spent all this time on the blood. And even more time on the semen and hair. And, sure enough, it all belongs to my client; we've never disputed that. However, those things add up to immoral behavior, not murder.

"I remind you that it is the *prosecution* that must stick something on the wall. And what must they stick? Plenty. Because it isn't nearly enough that they prove Ken Lawson *might* have been the killer, or that he *could* have been the killer. We don't need to stick a single thing, not a single speck of mud or a single speck of evidence. My client doesn't need to prove he didn't kill Chelsea Miles. And he certainly doesn't need to prove who did.

"So what has the prosecution stuck on the wall that proves Ken Lawson committed this murder beyond a reasonable doubt? Nothing. The only evidence relevant to the crime of murder is the partial thumb print. That's it. The rest is just hypothesis, conjecture, and speculation. And hypothesis, conjecture, and speculation simply will not cut it here.

"So what about the thumb print on the shovel? It belonged to Ken Lawson all right, but he didn't put it there. Eric Loebowitz did. Can we be 100% certain of that? Regrettably not. But does it create a reasonable doubt that Ken actually held the shovel? Of course it does. Loebowitz told you how he'd transferred the print from a coffee mug and no one was more surprised by that testimony than Ken Lawson himself.

"There is another important piece of evidence that puts another layer of doubt on the fingerprint issue. Javier Flores testified he didn't use the shovel again after leaning it against the house that morning. Is that credible? It is, because Javier testified that if he'd used it again that afternoon he would have put it back in the garage.

"If Ken had used the shovel to kill Chelsea, then his finger prints would have been all over it. So how does the prosecution explain just one small print? They have invented a scenario where Ken supposedly plastered the handle with his prints and then wiped them off, missing one tiny spot in the process. However, under that theory, they need to explain why *Javier's* prints are still all over it. So they claim, without any evidence whatsoever, that Javier used the shovel again after Ken had wiped off his prints. But Javier claims he didn't use it that afternoon, didn't even touch it.

"And while we're on the subject of prints, does it seem reasonable to you that Ken Lawson, this calculating murderer of the United States Senate, carefully wiped his prints off the shovel but didn't bother to wipe them from the bedroom?

"Ken Lawson did not kill Chelsea Miles. The killer was Eric Loebowitz. He knew inside information that only the killer would have known. His motivation for killing her is also reasonable, if not absurdly demented. He was paid to do it. He was paid by Susan Lawson, the wronged and shamed spouse in an act of outrageous retribution.

"Ken Lawson has suffered enough for his dishonesty and for breaking the commitments of his marriage. It's time to let him go."

Stew Franks had the last word, and he was eager to use it.

"There is no credible evidence against the defendant? Surely Mr. Bradshaw jests, surely he can't be serious. The defense of this case rests on two people. The first is an illegal immigrant who couldn't possibly remember what time he'd touched a shovel several months ago. Come on. He couldn't remember how many times he touched his spoon this morning at breakfast. His testimony was worthless.

"And Loebowitz? They pin their hopes on an admitted murderer with a ten-page rap sheet? He'll say anything to escape punishment for brutally beating a man to death with a tire iron. Did he kill Chelsea? Sure thing! Did he kill John Lennon? You bet! How about JFK? Why the heck not, if it means he won't be punished for a crime he really *did* commit.

"There is not one shred of evidence that connects Loebowitz to the scene of the crime. Nothing. Nada. Nil. Zilch. Loebowitz, in his own twisted and demented way, wants credit for committing the crime of the century. He'll get off for murder *and* become famous! Can't beat that! So deep in the bowels of jail he hears about this sensational crime and wants to take credit for it, and get a break to boot. Ingenious!

"Now, Mr. Bradshaw said 'but how could Loebowitz have possibly known the dark unknown secrets that only the real killer would know?' That is easy enough. All he had to do was look at the crime scene photos for something that he can say he saw or planted there. That evidence was available to Loebowitz and his attorney. There's no great mystery in that.

"So there are two narcissistic killers, Loebowitz and Lawson, and they have both conspired to get away with murder. Please, do not let that happen."

The twelve jurors were ushered from the courtroom to the jury room. Their verdict would have to be unanimous. Lawyers make it a habit to predict which of the jurors will be chosen as the foreperson, the one charged with keeping them on task. Stew predicted Juror #5, an outspoken businessman who battled gluttony. Bradshaw thought it would be #2, the blunt president of her local Rotary Club. Lawson bet that both of them had voted for him in the last election. He hoped they would vote for him now.

The jurors studiously avoided looking in Lawson's filthy direction as they filed out. This was an ominous sign, for it meant they were, at a minimum, grossed out by Lawson's behavior (even though Juror #7 was sleeping with his secretary, Juror #3 hadn't filed an honest tax return in thirty-six years, and Juror #11 had worn the same ugly sweater four days in a row).

49

ALL AFTERNOON THE JURY DELIBERATED, sitting around a large conference table covered with photos, jury instructions, notes, and Styrofoam coffee cups. The shovel also lay on the table, lengthwise, like a malicious table runner. The first order of business had been to select a foreperson. There'd been only one volunteer, Juror #2, the bossy woman on the front row who no one in their right mind would want to be married to. This uncontested victory went straight to her head, like she'd just won the Iowa caucus.

Myron stood guard outside the door, lest one of the attorneys stick his head in to give one more rousing pep talk. *Don't forget the thumbprint!* or *Remember, nobody's perfect!* Inside the room, the jurors were hesitant to come right out with their opinion. They acted like you do at a cocktail party when the subject of politics comes up; polite reservation before gently exposing yourself (and once you know you're in safe company, you let it rip, relieved to be speaking to someone with a freaking brain in their head). And so it was in the jury room.

The initial vote was six to six. So, they started at the top, going through every piece of evidence. Some of the jurors sat back, nodding agreement with whatever was said, whether they actually agreed with it or not. They just wanted to get along. I understand. Others argued every point, believing there was nobility in being the devil's advocate (but they weren't advocating for me, I can tell you that).

The jurors knew the magnitude of this trial; they weren't that dense. Even though they'd been sequestered for ten days, they'd seen the hordes of media and the occasional newspaper headline. They knew they'd probably be summoned to the Dateline studio a few months later to discuss these very deliberations (and no doubt Juror #2 would hog the floor there, too).

By six o'clock, it was nine votes to three. The coalition of three was stubborn, fearing if they caved in now they'd look like flip-floppers. So they dug in deeper. And it didn't help that Juror #2 treated them like they had dementia. The only unanimous verdict they could reach was that those who disagreed with them were total morons. This they could do beyond a reasonable doubt.

Bradshaw and Lawson's anxiety rose with every passing hour. They tried not to look at the courtroom clock, but did so every two minutes. What was taking the jury so long? If the jurors had believed Loebowitz, they would have voted for an acquittal by now. Bradshaw's hope for a quick acquittal was replaced by hope for a long, drawn-out hung jury.

The Gobbler sent a note into the jury room (even he couldn't just waltz in to chat). Were they close to reaching a verdict? If not, he recommended they finish for the day and resume their deliberations the following morning. No one was budging, so they voted for an overnight break.

There was someone else, yet to be introduced, who was also concerned. Alex Matsumara was a nerd who blended into the enamel at the county's forensic lab. He made about as much noise as a lab rat. Matsumara logged more hours staring into a microscope than anyone else in the department. He'd done the analysis on Lawson's hair samples and was familiar with the investigative file, so he'd been as surprised as anyone else with the testimony of Eric Loebowitz. He didn't want to believe the felonious bastard who was probably jerking the county's chain. However, maybe, just maybe, they'd overlooked something.

He scanned the evidence log again, looking for anything that might jump out. Nothing did, at first. Then he saw something that had been ignored.

There was one previously unidentified strand of hair.

50

DAY EIGHT. WEDNESDAY, MARCH 25TH.

Everyone arrived at the courthouse at 9:00 a.m., just long enough for the judge to bang his gavel. The jurors were then promptly escorted back to the jury room to resume their deliberations. Everyone else waited. They bit their nails and watched the clock. Those whose necks weren't on the line talked about their March Madness brackets. Others paced. No one paced more than ex-Senator Kenneth Lawson. It was like waiting for the results of a biopsy, only worse.

Two hours later, the jury had a question. It's not uncommon for jurors to have questions about the law or a certain piece of evidence during their deliberations. They're told to write it down and slip it to the bailiff, who then gives it to the judge.

When the judge got the question, he summoned the lawyers back to his chambers. Stew, Scott, and Bradshaw followed Beth, at a reasonably safe distance, to see The Gobbler. Lawson was left behind to fret. Once they were seated, the judge said: "Counsel, the jury has asked a question and I want your input before composing a response." He unfolded the small handwritten note. Stew saw that it appeared to be written in the penmanship of a female.

If we find the defendant guilty, do we have to stick with first degree murder, or can we do something else?

Bradshaw wanted to throw up. Clearly they hadn't believed Eric Loebowitz.

Stew was over the moon. "Your Honor," he said, "I believe the correct response should be that the defendant is charged with first degree murder and they aren't allowed to arbitrarily reduce that charge. However, you should tell them they get to impose the sentence and can consider any concerns they have at that time."

"Wait a minute," Bradshaw said. "That's nonsense. The jurors here don't get to choose the sentence. They only decide between life in prison, or death. I strongly object to telling them they can manipulate the charge by incorrectly believing they can give him a lighter sentence."

"But if they think it's all or nothing they might not convict him of anything," said Stew, who saw no virtue in *that.*

"Exactly," said Bradshaw. "You filed the charges, not me. Maybe you overreached and we'll get an acquittal, or a hung jury."

"I can only tell them," said The Gobbler, "that they have been instructed on all the law necessary to render a verdict in this case, and leave it at that."

Stew practically skipped back into the open courtroom. Bradshaw followed (but wasn't skipping). Ken studied Bradshaw's face, and what he saw didn't look good. When he heard what the jurors' question had been, he slumped over to the table and put his head in his hands. They were going to convict him. Bradshaw tried to console him. "Listen, Ken, it's not over. If they were so hell bent on convicting you, why didn't they just do it? Why the note in the first place? You never know." This pep talk lifted Lawson's spirits by approximately two percent.

Stew was busy congratulating himself. Oh, how he wanted to dash out into the corridor with a proclamation that he'd probably won! Instead, he allowed others from the department to tell him what a remarkable job he'd done. I thought his head was going to pop.

A few minutes later, Alex Matsumara, the lab geek, entered the courtroom with a manila file in his hand. He walked up to Stew Franks and tapped him on the shoulder. Could he have a moment of his time? Somewhere private?

"Matsumara, can't this wait? I'm in the middle of trial, for God's sake!"

"Mr. Franks, this is very important."

They retired across the hall to a small empty conference room and closed the door.

"I think we have a problem with this Lawson case," Matsumara said.

"What in the hell are you talking about? We're moments away from a conviction. The jury will be out any minute."

"Last night I reviewed the evidence again," said Matsumara. "I went through all of it."

"Why, Matsumara? Why would you spend your time going over this case again? We've gone over it for months." Stew didn't like the direction of this conversation. He knew Matsumara hadn't shown up to remind him he'd be out on vacation for a week in early July.

"I was troubled by that Loebowitz testimony, so I wanted to go over everything one more time, to make sure we hadn't missed anything."

"Not Loebowitz again. The jury saw right through that lying sack of shit!"

"But, Mr. Franks, we have a problem."

"What?" All that pride had been replaced by a whole lotta wrath.

"Remember there was that one strand of hair that didn't match either George, Chelsea, or Lawson? There was that one unidentified hair we found at the foot of the bed. Remember?"

"No, Matsumara, I don't. There were all sorts of fibers, dog hairs, and prints belonging to who knows who. The landscaper and those two-bit punks didn't give their samples either. So, no, I don't remember. But something tells me you're about to enlighten me."

"The hair was human, Mr. Franks. It was red and curly. I analyzed it against the hair sample taken from Loebowitz after he was arrested in the tire iron case."

Stew stared at him.

"I can tell you with near certainty that it belonged to him, Mr. Franks. Loebowitz was in that room."

Stew wanted to kill Matsumara—just flat out reach across the table and strangle him with his bare hands. Instead, he put his head down, and finally spoke to the floor. "The defense had equal access to the investigative file, Matsumara. We didn't hide anything. It was all there, available to them as well as us."

"That's true," said Matsumara, "but they obviously didn't connect the dots."

"And that's our problem?" replied Stew as he lifted his head to look at Matsumara.

Just then there was a knock on the door. It was Beth, the clerk, who opened the door and stuck her head just inside.

"I'm sorry to interrupt, but the jury has reached a verdict and the judge wants you in the courtroom. Now."

She closed the door. Stew and Matsumara looked at one another for several seconds. Stew finally broke the silence.

"It's too late, Matsumara. It's just too late." And with that, he opened the door and walked back to the courtroom, buttoning his suit coat.

"Has the jury reached a verdict?"

"We have, Your Honor," said Juror #2, who stood and spoke her line too loudly.

"Please hand it to the bailiff."

Myron waddled over to the jury box. His leather holster squeaked; the only sound in the room. He handed the folded piece of paper to Beth, who handed it to The Gobbler. Everyone in the courtroom studied his expression as he silently read the verdict. He gave away nothing. He handed the verdict back to Beth.

"Will the defendant please stand."

Ken and Bradshaw both stood; Ken barely remembered how.

"The clerk will now read the verdict. However, before she does, I must admonish everyone in this courtroom that proper decorum is required. This court will not tolerate any inappropriate display of character."

Beth stood at her table in front of the silent courtroom. A

dropped pin would have shattered the stillness. Ken wanted to throw up. She cleared her throat, and then read:

"In the matter of the People of the Commonwealth of Pennsylvania vs. Kenneth Lawson, case #93080. We the jury, in the above titled action, find the defendant, Kenneth Lawson, guilty of the crime of murder in the first degree in violation of penal code section 187, a felony upon Chelsea St. Claire Miles, a human being as charged in Count I of the information."

There was a moment of silence before the courtroom erupted. Ken dropped his head. Bradshaw did the same, shaking it back and forth. He put his arm around his client.

Stew had turned to face the gallery, fist pumping. The media bolted for the exit. Rebecca was sobbing and shaking. John stood and yelled "Bullshit!" at the jurors. The Gobbler banged his gavel.

Once order was restored, the judge announced the court would resume for the sentencing phase the following Monday morning. Until then, the jurors were told not to speak to anyone about their verdict. Sure. Fat chance. They'd be mauled like John, Paul, George, and Ringo, and they knew it.

"Mr. Lawson, I will allow you a few moments to be with your family, after which you will be taken directly into custody pending further order of this court. And, now, this court is in recess." One final gavel bang.

John and Rebecca leaned over the three-foot-tall partition that separated the gallery from their father, gathering into a tight huddle of three, sobbing. This had been a diabolical set-up. They were sure of it.

"It's not fair!" Rebecca cried. "It's not fair!"

"Mom wouldn't do that," John said. "It's the same bullshit, dad. They've got no proof."

"Where's your mother?" He needed to find her! "Have you spoken to her?"

"No. We tried but she won't answer."

"Where in the hell *is* she?"

John and Rebecca looked at each other.

"Talk to me, dammit! This is important!"

Finally, Rebecca said, "She's in Bermuda."

"She's *what!*"

"She went there before the trial started to get away from the media and all that. We've been trying to call her."

Ken looked away. "So she knows."

Myron peeled the children from their father and Ken was led away, to jail, and ultimately to prison where he would likely spend the rest of his life. If they didn't execute him, that is.

Susan Lawson knew the verdict was imminent. She'd been surprised that she hadn't been contacted by the police, or at least the media. No doubt they'd been trying to find her. She watched CNN, her stomach churning, when they announced that a verdict had been reached. A minute later they cut to a live feed from the courthouse. Susan sat at the foot of the bed, shaking, staring at the television next to the empty mini-bar. The reporter, wind-blown hair across her face, hand to her ear, announced the guilty verdict.

The relief! Trying to blame her for the murder had failed. Ken's conviction meant her liberty was assured. Thank the Lord!

Did she feel guilty? I suppose there was some of that. But the combination of wrath, pride, and greed trumped the guilt. He had it coming (and so had Chelsea). The pompous, ungrateful, cheating slime would never use her and her money again.

When the guilty verdict was announced, Maggie shouted, and kept shouting, causing the tenant below to jab the ceiling with a broom stick. She would have justice! She would finally be paid! She called Young Associate who feigned absence. She left him a message inquiring what time he wanted her to swing by the office for her check. Then it was back to the computer to browse cruise itineraries.

51

STEW FRANKS LUXURIATED IN HIS VICTORY. There were requests for interviews and congratulatory calls (including the pandering Governor who wanted to steal the vacated senate seat from him). He'd won fair and square. Or had he? And this was the thought that robbed him of his sleep.

Stew had to carefully avoid Matsumara the next day at the office. He was forced to take a slight detour on his victory lap (laps, really) around the office corridors. *Well, thank you, Lloyd. It was an uphill battle. I don't care about the accolades, I'm just glad to see that justice was done.* All day long he tried to push the thought away, but there it was, lurking. He didn't care a lick about justice for Ken Lawson, who deserved to be punished for his flagrant immorality, if nothing else. But what if Matsumara talked? What if Scott, that backstabbing upstart, found out? He'd tattletale. He'd rat him out to the bar association faster than you could shake a stick at it, blabbing like he was in a confessional booth. So the unpleasant thought loitered, not on center stage, but in the wings, peeking around the curtain, waiting to burst onto the stage for an inglorious curtain call.

Stew was convinced that Ken Lawson was a wicked man; an immoral hypocrite. But was he a murderer? Could Stew live with his own hypocrisy if he let the conviction stand? Come on, Stew, sure you can! It's easy! You're the hero! Lawson got what he deserved! I whispered, I nudged, doing all I could to let injustice reign.

But I'll be darned if Stew didn't decide to call Bradshaw the next morning. They would contact the judge to undo this minor injustice. He'd already proven his prowess in the courtroom, and now he'd prove his honor in a selfless display of magnanimity!

Now, having made the decision that would cause admirers to respect him even more, he slept, secure in the knowledge that he would have his cake and eat it, too.

Ken's first night in jail, this time *officially* in jail, was a long one. He tried to ignore the inmates who were guilty of three times what they'd been charged with. They bitched about the blasted unfairness of it all. Ha! He tried to ignore the smell of jail; damp concrete, metal, disinfectant, and body odor.

Bradshaw told him they could appeal—a loser's remedy that sounds better than it really is, like chocolate flavored broccoli. The Gobbler had made a few mistakes during the trial, but they'd been harmless errors; nothing blatant enough to warrant a new trial.

Ken heard from no one. There wasn't a single *Hey, bummer about that court deal.* Only his kids had been to the trial supporting him. No one else wanted to be infected by his radioactive shame.

Even fellow inmates were bored with the case. He was just another loser in a one-piece orange jumpsuit.

Ken tried to decide how he felt about Susan. There was the obvious loathing, of course. But did he feel pity for her? Surely she had her own demons to contend with (and he hoped they were vicious little bastards), and she must have shame over what she'd put her children through. Other than that, he simply wanted her to rot in hell.

Stew arrived at his office early the next morning. Matsumara's car was already in the parking lot. Stew assumed he was probably hunched over a microscope, trying to sabotage another remarkable verdict. He walked back to the lab.

"Are you absolutely certain that hair belonged to Loebowitz?"

"Yes," said Matsumara. "Certain of it."

"Can you think of any other plausible reason why his hair would be in the bedroom, other than him actually being there?"

"Uh, no. Can you?"

"I believe justice requires me to take the higher road and disclose this information to the court."

"The higher road, Stew?"

"Yes. I believe we have a duty to do that."

"You think?"

Stew didn't answer. He was so absorbed in his own self-righteous martyrdom that the sarcasm didn't register. I love how you can do this. He returned to his office and closed the door. He picked up his phone and dialed Bradshaw's number. What an honorable man he was! He'd be a shoe-in for the vacant senate seat.

"This is Andrew Bradshaw."

"Yeah, hello Andy, this is Stew."

Bradshaw would have preferred the caller be a solicitor. Stew was probably calling to ruminate about the trial, in a condescending tone no doubt. *I don't know, maybe I just got lucky. But don't worry, Andy. I've lost a trial or two myself.*

"Sure, Stew, what's up? I presume we're still scheduled for two days on sentencing?"

"Well, Andy, something has come up."

They met with Judge Franco an hour later. Bradshaw couldn't believe what he'd heard. No doubt the court would dismiss the charges completely, or at least give his client a new trial with this new evidence. Bradshaw had not yet dared tell Ken. He wanted to talk to the judge and Stew Franks personally; to be sure this hadn't been a prank call, or a dream.

Beth ushered them into the judge's chambers.

"Gentlemen, you said this was important."

"Your Honor," Stew began, "there's been an important development in the case. We've discovered there was a previously unidentified hair at the crime scene. My office has learned that it is a match to that of Eric Loebowitz. It appears he was in the bedroom where the victim was murdered. Even though this evidence was available to the defense from the beginning, they overlooked it. And, I'm afraid, my staff overlooked it, too."

"When did you discover this evidence?" The Gobbler looked squarely at Stew.

"I learned about it after the jury had reached its verdict." What a big fat liar. I suppose it was *technically* true, but very misleading. "I asked one of our lab techs to review the file again because we wanted to be absolutely certain of Lawson's guilt." There was absolutely nothing technically true about *this* statement. "He discovered the evidence and I wanted to immediately inform the court." Or this one.

"Your Honor," said Bradshaw, "I appreciate Mr. Franks advising me of this discovery. I now hope the prosecution will move to vacate the conviction and agree to have it overturned."

The Gobbler had seen it all, but this would surely make his Top Ten. "Mr. Franks, how do you wish to proceed?"

"Your Honor, I have no interest in convicting an innocent man. *Uh-huh.* That's why I immediately came forward with this evidence. *Uh-huh.* I presume the court will grant a new trial in any event, and if so, I believe the state would be unable to meet its burden here. Therefore, we are willing to dismiss the charges."

"Very well. Let's get something on the record. We will dismiss the jurors and inform them that additional evidence was discovered that appears to exonerate the defendant, and the state has voluntarily agreed to dismiss the charges. I don't think it's necessary to give them the specific nature of the new evidence at this time. Like everyone else, they'll be curious, but they'll learn about it soon enough."

"About that," said Stew, "we request the state be given another day or two to consider other charges before this is made public. Obviously we need to find Susan Lawson."

"I understand," said the judge. "Mr. Bradshaw, can you live with that?"

"Yes, I can. But may I be permitted to tell my client? I would tell him it must be held in strict confidence until the state makes it public. I presume he'll be publicly cleared within two or three days?"

"I consent to those parameters," said Stew with solemn officiousness that was quite unnecessary in this private conversation between the boys.

Bradshaw immediately took the secure elevator down to the jail. Visitors ordinarily sat across from inmates in three-sided booths—the functional equivalent to a row of urinals. Dirty sheets of plexiglass with small holes separated them from the inmates, who ranted about the injustice to their attorneys or friends on the other side of the glass. Bradshaw, however, was given permission to meet with Lawson in a small conference room within the jail for a more intimate conversation. An armed guard stood outside the door. He peered in through the small window in the door to be sure that Lawson wasn't going berserk with a gardening tool, or that Bradshaw wasn't passing Lawson a lemon bunt cake with a file inside it.

"I know you didn't kill her," Bradshaw said.

"Thanks, Andy. That means a lot. But I'm afraid you're the only one who believes it. You and my kids."

"No, Ken. I mean, I *know* you didn't kill her."

"I know it too, and I've been telling you that from the start. But obviously the jury didn't believe me."

"Ken, they found more evidence from the scene."

Ken looked at Bradshaw and cocked his head. "Really? That's good, right? Can we use it for an appeal?"

"There won't be an appeal, Ken."

"But...I thought you said if we could find anything else...."

Ken was so depressed he had no more fight in him. And now he didn't even have grounds to appeal?

"There was a single unidentified hair in the bedroom by the foot of the bed."

"What do you mean? Whose was it?"

"Ken, the strand of hair was red. It belonged to Eric Loebowitz."

Ken's mind desperately raced to catch up. New evidence? A hair? Loebowitz? When he could speak, he asked, "Does anyone else know about this hair? Is it too late?"

"The prosecution knows and so does the judge. It was discovered last night. I met with Judge Franco and Stewart Franks this morning at the courthouse."

"So can we reopen the case?" Ken asked so hopefully, so pleadingly, that Bradshaw could not have imagined any other response than the one he gave.

"Ken, the prosecution has agreed to drop the charges against you. The judge is dismissing all of it. You're going to be released."

When Ken finally allowed himself to believe this was real, he dropped his head, reached for Bradshaw, and sobbed. There was no hooting and hollering, only profound relief. But the relief was ambiguous, coming as it did with such a staggering cost.

Bradshaw explained this was all confidential and could not be disclosed to anyone for another day or two.

"Why?"

"Because the police need to find Susan and coordinate her arrest. You'll have to stay in jail a few more days, and you can't breathe a word of this. Seriously, Ken, not a word."

"Okay," Ken said. "But please, Andy, get me out of here as soon as you can."

52

SUSAN RETURNED HOME TWO DAYS FOLLOWING the conviction of her husband. Her plan had been risky and reckless, but she'd survived it. As her plane touched down in Philadelphia, after a celebratory glass of champagne in first class, she thought she had finally rid herself of Ken. She could keep their entire marital fortune (which should have been hers all along).

As she collected her Prada carry-on bag, she couldn't have known that she would never fly again. She wouldn't sip champagne again either. Her drink of choice forevermore would be tap water, or watered down apple juice.

Detectives Flygare and Olson approached her at the baggage claim area, looking like a couple of fifteen handicappers.

"Excuse me, are you Susan Lawson?"

"I am, but I'm not prepared to make a comment at this time. I hope you understand. Now, if you'll excuse me."

Flygare showed her his badge. "You are under arrest for the murder of Chelsea Miles."

Susan dropped her bag which attracted the attention of worn-out travelers at the revolving luggage conveyor belt. Flygare took her shaking hands, pulled them behind her back, and cuffed her. He read her Miranda rights (his favorite employment pleasure), and she was led away through the crowd of gawking onlookers.

Susan said nothing. She held her head high as they escorted her through the airport to the waiting patrol car, double-parked at the curb. By the time the rear-door closed she had lost all control. She'd cried hysterically, trying to make them understand that he'd cheated on her, that he'd been an abysmal husband who'd basically raped her. These were embarrassing indictments against her husband, to be sure, but even Susan knew they were wholly inadequate to justify murdering his lover (you didn't see Ken taking a gardening hoe to Susan's personal trainer).

With the evidence so overwhelmingly stacked against her (the forensic accountants traced her payment to Loebowitz), she pled guilty in exchange for a twenty-five-year prison term. She'd be eighty-three-years-old. All the chemical peels, cosmetic surgery, and hours on the goddamned elliptical machine had been a waste of time, unless she wanted to preen for her fellow inmates, many of whom were toothless and hard as stone.

Maggie fumed. She'd been on the verge of financial freedom, and now this latest sucker punch. She couldn't bear the thought of returning to the Guatemala commune, so she wrote George, appealing to his sense of decency for his former mother-in-law (twenty-five years his junior). But the goddamned greedy munitions dealer didn't even respond. Can you believe it? Family obviously meant nothing.

Young Associate also showed a callous disregard for her loss. Why pamper this dreadful client who wouldn't generate a fee? But, alas, he'd petitioned Susan's high-powered criminal defense attorney, the one who'd negotiated the twenty-five-year prison term on behalf of his client. Susan had eventually agreed to pay $15,000 from prison to settle the wrongful death claim. She'd done it to stop the old hippie from writing her three times a week, complaining about her misery in the wake of Petunia's death. It'd galled Susan to pay a red cent to the mother of the slut, but she'd grown weary of the pestering.

Maggie had been insulted by this paltry offer. But Young Associate insisted this was the best they could do, so Maggie plugged her nose and took it. She was outraged when she received her check for $2,130 (she thought she'd be getting the entire $15,000). Young Associate impatiently explained that was her share after deducting the attorney fees, costs, and re-payment to the firm of her two prior loans (which Maggie had conveniently forgotten about). Poor Maggie felt like Dante; pushing that stupid rock up the hill, day in and day out. When she returned to Guatemala, she was victimized yet again when her hippie sister, the one who'd loaned her the airfare, demanded to be repaid. Maggie was defenseless from the cunning and avarice of even the hippies.

53

ONE YEAR LATER.

Ken drove west on I-76 from Philadelphia. The drive to Muncy would take him three hours, time he could use to collect his thoughts. He still drove in luxury, the silver Mercedes humming along at eighty miles per hour. He was casually dressed to deflect the public spotlight that still shown upon his tarnished image. Ken was still one of the most recognizable faces in America, a fact he would have coveted years earlier. Now he lived in infamy as the pathetic womanizer who'd publicly embarrassed the United States Senate for being caught. All the other senators denounced his tawdry affairs and privately covered their own tracks.

His senate seat was now occupied by the spiteful ex-Governor. Stew Franks had been poised to run until word of his unethical conduct bubbled to the surface and he was disbarred (I wonder who'd orchestrated that little leak?). It was so unfair— "sour grapes" he called it. Did his magnanimous agreement to dismiss the case mean *nothing*? Those new suits now hung in his closet collecting dust. His wife told her friends he'd simply decided to retire while he was on top (they pretended this was sensible, but were grateful for something to gossip about behind her back).

Ken's divorce from Susan had been quite public. The press feasted on the story until their stomachs were taut, like vultures over a dead herd on the highway. The Lawson's fortune was carved up between themselves and their greedy lawyers. They didn't have much to show for all those legal fees either; one of them was now rotting away in jail and the other was a social pariah (he'd been offered a job on a raunchy cable channel but turned it down—because it was "unbecoming of a former senator").

Ken took the Muncy exit and drove to the outskirts of town. He turned down the long drive and approached the heavily guarded gate of the State Correctional Institution for Women. Even though the guard recognized him (you'd have to be Rip Van Winkle not to), he was required to show two forms of ID and state his business there. Ken told the guard he was there to visit Susan Lawson, his ex-wife.

He waited in a windowless concrete room. A metal table was bolted to the floor, surrounded by stainless steel stools, also bolted down. There was nothing else in the room, except for two iron hooks embedded into the concrete floor, used to chain inmates down.

The door opened and a female prison guard, who looked like a linebacker with a grown-out perm, escorted Susan into the room. She was handcuffed with her hands in front of her, but there were no chains around her waist or ankles, and she would not be chained to the floor. The guard told Ken and Susan they had twenty minutes.

In moments of self-pity, Ken had looked forward to confronting this woman who had ruined his life (it was totally her fault, obviously). Now, he could think of nothing to say. They just looked at each other. There was no love between them, of course, not even an ember that might've been fanned into some heat. But there was history.

Susan had aged by more than a year. She'd been stripped of her makeup, trainer, masseuse, hair colorist, nutritionist, and fashion consultant. Ken hadn't changed much—perhaps only a bit grayer to make him look more distinguished. Yet another cross for Susan to bear.

"You've probably heard that George Miles took most of what I have left in his wrongful death case," Susan said bitterly. "I presume you've come to gloat." George didn't need the money, but he was upset to learn why Susan had Chelsea murdered. It'd been so unnecessary.

"No, Susan," said Ken. "I didn't come to gloat. I came hoping for an apology because that's about all you can give me at this point."

"Then you've wasted your time."

"It might sound crazy, Susan, after what you've done to me, but—"

"After what I've done to *you*? You got exactly what you deserved. You're a pathetic egomaniac, Ken. Pathetic."

"And you?"

"So you did come to gloat."

"No. I only hoped for an apology. And you can't even do that. I'm actually sorry for you. I'm sorry for the kids and I'm sorry for myself. I don't think I can ever forgive you, but I'm sorry for all of it."

"Well, good for you, Ken." I was impressed that Susan could muster the will to be so haughty under the circumstances, inasmuch as she was handcuffed in orange prison apparel for doing the most despicable of things (orange wasn't her best color either—it tended to wash her out).

"I also came to tell you about the kids."

"My lovely children. Tell me all about them. Oh, please do." Of all the indignities, the fact that her children hadn't come to see her was the most bitter.

"Rebecca has found someone. He seems like a terrific guy. They're engaged and planning the wedding. And you're not going to believe it, but John and I have started a company that develops energy renewal technology. He's the brains and I'm the wallet." Ken didn't tell her that he'd also taken up religion, something you tend to do when you hit rock bottom. The id, the ego, and the Holy Ghost. Go Ken!

"Well how wonderful for you." She pretended this news didn't wipe her out, especially the news about Rebecca and her wedding.

They'd run out of things to say to each other and Ken stood to leave. "They'll be okay, the kids. Try to understand their pain. One day they'll be here to see you."

He tapped on the door from the inside and it opened. He stepped out into the hall, thirty feet below ground, surrounded on all sides by ugly, gray cement. He didn't look back, so he couldn't see her tears, or hear her final words.

But I could.

The final tally wasn't pretty. That usually happens after I've had my fun. These small characters all dabbled with one Deadly Sin or another. Of course, none of them believed they deserved what they got. That amused me. They plainly saw each other's clumsy faults, but couldn't see their own. That amused me, too.

You hide your sordid thoughts and black-market schemes, relieved that no one knows the mischief you've been up to, sneaking around with your lust, camouflaging your greed, and luxuriating in your wrath. You'll soon forget about me, but I'm still here, lurking, ready to pounce with my gothic thunder. You'll let your guard down soon enough; you always do.

BMc

Made in the USA
San Bernardino, CA
14 April 2017